MISCARRIAGE OF JUSTICE

A FARRAH WETHERS MYSTERY

ELIZABETH AMBER LOVE

The Riverside, New Jersey town used in this series is not based on the real town by that name. It's an amalgam of towns in the Warren and Hunterdon County regions along the Raritan River. All characters are fictitious.

Cover Art: Thomas Boatwright
Cover Fonts: *Champagne & Limousine*
by Lauren Thompson
and *Lemon Milk* by Marsnev

ISBN: 0-9980615-1-4
ISBN-13: 978-0-9980615-1-1

To all the heartbroken souls who have had to survive gaslighting and abuse.

CONTENTS

CHAPTER ONE

FARRAH sat at the dining room table gripping the maple planks as she sobbed. She heard Jackson clumping around upstairs for ten minutes before he came through the living room with the last duffel bag of his possessions over his shoulder and Gordon the bloodhound on his leash by his side.

"You don't have to go, Jack! We've had problems for years. Why is this it? Why won't you stay and try harder?" She wanted to stand up, but after three days of being sick from the fighting, the silence, the empty house while he was at the office, Farrah was running only on adrenaline.

"I have to. We've tried. Over and over, we've tried. I can't do it anymore." His bare brown arm shifted the weight of the overloaded bag when he stood up straighter to make his argument. "We have had problems for years, but I never cheated on you. I never abused you. You cheated and I'm tired of sleeping on a couch."

He commanded the dog to follow him out the side door to the driveway. The car rested lower on the tires from being filled to capacity and that didn't even include furniture. Jackson pulled out of the short paved strip and left to move in with Frank Morelli, his best friend and the ex-husband of Farrah's best friend June Cho. Farrah couldn't bear to watch him. Her face, wet from all the tears, stayed buried in the crook of her arms awhile.

The only one to watch Jackson leave was Miles the ginger cat who perched in the front windows probably grateful Gordon was gone and he once again had the house back.

Farrah took a couple breaths and stood, but in less than a minute the wailing returned. It was a cycle that repeated for hours. She used the few seconds between bouts to move from one room to the next. She managed to grab a bottle of water and her phone before landing on the couch curled in a ball with her face in a throw pillow clutched by white knuckle fists. Miles jumped up and curled himself into a circle at her feet. This wasn't the first time in her life that she wished she was dead. The death wish wasn't a feeling that she could recall emotionally like thinking about her happiest moments. It came on from time to time and lately, it was worse than ever.

He's gone, she texted to June. The two women knew each other well enough that they didn't need to elaborate. Their shorthand was usually enough. June was immediately out the door and arrived from her condo only a mile away at lightning speed.

Farrah sat up to make room for June then collapsed into her bosom. She received the comfort of having her head stroked and gently kissed by someone who loved her. Her tears created wet spots all over June's white t-shirt.

"Do you want me to make some tea, sweetie?"

Without words, Farrah shook her head still buried in June declining the offer. Her friend handed her another tissue from the nearby box that was almost empty.

"I packed a bag to stay here with you, but if you'd rather come stay on my couch to get out of here, that's fine too. Or you can be alone, but only if you really want to be."

"Thanks. I don't know what I'd do without you." Farrah straighten herself and swung her feet around to rest them on the coffee table.

"Does Janice know?"

"My daughter is still insisting on being called her new name, Nova. But, no. I only told her things were bad at home between her father and me and I don't know how to tell her this. I never told her about when he spent a few days at Frank's before."

"It might shock her then. But she's quite an incredible adult now. If you can explain to her that things have been leading to this split for so long and not to be afraid to give her some details - not all obviously - I bet she'll understand."

It was difficult for Farrah to take even a sip of water. Her stomach was clenched so tightly. For days, her body had decided to reject all sustenance. The bottle shook in her grasp until she placed it safely back on the table.

"I guess there's no hiding what I did when I worked at that retreat center. I have a feeling it would be better coming from me than if she heard from her father badmouthing me. I just don't know how. I still can't believe things were so bad that I was wooed by that psychopath Derek Davis."

"He took advantage of you, sweetie. He had some kind of target on you from the second he saw you. And then when you trusted him enough to talk about how bad your relationship with Jackson was, that slimeball upped his game and followed the pickup artist playbook until he got you alone in his room."

"I appreciate you having my back, but I did those things. I should have stopped it sooner. Hell, I should never have entered that room or kissed him in the greenhouse. I know what I did. I hate that it felt so damn good at the time."

June made herself a Jack Daniels and ginger ale in order to have a cocktail in a matter of seconds. She knew her way around Farrah's kitchen and found a box of crackers which she brought back to the living room. Farrah picked up a cracker but didn't have enough saliva to consider eating it. She dropped it back on the table and started crying again. Her breakdowns varied in length from long and tragic meltdowns to shedding tears while being able to speak that contorted language only other experienced criers can understand.

"I guess I have to go back to work even though that job is cursed. I barely make any money at this massage practice now!"

"Look, sweetie, Jackson is pissed and he left, but I doubt he's leaving you high and dry. You'll work out how to pay the bills once you can actually breathe for more than one minute at a time."

Farrah was plagued by guilt about her lack of success at Riverside Wellness Spa. First, she had one wealthy client die on her table — a murder for which she was briefly a suspect. Then she worked off-site at a retreat center for Caressa Lamour Cosmetics' conference where she had an affair with a psycho stalker that went beyond kissing but short of intercourse. Other than that, she hadn't established enough of a clientele

4

in the office to make even a steady part-time income. Jackson was the breadwinner and his support of her new career after her layoff was mediocre. He paid to support them, but he hadn't seemed convinced massage therapy was a viable industry.

June shook the box of tissues. There was no way it could last much longer. She went upstairs to the linen closet and retrieved a fresh box. As she walked through the long hallway of the Colonial, she counted the doors. Three bedrooms and a full bathroom upstairs. The master suite was Farrah and Jackson's of course; the second was their daughter's who showed no signs of coming back home from college. The third was mostly a messy storage area that used to be set up as Jackson's home office.

"I have an idea," June said back in the living room. She plopped the new box of tissues on the coffee table and picked up the soggy ones strewn all over. She pitched them into the fireplace, grabbed her cocktail, and presented a possible plan.

"You want to move in here?"

"It makes sense. You'll have the room if we can get rid of some of the clutter that you haven't looked at in years. Plus, Nova's things really could be boxed up and put aside for when she wants them. I'm not trying to erase your daughter, I know how you think. But honestly, sweetie, she's happy at college and she'll be looking for her own place wherever she lands a full-time job. It won't be here."

"I know I should've been clearing out old junk each year. I just kept holding on to it. I thought that if the house didn't change, we wouldn't change so much." Her puffy face sagged in despair from the reality. She and Jack had survived one separation, but it was truly over. She didn't know how to live life differently.

"It's never easy. Even for couples who hate each other, it's still never easy to split up." June knelt on the floor next to Farrah and gently rubbed her knee.

"How did you do it when you left Frank?"

"Well, Frank and I weren't fighting like you two. We drifted apart. It felt like our lives were no longer intersecting. I started spending as much time as I could stand at the office or taking workshops like that jewelry making class. I just kept myself busy."

"But eventually, you had to pack and leave."

Farrah knew the story, but she needed to hear it again. The validation that sometimes relationships just don't work no matter how hard you want them to was the thing gnawing at her. She did want it to work with Jackson more than anything in the world.

June kept patting Farrah's knee as she spoke. "One night, I got home from work and he was in the garage mixing up some mold casting rubber. I watched him for a while and then eventually I said, 'Frank, do you love me?' And he turned around and said, 'What?' So I said, 'Nevermind,' and I walked into the house and started looking up places to rent or buy. Once his kids were all grown up, Frank lived only for Frank. I felt like I was there because I was expected to be, but not because he wanted me to be."

"If we did this, if you really moved in here, what would you do with your condo?"

"I could rent it out. It would be great additional income which could in turn help us pay for things here."

Farrah couldn't think of any other options. She couldn't move into June's tiny one-bedroom condo and sell the house right away. They may as well try and make a go of affording it together, hopefully with some support from Jackson until they were forced to sell. Then she and June could downsize into a two-bedroom condo that would be more affordable.

"Okay. Let's do it."

CHAPTER TWO

SAMANTHA Waterston's email to all the practitioners of Riverside Wellness Spa inviting them to an important meeting wasn't something Farrah wanted to face. Though everyone worked as independent contractors, Sam was the boss. She was majority owner of the company and owned the commercial space in the business condominium complex. The meeting was mandatory, but there was no way everyone would attend. Most of the therapists preferred their autonomy and let Sam and her business partner Maggie Llewellyn make the decisions.

"Jeez, I don't want to deal with this crap," Farrah said reading the message from her phone. She accepted that she needed to get her head back into the desire to run her practice, but she wanted to put its drama behind her first.

"Do you think it's about the retreat center job?" June asked.

"I have no idea. I'm sure there will be some kind of disparaging comment about all that. It says it's to strategize ways to boost our business." Farrah turned off the screen and tossed the phone to the other end of the couch.

June picked up her empty glass and relocated to one of the comfortable chairs. She swirled the ice around and took a final sip despite having no more whiskey left in the melted cubes.

"The distraction will be good for you. I know you don't want to face it, but if you sit here, your brain has literally nothing else to do but think about Jackson. When is this meeting?"

It was scheduled for two nights from then at seven. That should have been enough time for anyone with day jobs to get there. Sam was going to host the meeting at her house instead of the spa in case anyone got booked for an appointment which she would never want turned down.

"I'm so tired, June."

"I know, baby. I know."

They agreed that for that night, June could sleep in Nova's room. Once all the moving and rearranging could be done, they'd move the storage junk into Nova's room and June would get the former office. She could include a lot of her own furniture in the condo when leasing it out and only take what she felt was personal like her bed, decorations, and everything in the bathroom and kitchen except the appliances.

Two days later, things were in disarray yet improved. The house had added touches from June's decor to replace empty spaces left by Jack's treasures like portraits of his family and hand-me-down furniture from his grandparents.

With June at work, Farrah and the cat had the house to themselves again. She inched through her daughter's bedroom and packed up everything Nova left behind when she went to college. June was right; chances of Nova settling down back in Riverside and wanting to live at home were slim. She wasn't afraid to live life like her mother. She had big hopes and dreams and would likely end up in Philadelphia or New York. Packing things would make it easier for her in the long run when she'd eventually be responsible for her own storage.

Farrah felt like she was invading her daughter's privacy each time she opened a drawer. If something was questionable, she simply moved it to a box labeled "miscellaneous". She focused on simpler tasks like all the folded clothes, shoes, and handbags; and then she addressed books and knick-knacks which were also easy to pack. June could hang her clothes in her own closet but the floor and shelf of Nova's closet would help.

After a few hours, it wasn't too bad. The boxes with Farrah's neatly handwritten labels were stacked. June would get the dresser in order to leave hers behind in the condo — Farrah couldn't drag it to the other room on her own though. That opened up a lot of the room for the rest of June's things that she didn't want renters to use.

The house may have been changing, but the person there wasn't ready to give up the life she had. She knew it had to be done. Farrah went to the kitchen to make a hot cup of herbal tea and call her daughter, but she got voicemail.

"Hi, honey. It's Mom. I don't know what to say here on voicemail. There's a lot going on that I need to talk to you about. Maybe your father has already called you. I don't know. I have a meeting tonight, but really need to talk to you. I love you. Just remember that."

June texted on her lunch break to make sure Farrah was functioning as best as could be expected. Instead of their usual long text sessions, Farrah kept things short. She wanted to soak in the tub and lie down. No amount of lavender oil would relax her. She hoped that wouldn't be forever though it definitely felt like it.

Fortunately, massage therapists and bodyworkers weren't held to dress codes of uncomfortable pencil skirts and pointy dress shoes. For a brainstorming session with only the staff, leggings and a couple of layered big shirts would do.

Farrah laid on her bed noting that two pillows were distinctly missing. She had changed the sheets the day before mainly because her pillowcase had enough tears and snot to be a runaway lab experiment on DNA. Other than expecting a call back from Nova, there was no one she thought she'd hear from. She felt compelled to hold onto her phone though. She kept opening up her photo galleries to look at pictures of her and Jackson together or him with Gordon. She never felt like she could equal his hotness. In her eyes, he was a ten and she was an average five at best. She considered herself a Plain Jane — a boring looking white woman with sandy hair over forty. She knew he lost interest in her ages ago. Once upon a time, he was everything she ever wanted in a husband. What the hell went so disastrously wrong?

She laid there intermittently crying, staring at her phone, and watching a sitcom hoping it would make her smile the slightest bit. Everything reminded her of him. She checked his social media every few minutes in case he updated. He didn't. But his profile at least retained "Jackson is married to Farrah Wethers" in the biography window.

The irrational power of social media grew to an obsession. She clicked back to her own profile and reviewed what she wrote about herself. As soon as Nova went to college, she was unlinked. Farrah's page listed her husband, an aunt, and a couple cousins in the family section. She wanted to make a profile for the cat believing his life was something people would read about before her own.

The last event listed in her milestones section was graduating from massage school. Being cleared of murder wasn't the sort of thing she felt needed memorializing publicly to people from high school she didn't care about. The snarky smartass side of her which was influenced by June, wanted to enter a milestone captioned: Officially became a bitter old woman with a cat companion. And under professional skills, she wanted to add: being depressed, crying, expert jumper to conclusions.

Until the past few years, everything seemed completely normal. Content even. No waves. Then their daughter went away to college and Farrah lost her job. The layoff? Could that really have been the spark that burned down their marriage? That's when Farrah made the biggest changes to her life which affected the entire family, mostly financially.

A couple quiet hours went by when finally, Nova called back. Farrah broke the news and fielded the questions she was comfortable with. When faced with, "Did Daddy cheat on you, Mom?" she didn't know how to say, "No, honey, I did." Farrah left it vague but mostly accurate telling her, no, Jackson hadn't cheated even though for a while she thought he had. She worried about what Jack's version would sound like when he spoke directly to Nova in their inevitable conversation.

She wanted to feel like she had a family again. Something had to fill the void.

CHAPTER THREE

MILES was curled up on the couch in a tight ball when it was time for Farrah to leave. She envied that cat. She wanted to come back in her next life as a chubby spoiled house cat with loving human companions. While she continued living her human existence, she forced herself to move through the motions of being a responsible adult.

June was at the gym trying to keep to her resolution to try something new. Kickboxing was going to be it, but Farrah had a feeling it wouldn't be a lasting commitment. She knew her friend preferred her exercise to come in the form of activities where she was doing something not in pretending to do something. June would've been riding horses or building snowmen before standing in a line with an instructor barking commands into a headset. She wanted new things and Farrah somehow still wanted old things.

The drive to Samantha's house gave Farrah time to listen a podcast interview of one of her favorite authors. She barely paid attention to it. Her thought processes weren't even alert to the curves in the road. It was more like being on auto-pilot even though she had been to the house once before (mindlessly following the GPS). The podcast gave her the feeling that she was with people who were talking about something other

13

than her marital trouble. The voice of Eliza Stewart spoke about how she was sick the month she wrote the first draft of her best seller and ended up tossing the whole thing and beginning again.

"I thought I couldn't possibly throw out the whole thing," Eliza Stewart said, "and it took days of struggling with the crap I created in order for me to realize that I had to slash and burn it. Raze it to the ground and start fresh. My story needed new life."

Okay, so maybe the author wasn't trying to speak to Farrah's wilted relationship, but the metaphor bit her in the ass anyway.

Jay and Samantha Waterston lived in an ostentatious development where the houses were too close together and an aerial view looked like a board game set. All the houses had three-car garages, most with basketball hoops. The shades of white siding were like a strip of paint samples: ivory, pearl, snowy, egg shell, and actual white. The personalities of the inhabitants were likely to match their cocoon exteriors.

"Come in." Jay greeted Farrah at the door. He directed her through the hallway and to the dining room where six practitioners sat around the long table that could fit twelve. "Can I get you something to drink?"

"Just water is fine. Thank you."

Small talk amongst the group lasted about fifteen minutes. Then Samantha decided to get started and anyone late could be brought up to speed.

"The reason I wanted to get as many of us together as possible is to brainstorm about ways to bring in business. I heard from a friend on the township planning committee that one of those new franchise massage chains is going to be opening up by next week in the strip mall on the highway. They will destroy independent therapists like yourselves and drive me out of business completely."

"I don't know anything about those places. What are they like?" asked Diane Phelps.

"They're cheap is what they're like. They offer people memberships like at a gym and they auto-charge people's credit cards whether or not they've been in for their appointments. It's a great business model and great way for the chain to make money, but I don't like to screw our clients. I want them to have quality services. We don't even charge for late cancelations. Never have and never want to." Samantha was fierce. She had a portfolio in front of her with a notebook covered in bullet points to address. Tucked into the leather cover were some of their brochures of services and informational facts.

Farrah wasn't business-minded and wanted to keep her mouth shut and ears open. But Samantha had a way of calling on everyone to get opinions.

"Well, I guess their therapists still have to be as trained as we are or they wouldn't be allowed to work, right?"

"Yes, Farrah, that's true. They have to meet the minimum requirements. Six hundred hours of education broken down into knowing the practical applications, ethics, and first aid. That doesn't mean they're offering what we are."

Christine, the therapist who had been at the spa since Samantha opened it and the busiest one of the bunch, explained what they had been discussing together for a few days.

"Take my services, for example. No one at Pinnacle Massage will be the type to travel to China to study in depth. Everything they do will be an add-on like in a hair salon."

15

"So you mean when I use my aromatherapy oils in my sessions, that's the sort of thing they'd charge extra for?" Farrah said.

"Exactly." Christine pulled out her own notes which looked like they were printed pages from a website. "I downloaded this information. What people get when they have their monthly massage is only a fifty-minute appointment and doesn't include anything like aromatherapy or the hot towels you do, Farrah. And speaking of, their hot stone massage is fifteen minutes shorter than ours so it looks like people are getting these big discounts when they aren't."

Samantha resumed the reins. "Customers there are getting fifty minutes of Swedish massage. They aren't getting neuromuscular therapy or myofascial release like we offer. We pad our appointment times so that there's time for people to get dressed and time for the rooms to be cleaned. So when Pinnacle Massage has commercials for massages that cost under fifty dollars, people are only thinking about the dollars not the services."

All the faces around the room carried the weight of worry. They didn't know how to be competitive in a lousy economy. Tourists and bridal parties were likely to be the only people indulging in expensive services so spas located in hotels and casinos paid off well for the staff. Running a small town business, however, was a different beast. Half of the appointment income went back to Riverside Wellness Spa, LLC to cover overhead like the real estate, utilities, advertising, and linen service. Lowering their rates was out of the question. Part-timers like Farrah barely made enough to fill their gas tanks for the week.

"Maggie will of course continue with the off-site events and she's going to be looking for people who want to help her expand that side of the business. I'm asking each of you to come up with two proposals for boosting business. It doesn't need to be elaborate - just good, solid ideas. Even the staff who couldn't make it tonight are going to be doing this. We need to be united in being successful. Now, I'll let Christine take over for the final agenda issue."

Christine explained that she was leaving on another trip to China for two weeks and would rather have some of her appointments covered by other practitioners who had the training instead of rescheduling them since it was so important to bring bodies into the bottom line. Farrah was assigned one pre-natal client and one hot stone session. Diane took the reflexology and neuromuscular therapy appointments. And Samantha split the rest of Christine's appointments with Jordan.

It was good news for Farrah who would get some guaranteed income. It still wasn't enough to buy food for the week and keep the lights on. She prayed her new living arrangement with June would solve those problems. She could still be a housewife. She would just be that for her best friend rather than her husband.

Before leaving, Farrah talked to Christine about the needs of the pregnant woman she'd be working on in her absence. Lenore Lexington was getting regular pre-natal massages for the past month. She booked Christine for bi-weekly appointments from the moment her doctor gave her the clearance. She was at eighteen weeks last time Christine saw her and barely showing.

"I blew up like a whale with my third," Christine said. "Lenore is tiny, but she has time to put on some weight."

Farrah had quite a number of pre-natal clients since they were often looking for appointments during the hours she preferred to work. Plus, they usually had the best medical attention and as long as they had a doctor's note, Farrah didn't have to charge them sales tax. It wasn't what she expected to specialize in; it just happened that way. She could still use her athletic wellness techniques on pregnant women who were particularly active to integrate both areas of interest. Pregnant people with back and hip pain needed assisted stretching even if they weren't particularly active.

*****

"How was the meeting?" June sat on the couch, her long hair wrapped up in a towel turban fresh from the shower. She had a bowl of soy ice cream in her hands that Miles was eyeing like prey.

"Interesting. How was kickboxing?" Farrah left her purse and keys on the dining room table and took a seat in a chair next at the end of the couch close to June.

"I think I hate it. But I'll give it a month. The instructor is hot so at least there's something to look at." The cat pawed at her bowl hoping June wasn't paying attention. "So tell me, did they welcome you back with open arms or what?"

"Sort of. Christine is going away for a couple of weeks for more training so I'm getting two of her appointments. We split up her sessions so no one would have to be canceled."

Farrah brought June up to speed regarding the unfortunate news about Pinnacle Massage opening up in the same town.

"They'll put us out of business. It's only a matter of time." She leaned over and took the spoon right out of June's hand to help herself to the ice cream. "Is there any of this left? I think this is what I want for dinner."

"I left half the container for you."

Farrah prepared a bowl of the vanilla soy ice cream, drizzling it with a dark chocolate syrup and topping with a maraschino cherry.

"If you don't mind, I'm taking this to bed. You're okay, right?"

"We're fine, aren't we?" She rubbed Miles on the head. "I'll be up for a while. I don't want to miss *Scandal*. Some of the actors live tweet during it."

Farrah turned on the TV in her bedroom and devoured her untraditional dinner. She changed into a huge oversized t-shirt for bed. After brushing her hair and teeth, she closed the door most of the way, leaving it ajar for the cat. She was oddly worried he'd choose June's company over hers despite all their years together. She didn't have a husband next to her anymore and the lump of a cat could remind her that she was still lovable. She hadn't been feeling worthy of love for a while.

The fatigue wasn't enough for her to fall asleep. The late meeting had her stressed and ramped up with energy, but not the kind of productive energy that could be used to accomplish anything. It was the kind to keep her brain from settling down.

CHAPTER FOUR

LENORE Lexington was a petite young woman covered head-to-toe in purple, a stark contrast to the earthy shades of tans, golds, and maroon in the Riverside Wellness Spa lobby. The modesty of her tight leggings and billowing clouds of fabric from the dress, aged her by a couple decades. Her smile radiated life — a force or aura or something unexplainable that seemed to float through the room when Farrah came out to greet her.

"Did you complete your intake form when you began seeing Christine?"

"I did. Oh and there should be a doctor's note on file from my ob-gyn saying I'm okay to get massages." Lenore's smile was captivating. She reminded Farrah of a maiden from an Arthurian tale about princesses and knights.

"Okay then. Let's get you started. Come in my room and I'll explain how my sessions are."

Farrah lead the way to Room Five, her assigned home for the day. She specifically requested never to have Room Three again after a client died in there. She wasn't guaranteed to always get Room Five in case there was a conflict with any other therapist who may be booked first.

Farrah had to carry her supplies in a basket and kept her reference books in the back of the office suite with her name in them.

She explained her routine for pregnant clients and double-checked to see if Lenore could be allergic to any of her products. Everything was agreeable, so Farrah began with Lenore on her back. Despite the barely noticeable baby bump, Farrah was too nervous to have her prone. Pregnancy isn't an illness, but Farrah's anxiety about her skills probably could be considered one.

It's just a massage. It's just a massage. It's just a massage.

She repeated that in her head hoping the voice would get through to her own psyche. Confidence was something Farrah couldn't wait to possess. She had spent a couple years working on a variety of bodies and plenty of them were pregnant women. The responsibility for someone else's possible future kid made it that much more worrisome.

"Have you experienced any swelling in your fingers or ankles? It's pretty early on, but I figured I'd ask."

"Umm no, I haven't noticed swelling yet. I get the absolute worst morning sickness though. And the thing is it comes at night not in the morning. My boyfriend says it's because I'm not eating right."

Farrah stretched one of Lenore's wrists, moving it all around and then stretched each finger. The absence of any engagement ring was silently noted — not that it mattered. A lot of people were non-traditional. But it was something she wasn't used to seeing with most people in their conservative, suburban demographic.

"You've talked to your doctor about the nausea, I hope?"

"Yeah, we're keeping an eye on it. If I can't keep anything at all down, then I have to be admitted and get checked out. But most of the day, I'm fine."

Farrah skipped the abdominals but made sure to work all the hip joints. With an expanding pelvis, there was more pressure on the lower joints from the constantly changing pregnant body.

"I had Reiki done a few days ago. I don't care what people say about energy work being a hoax. It makes me feel better. Plus, Joel paid for it. He pays for these sessions too. Says I should do whatever it takes to feel my best and deliver us a healthy baby."

"I love energy work too. Acupressure. Jin Shin Jyutsu. Reiki. It's never going to harm someone, so people who don't like it, shouldn't discourage anyone from treatments if it's what they want. It should all be complimentary. As long as you have a doctor who says it's fine, you should keep doing it." Farrah moved on to Lenore's feet which were adorned in adorable toe rings and blue nail polish. "Who did you see for the Reiki if you don't mind my asking?"

"Oh, my friend Star. One of my part-time jobs is doing tarot readings at her shop, Star's Blessings."

"I love that shop! It's filled with such interesting things. I'd love to know more sometime. But you don't have to keep talking if you want to rest."

"I love talking. I feel so isolated sometimes. I live alone still — Joel hasn't moved in. My jobs at the book store and the new age shop give me lots of contact with people though. I love it!"

Lenore was shifted to lie on her left side properly bolstered with pillows to support her limbs. It gave Farrah access to her back and glutes safely.

Farrah added some essential oils to the cream. The fragrances of rosewood, ylang ylang, lavender, lemon, and a few other carefully blended herbs filled the small room.

22

"Oh that smells so nice." Lenore was facing away, but Farrah could tell she was smiling just by her tone. "I drink so much ginger tea, sometimes I forget what other scents are out there."

Farrah thought back to the last time she actually went out to a Thai restaurant. It had been quite a while. She told Lenore that she also loved the spicy tang of ginger tea and how she used to order a Pad dish that had a lot of the sautéed root in it also.

"We're naming the baby Ginger if it's a girl which I'm pretty sure it is. You know how those ultrasounds are. They've gotten better ones recently, but the little babies still need to be positioned just right to see." Lenore's hands went instinctively to her belly while she beamed a radiance that Farrah recognized from the days when she was young and in love.

"That's beautiful. You're all done for today. Take your time getting dressed. I'll get you some water and meet you out front."

Farrah sat at the reception desk to enter the details of her appointment noting significant anomalies like Lenore's nausea, possible reasons to be concerned about her eating, and that she holds down two jobs where she's on her feet a lot. She also included the list of products she used with a notation that the client responded positively to them — no adverse reactions. Allergies could be unknown or spontaneously pop up so it was always safest to give a lot of details rather than brief meaningless notes especially on a regular client.

"Here's some water. Stay hydrated and please eat well. Your boyfriend is right about that. You need to nourish yourself and your baby."

The little paper cup of water was small enough for Lenore to drink completely in one gulp.

"Thank you for everything. I enjoyed our time so much. I'm all loose and relaxed now, but I have to go to work."

"Which one?"

"Star's shop. You should come by sometime soon. I'd love to give you a reading."

Farrah never cared about religion much, but she embraced the magical thinking of spirituality for the way it made her feel. Faith couldn't be meaningless. She believed even if all it gave was comfort, it served a purpose. Jackson would have scolded her about wasting money for even considering a spiritual adviser.

"You know something, I think I will. My friend June gets home around five-thirty. Will you be there then?"

"For appointments, I make myself available. Two of you? Half an hour each?" Lenore bundled up in her long coat and pulled out earmuffs from the pocket.

"We'll be there."

*****

The bells above the door made a soft jingle when Farrah lead June into Star's Blessings new age shop and botanica. The shop was so jam-packed, they had to be violating ADA laws. A baby buggy couldn't fit in there no less a wheelchair. Farrah was afraid that if she turned around too quickly, she'd knock several hundred dollars' worth of merchandise onto the floor.

A long haired calico cat in the front window didn't so much greet them as monitor their entrance like a sentry. She must have felt they were acceptable customers because she turned away and resumed her gawking at the passersby on the sidewalk.

"Hi! Welcome to Star's Blessings. Is this your first time here?" The woman behind the counter finished ringing up a young couple who had a small shopping bag filled with incense sticks and packets of dried herbs.

Farrah introduced herself and June while they slowly made their way around the couple trying to exit. "I've only been in here once before. We're here to get readings by Lenore."

"Oh right. You're on the schedule. She should be finished with the person in there now in about five minutes." They were instructed to look around and ask questions on anything they found interesting or confusing.

"Wow, how do you sell hard copy books in this market with a big box store a few miles away?" June's interest in the economy was probably not what Star had in mind when said she'd be happy to answer questions.

"Well, it's not easy. Everything is available online too. But we cater to authors we know personally who have come in here for workshops and signings and for ones I've met in my travels. I think it matters a great deal when our community can support from within."

Farrah whispered to June, "Happy now? She handled you more gracefully than someone at a big box store."

"She said to ask questions." June shrugged it off. "In fact, I like what she said. I believe we should support local artisans and businesses as long as we can afford to."

"Well that's another story." Farrah still didn't consider her roommate's financial resources to be a joint asset.

Lenore came through a curtain separating her cozy nook from the main part of the store. She spoke parting words to a short Hispanic woman who was crying. Lenore took the woman's hands in hers even though the customer was gripping balled up tissues. They hugged and the woman made her way to the display of candles without making eye contact with anyone else.

"Farrah! You made it. I'm so glad you came."

Lenore extended her hand to Farrah and then tried to duplicate the effort for June, but she was too busy observing the Hispanic woman, too curious to be polite.

"I guess I'll go first while June keeps looking around."

Lenore showed Farrah into the closet sized room. On the round table, there was a tiny lamp, Lenore's deck of tarot cards, a few crystals, and an empty tea cup. The space was contained by indigo curtains and black scarves with white fairy lights crisscrossing between branches and fake vines on the ceiling.

Farrah removed her bulky coat and scarf but left her knitted hat on because she knew the static electricity would have made her already moppy hair look ridiculous.

Lenore instructed Farrah to shuffle the deck of tarot cards thoroughly. When she felt she was done, she asked her to make three piles and put them back in any order.

"Let me give you a little explanation as we begin. This deck is pretty different than some others out there. It's based on elements of nature and mythology. And for me, I try to interpret them using my intuition and their folklore. There are all kinds of plants, for example, and the herbs and flowers have all kinds of history to them for healing or magical uses or as omens. The one thing I apologize for in advance is that most cards that are available follow some old-fashioned rules on gender and sexuality. So if I see a card that comes up as an older man, it could truthfully mean a woman. I believe we aren't beholden to strict labels, if you know what I mean. And other decks deal with reverse or upside-down interpretations. This deck doesn't do that."

"Yeah, okay, sure." Farrah had an inkling of what the mystic was talking about, but she wasn't a hundred percent certain. She was there to be entertained and hopefully enlightened by the young woman. If things didn't make sense, she wasn't writing it off as a waste. She was there to relax and maybe have thirty minutes of enjoyment.

The last thing Lenore said before beginning was that Farrah could take notes if she wanted and she handed her a small pad and a pen. The cards were spread with the first one in the center and six cards around it.

"Hmm... Chiron. The Knight of Grains. You're going to be focusing on your health and wellbeing. He's a good sign for this and when you make a call to see an expert about it, you'll know you've made a good choice."

"I don't have any money to see experts about anything. Your fee is the biggest indulgence I've allowed myself in a long time."

"You will be fine. Now let's look at the reason why Chiron is your guide today. In your roots you have the major arcana of Orchis, the magical orchid. Even though we see the flower as a whole to be beautiful, these specks inside indicate that there's damages and wounds which have piled up one after another, year after year. The Orchis is telling you to use your knowledge and be wise so that you can be free."

Lenore told her that there would be daily struggles soon which will cause Farrah to change strategy before being victorious. After the long transition, she would face what the number thirteen card said would be visible change and the end of a situation.

"Well, I guess that's most likely going to be my divorce. It could also mean the business. I shouldn't say much, but the spa isn't doing well and we don't know how to keep the doors open. Basically, my life is chaos."

"Let's see what the harvest says. Hmm... the Three of Flowers. Financially, things will work out. I can't tell if that's about the business though. Flowers are more about love. So if you're worried that your divorce will leave you in poverty, I believe you'll pull through with a plan that works."

Farrah wanted to believe her so badly. She wanted to have all the faith available to feel safe and secure. The next card read to her, Lenore described as the compost of her life.

"This tells you what you need to get rid of in order to move forward. You pulled the Waterlily. It's about regaining the love of a partner who was unfaithful. You need to show both diplomacy and harmony in order to accept this situation."

"I've tried, Lenore. Oh how I've tried. The guilt kills me more each day."

"I'm sorry to hear that. Your final card is the result of the work you'll put in. It's the Valet of Flowers showing the Danaide. They were known for killing their husbands. This tells me that whether your situation is based on a useless fight or truly a dangerous situation, you'll face more discord. Remember the compost on which you are growing. You need to make peace with yourself and find your dignity because you could lose your self-worth from these fights. After all is said and done in your marriage, what your ex-spouse thinks of you doesn't matter. It's a new time to harvest and grow a new version of yourself that you can love."

Lenore handed Farrah a tissue which surprised her. She didn't realize she had tears running down her cheeks. She was told to sit for a minute to breathe and ground herself before trying to stand up with all those emotions whirling through her. When Farrah was ready, she left the cozy nook through the curtains. Lenore took a short break to stretch and use the bathroom before beginning June's reading.

"Wow. You're crying. Was it that good or that bad?"

"I'm okay, I guess. It was just so remarkable. How could those pieces of paper tell that much about me. It's bizarre, I swear! And she knew things. She just knew them."

"After this we'll go the cafe and you can give me the details."

When June came out of the nook after her reading, she wasn't crying like Farrah. She looked like a deer caught in headlights. Something said in there shocked her.

"What happened? What did she say?"

June shook her head to come back to reality. "She told me to call my mother. That it was important. I haven't spoken to my mother in years. I don't know if I want to."

"Well, you don't have to. It's a suggestion."

"No. There was something deep in the way she said it. It sounded like something I couldn't avoid any longer."

"Okay. Tell me the rest when we get out of here."

They were about to pay for their readings when Lenore came over to the register with a pink candle. She gave it to Farrah in a small paper bag.

"You'll want to burn this on the night when the moon is waxing, after the new moon." Lenore rang Farrah up for the reading and then applied her own employee discount for the candle.

They got outside and June still looked a little stunned.

"Did she tell you the name of the tarot deck she was using?"

"The name? No, I didn't realize they had names. She said it was a nature deck."

June fished inside her coat pocket for the keys and pressed the remote start button. "She called it the Tarot of Hellen. Farrah, Hellen is my mother's name."

CHAPTER FIVE

AT their favorite coffee shop, Toast & Roast, the barista prepared Farrah's dark roast, hand-poured drip with a dusting of cinnamon on top, almond milk and agave and June's peppermint skinny latte.

"You haven't talked about your mother since then. It's been years, babe. Maybe it is time to figure out if you can patch things up."

"I spent a long time soul searching and trying to forgive her. I thought it was behind me. I thought my life would no longer involve her. Now, all those memories are flooding back."

It wasn't like June not to look Farrah in the eye the way she was. She gazed at the coffee cup then watched the line of people at the counter. Farrah recognized the signs of nervousness. She oftentimes had them herself.

"A lot of time has passed. Maybe there's new information. Maybe she's too afraid to call you and tell you what you've been waiting to hear."

"I know I don't acknowledge my roots much, but what Hellen did made me obsessed for a while. I had to distance myself. I had to create a new version of myself."

Farrah reached over and put her hand on top of June's still gripping her cup. "Maybe it's not a new version of you. Maybe it's a more complete version of you."

"I searched for a couple of years for my birth father and my half-sister. I don't even know what country they're in. Han Kwan-ho could be anywhere. He could be using an anglicized name. I don't even know my sister's name."

"Do you still talk to your dad? Jae-sung, I mean."

"I do. Not often. For some reason, I'm not as angry with him about keeping this family secret. He married my mother and raised me. I feel like he was noble where she was deceitful. I don't know. I can't make sense of it."

The cup was empty, but Farrah kept her hand on it. The void where her phone usually was needed to be filled with something.

"How do people stayed married through that kind of turmoil and drama? Jack and I made each other miserable."

"Honey, it's not like couples have much choice. Every household needs to be two income and people can't just leave no matter how much they want to."

"Speaking of incomes and surviving, what about Lenore? Can you believe she manages to have her own place on shitty retail wages?"

"Maybe she gets help from someone. We don't know her that well. I need pie. Do you want anything?"

Farrah declined and June went back to the counter to get a generous serving of a deep dish Dutch apple pie embellished with caramel drizzled around the plate. Farrah wanted it once she saw it, but refrained. She may not have had anyone to impress with her figure, but she couldn't afford a new wardrobe if she put on another five pounds. She was making due with a few discount store staples now that she wasn't wearing office attire every day.

As if by fate, Lenore entered Toast & Roast to order herbal tea and a bagel. June almost collided with her and asked her to join them.

"I have about thirty minutes before I have to get to my other job. I offered to cover for a coworker from seven to closing so he could pick up his daughter from a school thing."

"Wow. You run yourself ragged, don't you?" June jumped right into personal questions without so much as a preamble.

Lenore smiled and said she was going to work as much as her body allowed her to before the baby arrived. Sixty hours or more a week was her average so she could save up as much as possible.

"Hopefully I won't have to wear myself out like this for too much longer. Joel will eventually get us a place together and he'll be so great as a dad. I just have to wait."

"For what?" Since Pandora's box was opened, Farrah didn't see any reason to hold back either.

"I really shouldn't say." Lenore looked around. "Um. No one knows this, not even Star and I don't have any other close friends. But, the truth is… Joel is still married."

Red flags went up all around Farrah's mind and she knew telepathically that June had the same reaction.

"He's getting a divorce. He really is, but because he has a lot of stocks and funds and things like that which I don't understand, not to mention things like their house and cars — he said it would be complicated to work out all their assets. But he promised me it would be done by the time our baby is born."

"You're in your second trimester now."

June laid out some truths. "Lenore, if his estate is that complicated, it's not going to be resolved in three months. Not unless he's already in the middle of the mediation process."

Farrah hoped to take a gentler approach. "Sweetie, has he filed? Has she been served already?"

"Well, no. Not yet. But he said I shouldn't worry because the stress I'm under is already more than I should have. I have to trust in him."

"As one of your healthcare providers, what did he mean about the level of stress you have? Is there anything more than the amount of hours you work? Is there something else I should have known about?" Farrah probably shouldn't have asked in front of June, but their conversation was casual and friendly.

"I don't know if it's anything. I told you whatever was relevant that we're monitoring. Usual stuff: blood pressure, sugar, the fetal development." Lenore looked down and shook her head ever-so slightly.

"And?" June pressed.

"And I had Star give me a reading. She uses a different kind of deck. One that has a lot more negative interpretations when the cards give warnings."

She had been tense, but Farrah loosened up when she realized Lenore's concern was about something read in tarot cards.

"One of the cards was an inverted queen of pentacles. Along with other cards around it, Star said I should be cautious about things that could lead to miscarriage." The young woman's worry was all over her otherwise flawless face.

"Oh, sweetie. As much as I loved your cards and the reading you gave me," Farrah said, "you can't allow them to make medical decisions for you."

34

June chimed in, "Besides, that's a vague statement. All pregnant people should be careful. I mean, they're not fragile glass statues, but still. All of them should be careful not to do anything extreme or dangerous or slack off on their health checkups."

Lenore sipped the tea in the travel mug she brought in for a refill. "I know, guys. But the cards are important to me. Other people turn to churches and sermons and Bible lessons. This is our thing. Our candles. Our incense. Our divination. It's what we do. I'm sorry outsiders think of it so lightly that they can brush it off." She stood up, but Farrah and June apologized quickly before she walked out.

"Were we terrible jerks just now?" June said.

"Yes and no. We're concerned for her health. Maybe we could have said so more delicately."

"What about all the bull her boyfriend is feeding her? A married man that gets a mistress pregnant and then swears he'll leave his wife? Come on."

"Oldest lie in the history of romance."

They walked back to June's SUV parked on Center Street. They had to side step three pigeons enjoying a cranberry scone. Gentrified suburban pigeons.

"Do you want to talk more about Hellen and your fathers?"

The ignition turned over with a delicate hum. There were so many lights and switches on the dashboard, Farrah called it the *Enterprise*. June corrected her and said if anything, it would be *Voyager*, the *Star Trek* spacecraft with a female captain at the helm.

"I'm surprised you know that."

"Hey, I didn't always watch dramas about spoiled rich people. Plus, I'm Asian. A bit of nerd is expected or racist people get disappointed."

They made plans to sit on the couch together with a bottle of wine and the laptop. Internet searches on common names were difficult, nearly impossible, unless you had something to narrow it down like a city or place of employment. June didn't have much of anything to go on.

"I know it's a long shot, but maybe I should register on one of those adoption websites where parents and kids can try to find each other. I mean, my circumstances aren't quite the same and it'll probably be fruitless, but it's something. There are so many sites now than when I looked before."

"It can't hurt. The only thing that may be unfortunate is if you get any false matches. It could be really emotional if you got your hopes up and then DNA proved it wasn't a match."

June's chipped peacock blue fingernails clicked away at the keyboard. Farrah took the moments of interlude to check her social networks and it only depressed her more. Jackson wasn't one to share any emotional updates on his profiles. He used it for the occasional proud father moments and posts about politics, especially local issues. And, of course, more pictures of his dog than the two of them. It was like he never wanted to acknowledge her publicly.

"Hey, there's a section in here that's about reconnecting with estranged siblings for people who aren't looking for their birth parents. This would probably make more sense if I knew anything about my sister. I don't know where she was born or even when."

"Would your mother know?"

"I don't know. She might. But it's not like she's open about any of it. She kept this family secret for decades."

With nothing more possible to do that night, they closed the laptop and turned in. Farrah hugged her pillow and cried herself to sleep with Miles curled up in the crook of her knees.

CHAPTER SIX

EVEN though she was incapable of sleeping late, Farrah wanted to stay in bed. It was pointless though. The logic pathways of her mind that still worked convinced the rest of her to get out of bed, do her basic bathroom necessities, then venture to the kitchen. She fed the cat and started the coffee. June wasn't likely to wake for the next couple hours.

Miles sat comfortably in his mini greenhouse style window and showed off the yoga skills necessary to clean himself. For two seconds a neighborhood cardinal caught his attention, but not enough for Miles to put his hind leg down.

There weren't any appointments on Farrah's schedule for the weekend even with picking up some of Christine's clients. Her eyes panned across the shelves of cookbooks. The thought of cooking and food shopping didn't interest her either.

There was nothing to occupy her time. Her thoughts were consumed by the failure of her marriage and the loneliness which had been her burden for too long. She was ashamed to think that she had been lonely while living with a spouse. Other people were truly alone. They were all by themselves. But she became undesirable to Jack — she assumed it was her natural aging or the resentment over her career change. She grew out of love with his judgmental personality too. Whatever it was properly called, it fundamentally came down to two people who didn't belong together occupying the same space. Without his presence and his possessions, she felt like his ghost was there. Most of the tension was gone, for sure, but there was an invisible miasma that kept her from feeling free.

The computer in the corner of the living room that she used for home office space called to her. The space was nothing more than an offshoot of the foyer which should normally be used for a mudroom with coat hooks and dirty shoes. She revamped it herself with paint colors that made her happy and kept the white glossy trim. Her desk, such as it was, was only an extra wide wooden shelf. The chair was one she bought at a yard sale, repainted it, and tied a floral patterned cushion to the seat.

With her coffee mug on its electric warming plate, she was ready and opened up her browser. It defaulted to her inbox and calendar which she ignored and navigated to LetMeShare, the popular social networking site.

The LMS site as it was often abbreviated when microblogging, became a huge part of divorce cases because of the ease with which it allowed public displays of stupid behavior. People would use the geo-tagging to check into locations like hotels or restaurants which seemed innocent enough; that is until a suspicious wife could see that another woman on her husband's friend's list was also checked in there posting a photo of her dinner. There was plenty of harmful lashing out too and despite the ability to delete posts, there was always enough time for another person to screen capture it and present it in mediation or in front of a judge.

Farrah bore the guilt of her own actions, but that didn't mean she felt Jackson was completely without fault in their separation. He pulled away from her years ago and his lack of support with her career choice had constantly caused her emotional pain. She was angry too and sometimes, though not always, she believed she had the right to be.

Jackson's LMS page didn't give her any new information, but she kept digging. Maybe it wasn't the healthiest thing to do, but she was alone and grasping at straws wondering if they still had anything to salvage. She viewed the profiles of several of his friends to see if there were any women who may be spending time with him that he wasn't openly talking about. She found one.

A woman named Heather O'Hara seemed a bit flirty in her photo comments. According to her profile she also worked at Wharton & Finkle where Jackson worked. She was beautiful and only thirty-three which made Farrah burn with jealousy. A significant amount of her photos showed off her bikini collection, her athletic butt, and perfect abs sculpted in her dark skin.

Farrah didn't realize that her grip on the mouse was so tight she was cramping her own hand. The other was unconsciously placed on her squishy belly roll.

On a photo of Gordon, Heather had commented: "Our dogs should have a play date! Peeta loves the beach at the lake!"

Peeta? Dear god, she reads too? It's not fair. You shouldn't get to look like that and be smart too.

She snooped more. These networks made it easy unless someone had their profile locked down and private. Heather O'Hara didn't. Her life was an open book. She was active, outgoing, always smiling and well-educated. Her graduate degree from Rutgers was just one more thing that made Farrah feel inferior.

There was a photo album from a company event. The description said it was a holiday luncheon. Women were dressed up more than their average casual office attire in a lot of Christmas red and green. The finalists of the ugly sweater contest were in a series of photos showing off their giant grins. Jackson popped up in the background of a lot of the pictures, but he was only the main subject of two — one with Heather and one by himself wearing a Santa hat.

The online snooping ended when Farrah heard the hum of her phone vibrate on the desk. She didn't recognize the number, but answered it anyway. If it was a scam caller, she had a litany of ridiculous things to say to them.

"Farrah? It's Lenore Lexington. Can you talk?"

"Sure. I'm not doing anything." She closed the browser window on the desktop. It wasn't common for a client to call after a visit. In fact, she couldn't remember it ever happening before.

"I was having more morning sickness, but there were some other symptoms too. I have a call in to my doctor, but I wanted to check on some things with you too." Lenore asked Farrah to go over the products and ingredients that could have possibly caused adverse reactions like an allergy.

"There's nothing toxic in them. I recently had my eyes opened to some of the misleading practices that allow companies to label cosmetics in questionable ways. I've done what I can to make sure all my products are nut free and most are as animal friendly as possible. Do you have a specific allergy that maybe you didn't remember when we talked about it before your session?"

"Not that I can think of. I'm not the healthiest person around. I know that. I was always called sickly. I'm anemic and Joel says I don't eat well, but I'm far from starving."

"I'm not saying an essential oil couldn't affect you the wrong way, but I don't think it's likely unless you're allergic and that would normally present as a rash or hives. There are other ways they affect people because of the olfactory sense. People have strong connections to their memories, even buried ones, which can come back to the forefront of their minds because of a smell. Is your dizziness maybe something like that? Did you sleep poorly or have any bad dreams?"

Lenore couldn't think of anything that fit what Farrah was talking about. She admitted that she felt stressed because of her boyfriend Joel. He had made promises to her that he'd be there for her and he hadn't been.

"Oh, honey, I think you're under a lot of stress. I'm sorry he's not living up to his end of things. Stress can take an incredible toll on the body. People don't like to think so, but hormones get released and go haywire and then you have headaches, upset stomachs, and tight muscles that clamp down on your joints. It's just something that's hard to separate the real science from the pseudo-science. But believe me, stress can cause a lot of problems."

Farrah feared that her attempts to sound comforting yet concerned were only adding to the poor woman's anxiety.

"There is something I didn't tell you during our appointment."

More red flags were thrown on the imaginary sports scene playing out in Farrah's mind.

"Go on."

"It's about my doctor. You know how I said I've been carefully monitored?"

"Yes." This didn't sound good.

"Joel is my doctor. He's my obstetrician and my boyfriend. That's why I can say that I'm getting the best care possible. I don't like people to know because they react badly to pretty much anything I say about him."

Farrah knew exactly why people would react badly to details about Joel. It's not that doctors don't treat family members — they do as long as they can think clearly about it and not violate the policies of their hospitals. This guy, though, was already feeding Lenore a load of crap about leaving his wife and making excuses for why he hasn't moved in with her yet.

"Um... okay. Well, I don't think it's my place to have an opinion on your boyfriend also being your doctor. If he's board certified and you trust him with your care, that's what matters."

"It sounds like you have a 'but' coming. But what?"

"I am concerned about what kind of boyfriend he is, not what kind of doctor he is. Although a doctor that has an affair with his patient doesn't sound like a very ethical doctor either. However, he could still be good at his job, clinically speaking."

"Look, I didn't call you for a lecture. I get plenty of those from Star. She's my boss and my best friend. Pretty much my only real friend. She's my family. And I promise you, she's said everything you're thinking. Now you can see why I never told her he was also married."

"Why did you call, Lenore? Not that I mind the conversation. I'm happy to talk to you anytime."

While Lenore talked, Farrah open up the browser window again. She typed into the search bar "Joel + ob-gyn + Hunterdon" and found a lot of hits. Lenore's Joel was most likely Dr. Joel DeSantos who had offices in two towns near Riverside and he had privileges at the local hospital. As far as she knew, the only infraction he was guilty of was having sex with a patient.

"Hang on a minute. Was Joel your doctor before you got pregnant? Is that how you met?"

"Yes. I'd seen him for a couple years for regular exams. But it's not like he asked me out while my feet were in the stirrups! I ran into him at the book store. Rather he ran into me while I was working. We got to talking and it became a regular, casual thing. He would come visit me all the time."

"But you felt like you couldn't fight the attraction to him or something like that?"

"Yes, how did you know?"

The surprise in Lenore's voice would not get the crystal clear truth out of Farrah who knew all about the temptations of handsome, charming men.

"Lenore, if you're not feeling well and if your ob-gyn isn't someone you want to see about it, the best thing I can suggest is that you call your regular family doctor or go to the ER. Are you afraid to tell Joel that you don't feel well?"

She explained that "afraid" wasn't what she'd call it. Lenore said she felt like a burden on him and he had already said she made too big a deal about her first trimester symptoms. He believed that she had them, but that she complained too much when they were perfectly normal things for the body to go through.

"Oh, sweetie, maybe you need to speak to a women's crisis counselor or something. I think you should be getting all the support and compassion possible from your doctor and especially from the father of your baby. The fact that it's the same person does make this more alarming. He's lucky no one has reported him to the board."

Farrah heard movement upstairs. A few moments later, June descended the stairs next to Farrah's office area.

"What's going on?"

Farrah pointed to the phone up to her ear and held up one finger. She'd be another minute and then fill her in on the details. She told Lenore to call her back at the end of the day to let her know how she was doing.

"I know I'm breaking my own rules about client privacy, but you will not believe what I just learned!"

"Are you going to tell me? Do I need my coffee first?"

"I can't really tell you. However, if you happen to put two and two together by my vague statements that don't disclose anyone's identity, well, there's nothing I can do about that, is there?"

"No. Okay, go ahead." June lead the way into the dining room so that she could fix herself coffee from the mini barista bar.

"Get your milk. I'll wait for you." Farrah sat at the dining room table almost ready for her second cup.

June took the seat at the head of the table, sipped once, and said she was ready to hear the vague gossip.

"I have a pregnant client who's baby daddy is not only married, but also her doctor that had an affair with her!"

"Oh. My. God."

CHAPTER SEVEN

"NOW what?" Farrah said when her phone chimed again. It was a text from her daughter.

"Something wrong?" June scrolled through her own phone as well out of habit. Scrolling and scrolling without even absorbing anything just to see if there was something that would catch her eye.

"No. It's Janice."

"Nova."

"I'm sorry, but I named her Janice before she came out of my womb. I, more than anyone, try to respect her new name, but I will forget."

"Edit the contact info on your phone so that you get used to seeing it every time she calls or texts. Anyway…"

Farrah realized June had a point and edited the entry so that it would say Nova instead of Janice. "She wants to come home for a long weekend to go through her things here."

"What's wrong with that?"

"Nothing. Technically." Farrah explained that she missed her daughter and enjoyed that they could occasionally spend time together as adults, but she hasn't seen her since dropping the bomb about the separation. "She'll probably have a million questions and that will probably lead to arguments. I don't want to fight with her. I don't need her taking sides. I just want her to know that we tried pretty damn hard to stay together and it still wasn't enough."

"I think you'll have to have this moment sooner or later. May as well rip off the Band-Aid and get it over with."

"Oh no. Oh no!"

"What?" June looked up from her own screen after Farrah's voice became more alarmed.

"She's here. Already! She went directly to Frank's last night to have dinner with her father. She spent the night at a friend's house. She's coming here right now!"

"Does she know I moved into her room?"

"Yes, I told her about how I packed up her things. Maybe with an extra set of muscle, she'll help us set you up in the other room now."

"It would be nice to unpack things, that's for sure. But sweetie, if you guys need to be alone and hash things out loudly, I can take off."

June was more family than most people's blood relatives. If there was going to be a family fight, she'd find out all the details anyway. If she got to witness it, perhaps she could be a referee. They had about fifteen minutes to brace themselves.

Farrah watched as Nova's head swiveled to take in all the changes to the house. Shit became real. Jackson's things were gone and June's things were there.

"I like your serenity fountain," Nova said.

"Thanks. It's June's. She didn't have much in the way of decorating, but I always liked that piece." Farrah's words drifted off when she realized her daughter didn't really care about the fountain at all. The ice-breaker was the best they could expect since it wasn't aggressive.

June waved from the living room and said hello with other mundane, "haven't seen you in so long" small talk.

"So," Nova kept a cautious distance from both women, "Dad says you're a lesbian now. With her."

"No. No. I wish he hadn't filled your head with lies." Farrah knew her daughter was the most open-minded person in her life. And despite June expressing her love for Farrah previously, no one was being converted, as if that were possible. "That wouldn't bother you anyway. Why do you seem upset?"

"Are you honestly telling me that you two being so close and moving in together isn't a romantic relationship?"

"Hey look, I respect the shock you must be going through right now," June said, "but your father is also living with my ex-husband. Did you ask him if they were gay?"

"No. Because my father wouldn't lie to me. And Dad and Frank are nothing like the two of you. You're practically attached. You're more involved in each other's lives than married people."

"Well that ought to show you why marriages fail, including ours," Farrah said. "June is my closest friend and she is family by choice not by obligation."

June stayed planted where she was even though Farrah tried to close the gap towards Nova.

"Not that it's any of your business, but I am bisexual and your mother is straight. We are not a couple. I'm only telling you in the spirit of openness and being part of this strange nuclear family because I want to be here."

"Uh huh."

Farrah thought it could've been a whole lot worse. Indifference and perhaps disbelief were preferred to anger.

"What else has your father said?"

"Oh, he said you had an affair. I assumed it was this right here."

The defeat and shame took hold of Farrah once again. Her head dropped, her eyes closed. She grabbed the back of a chair for stability and took a seat.

"Sit. Please."

"So it's true?"

"Yes." Farrah proceeded to have the most difficult conversation of her life. It didn't matter how strongly she tried to convey that they had been unhappy for a long time. No child who believed their parents were in love wanted to face the reality that they might not be.

After a lot of crying and yelling, Nova stormed up the stairs to see the status of her possessions. Then she yelled about that and threw boxes around to release the tension inside her. Farrah kept asking if she wanted help or what they could do to assist, but Nova didn't want them near her. She carried several of the boxes and armfuls of clothes to her car.

"Where are you taking all that?"

"I don't know but not here. I'm taking as much as I can because there's no way in hell I'm ever moving back in here. I'll see if Dad has room. It can all stay in his goddamn garage for all I care!"

"I do not want you driving angry!"

"Go to hell, Mom."

Nova sped off. At least she clicked on her seatbelt first. Farrah texted Jack to let him know that their daughter was furious and probably on her way over to him. She added sarcastic, "thanks for telling her I'm a lying, cheating lesbian instead of letting me talk to her," which only resulted in him lashing out back at her.

"Put the damn phone down." June tried to be the voice of reason. She knew nothing good would come of the two of them harassing each other, especially not if it was in writing. "He can screen capture all this, you know?"

"I don't care! I don't care about anything anymore! It's not like he can take anything from me. I don't have anything!"

June took the phone from her and turned it off and swore it would only be for fifteen minutes before she could turn it back on. Farrah was not reassured that Nova would calm down in due time regardless of June's effort to get through to her. Farrah's family was ruined. She couldn't even move on cleanly because of all the baggage left in the wake.

Her daughter would probably never understand that things fell apart long ago and they had been acting as passable husband and wife when it counted, but never without arguments. Before or after every event they attended together, there was a fight. When the routines became silent, Farrah felt even worse. Silence and apathy meant there was nothing left to fight for. The problem was that they never told their daughter. She wasn't prepared at all. The rug was pulled out from under her while she was oblivious and happy at college.

"How do I fix it?"

"I don't know, babe. I just don't know. I only had step-children. I can't imagine what all of you are going through."

"You and Frank may not have had kids, but you are well-versed in screwed up family dynamics."

"That is true. Speaking of which, I'll log onto that website and see if there are any comments on my post about finding my sister and biological father."

Farrah turned to food while processing her turmoil. She whipped up a batch of oatmeal and banana muffins while June looked to see if there was any news.

CHAPTER EIGHT

A frozen veggie pizza with crust akin to cardboard was going to have to satisfy Farrah and June for lunch on Sunday. June managed to pull together a couple of small salads with bib lettuce, a chopped apple, almonds, and slices of a mandarin orange on top. Their budget wouldn't always be as tight as it was operating that big house, but until it sold and they could get something more suitable, they dealt with it.

"Do you ever wonder how the cat feels? I mean, if he's realized that the dog and Jackson are gone?"

"I'm sure he's noticed, but I have a feeling he's more happy about it than I am."

Miles took the empty chair around the kitchen table and unceremoniously lifted his leg to clean his private neutered parts. Even in his advanced age, he was still a master yogi.

"Can you grab the water pitcher while you're up?" Farrah wasn't used to someone helping out and sitting down to a meal with her.

June took the pitcher from the refrigerator. "Ice?"

"No, thanks. Any word on the family registry site yet?"

"Nothing today either. I don't know why I was expecting better. I mean, the searches must be monumental. It's filled with people all over the world looking for lost family members. Some of them are estranged because of disasters and bombings making them refugees, not just adoptions and broken marriages." June picked at her pizza toppings. She plucked them off individually and ate them like a squirrel before lifting the slice up to her mouth.

Farrah mindlessly ate half the pizza, not that it was a surprising result. Those things aren't that big. Ways to comfort June escaped her. She tried distraction instead.

"I'm worried about Lenore. I know I probably shouldn't be. Maybe it's because Nova hates me right now so I'm displacing my maternal instincts onto someone else."

"Well, that baby daddy of hers sounds like a piece of shit. But you saw her — she looked healthy enough. Some people can carry babies to full term when they have addictions and diseases. She's stressed and thin. I'm sure she'll be fine."

"Miscarriage happens more often than people realize. Partly because some women think they're experiencing something else like a heavy period and partly because no one talks about it. You'd be shocked how many women don't even know or admit to themselves that they're pregnant. They think it's irregular periods."

"Oh, it can't be that many." June finally got around to eating her second slice of the pizza, the last one. Both of them were still hungry.

"All I know is what we were told in pre-natal class. As many as fifty percent of pregnancies end in miscarriage before twenty weeks. It certainly doesn't help that the home pregnancy tests can be wrong. A blood test is the only sure way to tell." Farrah's eyes followed the pizza to June's lips. She was speaking on auto-pilot to a degree because there was a part of her brain still thinking about food.

June never experienced pregnancy first hand. Years ago, she confided in Farrah that it wasn't something she ever wanted. At the time, Farrah hadn't realized the differences in bodies, sexualities, and gender roles. June wasn't opposed to raising children; she simply never had a longing to give birth which caused her deep feelings of guilt only Farrah knew about.

Needless to say, Farrah was taken by surprise at most of the information presented in that portion of her class. Giving birth a couple decades ago hadn't equated to expertly knowing biology and how miscarriages were so common.

"My mother never talked about being pregnant with me." June circled back to her family problems. "Then again, most of the time I question whether or not she ever loved me. I doubt she felt connected to me in the womb."

"June, you don't know that. I'm sure your mother loves you."

"It's a fallacy that only fathers don't feel connected to babies and can run off. Trust me, I think this Joel guy that knocked up Lenore is one of them. But that doesn't mean women don't abandon babies every day. The difference I'm talking about with my mother and women like her are that they are physically there but not emotionally. My mother loved her work."

"Do you think I should call Lenore and check on her?"

"I don't think it's a bad idea. She should know people care. I'm glad she has her friend Star, but it sounded like she didn't have anyone else besides that boyfriend of hers."

Farrah left a voicemail for Lenore and waited a few hours. She never got a call back. She tried again.

Still nothing.

She left another message. She attempted to soothe her worry by coming up with plenty of legitimate reasons for not being able to get a hold of her: she could have been in the shower then busy; she was at work and couldn't take calls; or, maybe her phone was dead. It didn't matter. Once Farrah began to worry about something, the thought patterns were in place and couldn't be detoured.

Unfortunately the call that did come through wasn't one she wanted.

"Hey, it's Sam." Farrah desperately needed appointments, but every time Samantha called, she got butterflies in her stomach. "I'm sorry to say that Lenore Lexington had to cancel her appointment with you this week."

"Why? Did I do something wrong? Was she unhappy with the service?" Farrah thought it would have been bizarre for the young woman to have canceled for being dissatisfied when they spoke on the phone Saturday and she didn't mention it directly.

"No. I'm sorry to say she's been admitted to the hospital. There's a problem."

"What happened? Are she and the baby okay?"

"I don't know anything except she had her boyfriend call both of her jobs and cancel everything on her calendar. He didn't tell me anything else."

"Do you think it's all right if I go down there and check on her?" Farrah was already on her feet and looking around for her purse and keys.

"You could try. If you do, please keep me posted. She's a sweet kid. And by the way, how are you doing? I know you must be dealing with your own problems." Samantha knew about Farrah and Jackson breaking up. That's all Farrah willingly told her. However, the Riverside grapevine and the internet could be rife with misinformation.

Farrah admitted things were rough, but left it vague. "You know, I'm fine, considering everything. My daughter is upset as expected. But we're moving on."

She didn't want to talk about herself. She wondered if Samantha knew that Lenore's boyfriend was also her ob-gyn. If Sam knew then it was one of the only secrets she ever kept. She was a huge link in the gossip chain.

"Um, Sam, do you know Lenore's boyfriend personally?"

"I don't think so. Don't think I ever met him. We only spoke on the phone for a minute when he called to cancel."

"She mentioned that he pays for her medical bills and for the massage appointments."

"Maybe he pays her credit card bill at the end of the month. I don't know. Why?"

"No reason. I was just curious about him. Me being nosy. The usual!" Farrah pretended to laugh it off.

When she got off the phone with Sam, Farrah asked June if she wanted to go along for the ride to see Lenore. At first, June hesitated. She was glued to her computer scrolling through the posts of all the people on the GlobalReach website.

"There are so many people out there. All of them looking to connect with someone because of biology. Maybe I shouldn't bother. My mother might not be the most nurturing woman, but she and Jae raised me. I think I turned out all right."

Farrah slid her purse back onto the table and sat down. "What if people don't want to be found? For their own reasons, I mean."

"The way this website works, their policies when you sign up and agree to all the fine print, state that you are only representing yourself or someone you legally can represent, like a lawyer or investigator or a legal guardian. There are valid concerns that people with protective orders against someone could be tracked down merely because they happen to be searching for their family. It's probably a one in a million chance, but you never know."

"So if someone is registered, it's because they are agreeing to be found, regardless of by whom?"

"Basically, yes. But only registered users can even search and post. I guess it legally protects the site owners and developers."

"Let's get your mind off it for a little while. Come with me to see Lenore."

*****

At the hospital, Farrah was able to obtain Lenore's room number without any verification. She was fully ready to explain that she was the woman's pre-natal massage therapist, but the receptionist didn't even ask.

The television was on, but Lenore wasn't looking at it. Her head was turned to the side away from the door as if she couldn't handle hearing the bustling excitement of the maternity ward. Farrah and June knocked softly and entered quietly. June closed the door behind her. Farrah walked around to far side of the bed to look at Lenore directly since she hadn't moved to see who came in.

Farrah said hello to her and asked how she was. Lenore didn't speak. A tear ran from her eye over the curve of her face and onto the pillow.

"June is here too. We were both worried and wanted to see how you were. Um, has Star come by? Do you need us to call her or call anyone for you?"

She shook her head no ever so slightly. Star was probably busy covering Lenore's shifts at the spiritualism shop. Farrah didn't recall the names of any of Lenore's bookshop coworkers. They wanted to be helpful, but there didn't seem to be much for them to do.

"Did they give you something?"

She shook her head yes while refusing eye contact.

"Has something happened to the baby?"

Lenore shrugged her shoulders. *How could she not know? How drugged was she?*

Her voice was cracked from hours of crying. "I don't know if she'll make it."

June got closer. "What have they told you?"

Finally Lenore turned her head and looked at them. Her features were so lifeless.

"I thought it was the morning sickness again. I couldn't stop vomiting. I felt dizzy and weak."

"How's your blood pressure?" Farrah asked.

"High. Way too high, they said."

"Joel brought you in?"

"No. I texted him and he called 9-1-1 and sent an ambulance to my place."

"But he's your doctor, right? Has he seen you?" June asked.

"Yes, he's here. But, please don't say anything that you know he's my boyfriend. It's still important to him to keep that on the down low until he serves his wife with the divorce papers."

The ladies reluctantly agreed to let him have his secret. For now, anyway. Farrah still wanted to turn him in to an ethics board or whomever would be in charge of doctors sleeping with their patients. It was time to focus on Lenore and keeping her stress under control.

CHAPTER NINE

"I'M glad Lenore agreed to add me as an emergency contact." Farrah said to June when they got home. "Someone needs to look out for that girl and there's something awfully shady about Dr. Joel DeSantos."

"Do you think we should find a way of getting the information to his wife or the hospital administrator secretly? The guy is clearly an asshole." June was approached by Miles and she bent over to pick him up. She nuzzled him close as she walked into the kitchen behind Farrah.

Farrah popped open the laptop on the kitchen table. "Ya know, you and I have a knack for finding ourselves tits deep in trouble. I want to keep my nose out of this if possible. My only concern is Lenore's health and wellbeing."

Miles jumped from June's grasp and sauntered across the table. Neither of the women cared. The cat was the only masculine energy in the house and he wasn't a jerk so they gave him liberal reign.

June made them hot mugs of orange pekoe tea. Nothing fancy. Just supermarket teabags rather than the imported loose leaf offered in the Victorian teahouse they went to on special occasions.

To pause from Lenore's problem, they sat and brainstormed ways that Farrah and her colleagues could bring in business. On paper, it appeared that they were already doing everything right. They had on- and off-site services because of Maggie's mobile clients. They offered a wide range of modalities from the classic relaxation of Swedish massage to Chinese methods Christine learned to the gentle energy based bodywork. Plus, the other special options on their menu of services like the hot stone massages and pre-natal were half as expensive as the prices inside large hotel spas but still higher than the franchises.

Farrah shot off a text to Samantha and asked when they could go over her list of ideas. She didn't really want to meet up with her, but she knew she needed to make more effort to be involved with the business if she wanted be given the appointments she needed to pay her bills. Of course Samantha made a dramatic display about how she never has any time to herself or with her family despite her ability and success which allowed her to take family vacations. Farrah was used to Sam's *woe-is-me-I'm-successful* attitude.

"I need to take my son to Lambertville. Can you take a trip and meet me out there?"

"If you want, I can just email these ideas." Farrah didn't want to use the fuel to get there, but she didn't know what alternatives to present to Sam.

"No. You know what? We should get the staff together again and go over this as a group. I don't know how many I can get to show up at the last minute though." The Bluetooth connection wasn't the best. Sam's sentences cut out, but Farrah could piece the words together to figure out what she said.

"You sound busy. Why don't we all do an online chat or something?" Organized chatroom discussions composed of cohesive trains of thought were nearly impossible with this group. The lengths Farrah would go to in order to avoid driving another forty miles.

Samantha claimed she didn't know how to set up a private chat and said she would agree if Farrah took the helm. A few hours later and she had Samantha, Maggie, Diane, and Jordan logged into a chat session. Everyone else said they were busy and Christine was on her trip. June showed her where to turn the text log option on so that they'd have a transcript.

Diane offered the first suggestion about coming up with a bridal package and advertising it in local hair salons and bridal shops. Samantha and Maggie agreed it was a good idea. Sam's connections at the country club meant that she could try and work out an arrangement where the club's event manager would allow them to have brochures in their office where they had other favored businesses featured.

Farrah typed to add more to the premise. "While we're talking about the club would it be possible to open a satellite location there? I know it would require investing more money, but instead of cutting back maybe we should be growing. Ya know, to compete with those chains popping up everywhere."

Her idea wasn't immediately brushed off. Samantha wasn't jumping for joy at the thought of investing more money. The way her brain worked for big ideas, she needed to believe that she came up with them. Farrah knew it. She expected to be rejected and have the plan come back around some other time. And that's exactly what happened.

Samantha said she would discuss an expansion privately with Maggie and her husband (a silent partner) and their accountant. Getting a loan to expand would probably count as a tax incentive. It would also look better within the community that with more opportunities for appointments, there would be more staff needed to work. Jobs always made the locals happier.

Farrah sent Samantha a private message no one else in the chat could see. She expressed her wishes to be the manager of the satellite branch if they really go through with it. It would be a full time job and even at a low hourly wage, it would help her with steady income to compliment her higher but rare income from taking clients.

"What else have you got?" Sam typed in the public window.

Did that mean she was ignoring the private message or did she honestly not know how chats worked?

Publicly, Farrah threw out another idea. "How about we partner with a local chiropractor to have him or her come in for appointments here once or twice a week? Then we'd have better access to their patients and our clients could consider adding service while under our roof."

That was something everyone agreed on. Maggie said they'd had to figure out which room could be used and find out what renovations would be required to allow for a medical service like that. Overall though, everyone felt it was a more immediately accessible plan.

"This has been a good meeting. Farrah will forward me the transcript. I still have things to do tonight so I need to go." Samantha signed off. Everyone else said goodbye and logged out.

She closed the laptop and stood up to stretch. June pointed out that Farrah spent two hours in the brainstorming session. Next on the agenda was to come up with something for dinner.

"More pasta?"

"I don't even care anymore. I could eat a bag of chips in front of the TV and call it a night." Farrah stood by the pantry closet depressed by the options. It was sad, but they opted to eat like college students instead of expending the minimal effort on boiling noodles and opening jarred sauce.

"I found the salsa. Let's go."

"Should we melt some veggie cheese on them in the oven?"

"Oh, I suppose. It wouldn't be that much to clean up. You preheat the oven. I'm going to get my pajamas on." Farrah headed up the stairs lined by the wall of family photos. She felt like all the people in the pictures had moving eyes that followed her, including her younger self with an unfortunate short haircut that made her face look twice as round. Part of the banister wobbled. It was supposed to be a home project for Jackson to fix, another thing that would never happen now.

CHAPTER TEN

WHILE Farrah sat in her home office trying to make a "TL;DR" version of the brainstorming notes to accompany the transcript of the online meeting, her text notification buzzed. It was June which wouldn't have been a surprise, but the message itself was.

> JUNE: Frank asked me to meet for drinks after work.
>
> FARRAH: What did you say?
>
> JUNE: I didn't have any real reason to say no.
>
> FARRAH: He's your ex. That's a reason. Did he say what he wanted?
>
> JUNE: To catch up. WTH?

Frank and June's divorce had been more amicable than most, but still, they were divorced. They had moved on. June had dated people since. They only saw each other a few times.

She and Farrah theorized what he wanted to see her about. Both agreed was not about rekindling their relationship. It was Frank who had put it into Jackson's head that the best friends were having a lesbian affair. At least that's how Jackson made it seem during all the fighting.

Even though June's hours at the county records office ended at four, she used to stay late often. When she lived alone in the condo, there was no reason to bolt out of there except for her sanity. To stop the habit of overworking, especially since her salary forbade overtime pay, she wanted to have a personal life. She had begun some new activities like a weekly pottery class and kickboxing. The previous summer, she even tried a couple months of archery. Nothing really stuck.

Part of the town of Triumph around the county courthouse and other government buildings was laid out in a grid around a beautiful square park. There were plenty of places to wine and dine within walking distance ranging from cheap places frequented by the locals to upscale joints where judges and attorneys would enjoy long lunches or dinners with whomever they were having affairs. There was a speakeasy code of conduct: you kept your mouth shut if you spotted anyone dining with someone other than their spouse. Same rule applied if an officer of the court was seen with someone known to have questionable connections or infractions. June had only been to one of those places when a defense attorney from a different county noticed her in the courthouse and asked her out during a trial.

The real dive bars were away from the square and walkable only if you didn't mind putting in the couple miles on a full stomach or needed to pee from all the beer consumed. Since June was shocked by the invitation, she wasn't going to succumb to drinking cheap beer. Instead she told Frank to meet her at Elixir near her office. It was a step up from cheap dives without seeming like she wanted to be impressed.

Elixir's bar had a high sheen varnish. The brass was shiny and the vinyl on the seats wasn't cracked and patched with duct tape like June's regular Riverside bar, Happy's. It was newer and had a decent reputation for American-UK fusion cuisine. They didn't just serve mashed potatoes; the delectable spuds were creamed with lots of butter and piped into tall mountains in martini glasses and could be topped with bacon, cheese, corn, gravy, chives, and/or sour cream. Paired with the right beer, the potatoes were a meal on their own. It was probably the only pub where the mashed version was ordered more than French fries.

Frank's blurry figure approached her as she watched him through the glass raised up to her mouth. His jeans were clean and he wore a striped dress shirt over his t-shirt. In other words, Frank was dressed up.

"Thanks for coming. I didn't think you'd meet me."

"No problem. I gotta say, I'm here because I'm curious. It's not like we keep in touch."

A waitress came over to take his order and looked over to June. "Did you want something to eat?"

"I would love a loaded potato martini. The works." June was used to Farrah's meat-free home, but when she was out, she ate whatever she wanted.

"I'll take one of those and the Triumph deluxe burger medium-rare with Swiss instead of American if ya got it."

"Sure thing. I'll get those orders right in for ya. And another pint for you?"

"Yes. Thank you." June spun the coaster around with her fingertips.

Once the waitress had gone about her business, Frank opened up with some small talk. He covered the bases of how his children were doing. Cate was pregnant and he was looking forward to being a grandfather. He spent his winter organizing the chaos of his prop inventory after Halloween and began sculpting new things based on popular video game characters that fans wanted to buy.

"Is that legal?"

"No. It's unlicensed for now. But I'm taking orders and making each an original piece in a way. The molds are good for a while but it's not like I'm running a factory in China and taking advantage of workers. I definitely have licensing them officially in my future. Need to sort out with a lawyer what it would take."

He downed his pint too quickly trying to give his mouth something to do between conversation points. June didn't offer up much.

"Frank, what did you really want to see me about?"

The waitress had passed by on her way to another table. Frank held up his empty pint and she returned with one for each of them.

"It's about Jack and Farrah. I'm worried."

"They're separated and on their way to divorce. I think we're all passed the point of worrying. Or is this because you don't want him as a roommate indefinitely?"

"No-No. He's great as a roommate. He's around more than Jesse who is still living in the small room. Jack helps me take care of everything. Has a real interest in the special effects work."

"So what's the problem?"

Their mashed potatoes were delivered with a bit of a flourish. Each glass was three times the size of what some bars use to serve martinis. There were probably three times the amount of potato one would normally have too, not that June cared about serving sizes or the food nutrition wheel. At the end of the booth, the waitress left a pile of paper napkins knowing that a single linen one for each person was never enough.

"That mountain of potatoes is the size of your head."

"Yes. And I plan to enjoy all of it." She savored the masterpiece of fat, cholesterol, and carbs. It was the best experience of happy hormones in a long time.

"This is really good." Frank noticed that June wasn't going to say another word until he started to explain himself. "It's, um, hard, ya know? On him."

"Don't you think it's hard on her too?"

"Well, I mean, come on. I'm sure she's upset, but she's the one who cheated."

"Frank, did you seriously call me to bad mouth my best friend? Because let me tell you something, that's not going to happen. I won't sit here while you trash her."

He backpedaled a little regarding his choice of words. Unless one of them got up and walked out, they'd have to listen to each other. He was lectured on how their friends' marriage had fallen apart long before Farrah's infidelity.

"What is Jack so upset about? He basically checked out of their relationship years ago."

"Doesn't mean he's a callous bastard. He does care. And he's got a lot of other things on his mind."

"Like what?" June was not going to find pity for Jackson so easily.

"I don't think he wanted Farrah and their daughter to know." Frank lingered. He took a huge bite from his burger to buy some time. The melted Swiss stretched out like a zipline to his mouth. "It's his job. They've been making cuts."

"Oh. And he's afraid he'll be downsized?" This was the first thing interesting enough to pause her gluttony.

"Look, June… those two have always been different than we were as a couple. You've always been as independent as I was. Now, I have no doubt it was an adjustment for you just like it was for me, to cover living expenses on your own. But Farrah and Jackson have had to rely on each other in different ways."

"You mean since she became a massage therapist and he's been paying the bills?"

"Yeah. I mean, you gotta know how much he hated it."

"Oh, I do know. I knew because she said so. I knew because he threw it up in her face all the time. He never supported her dreams of doing something different with her life besides sitting behind a desk answering phones and typing email. She wanted a life that was more rewarding and she went out and got it. She's been struggling and working her ass off trying to build up a clientele. And where's her husband been all this time? Giving her grief for it because he doesn't believe in her work. The very basic foundations of why she enjoys it, he can't even have a conversation about without rolling his eyes and negating half the philosophies!"

Frank held his empty pint glass and examined it for no reason. *Get another or get something stronger or just get out of there?* He held up his hand to get attention and ordered a whiskey.

"Look, I don't need the lecture. I heard his side. All I wanted was to have someone else to talk to. It made the most sense, in my head anyway, to talk to you since you have the other half of the pie so to speak. I don't think it's betraying anyone's trust if you and I talk about them since we're the two who would know all the information anyway."

June dug out the last goopy remains of her mashed potatoes. The tall glass of ice water helped her feel less like a potato herself with its refreshing relief. However, if she was going to stay and continue a heated discussion with her ex-husband, water wasn't going to be good enough. She excused herself to use the bathroom and when she returned, she ordered a matching whiskey. She downed it in two gulps and felt guilty about maintaining her buzz when she would need to drive home. They'd have to sit for a while. The last drink had been a stupid thing to do. She ordered them both coffee.

"Maybe you're right. Maybe we do need an alliance to be each other's sounding board. Typically I tell Farrah everything, but I have to bottle up everything she tells me."

"Right. But I already know the sordid details. And we keep this between us."

"I guess. I'll think about it."

They needed time to process the beer and whiskey which meant several more trips to the bathrooms. They needed to pass the time. She asked him about his work and how the haunted house season worked out. Frank never failed at talking extensively about that.

"I don't expect Jesse to board with me much longer. He has a girlfriend now. It's new, but he's smitten." He went to talk about how he started giving Jackson some lessons in casting the molds and plastics for the props. Frank was the artist and he loved the messy parts of the job too, but having someone around to help would speed up his processes. "We've talked about becoming official business partners. I think it'd be great."

"And if he gets laid off? Would you be able to pay him a salary?"

"Not much, no. Certainly not at first. But we have those big dream conversations too — like you said Farrah had about starting her new line of work. Jack is a smart guy, great friend. And he has some cool ideas about products we could sell for the haunted houses and horror conventions."

"You can't bank on seasonal work though."

She sat and listened to him go on about things. His eyes got big talking about the soaring popularity of costuming by gamers and comic book fans called cosplay. As a longtime fan of *Star Trek*, she knew exactly what he was talking about, but let him talk anyway. Bringing something else into the conversation alleviated some of her guilt for talking about Farrah behind her back, not that she divulged anything secret.

"With these cosplayers, there's never a real season for costume accessories and props. Winter is the slowest, but from March through November, people are excited to show off their outfits. Plus there's a massive show in LA."

"And this is something you think you and Jackson can do as a full-time business?" She finished her coffee, but continued to play with the teaspoon on a paper napkin.

Frank smirked. It looked like he wanted to say something and knew better. "Not exclusively. My job is fine. But it would be a great way for me to expand my side business and he could help out just in case Wharton & Finkle cut through his department."

"I better get going," June said when she realized he too had finished his coffee.

"Are you going to tell Farrah we met?"

"She already knows. I'm not lying to her."

Their check was set down inside a black vinyl holder with the Elixir logo in gold on the front.

"Can you keep the part about Jackson's company to yourself?" Frank stuck his credit card in the check and pushed as far to the edge of the table as possible.

June stood and looked around to see if the waitress was in sight. She pulled on her coat and scarf before sitting back down at the booth.

"Fine. I won't tell her that part since, truthfully, there's nothing to tell. He's worried. I'm sure if something happens, he'll tell her directly."

With the bill paid, they went to their cars and parted ways. June used her SUV's speaker system to call Farrah to say she was on her way home.

"What's wrong?" June detected the shakiness in Farrah's voice when she answered.

"It's Lenore."

CHAPTER ELEVEN

FARRAH knew June had a few drinks with her dinner. She hoped the starchy carbs would absorb it enough so June could drive home safely.

"Don't speed. And watch for deer."

"Sweetie, I've lived here long enough to know to watch for deer. I'm being careful. I promise. Now tell me what's wrong."

The SUV turned the corner of Walnut Street onto the county road that would take her most of the way home. It was curvy and on a small mountain. Luckily for June, only sparse evidence of snow and ice were visible in people's yards but not a danger to her tire traction.

"She lost the baby. I'm not entirely sure what happened. They said it was eclampsia which was a concern because of her blood pressure and other symptoms."

Farrah had taken the news especially hard. In such a short amount of time, she grew to care for her. June said she felt terrible for the girl too.

"I know you said she doesn't have any family around, but who called you?"

"Someone from the hospital called. A nurse, I think. I want to go over, but she said that they were keeping her sedated for the rest of the night and that I could visit her tomorrow."

When June finally walked in the door safely, Farrah popped out of her chair in the living room and quickly greeted her with a big hug.

"You've been crying. Sweetie, I'm so sorry. I know you're sensitive about other people."

"I know. It's crazy. Not like her baby was going to be anything to me. And hopefully Lenore herself will be okay, but I don't know. It was just so sad and I felt something that I can't stop from eating me up inside."

Both of them needed to decompress. June immediately changed into comfortable leggings and an oversized flannel shirt that could have fit three of her in it. Farrah was already in her pajamas and returned to her afghan cocoon using the blanket her mother crocheted many years ago.

"I hope you ate something," June said from the end of the couch.

"Nothing great. I microwaved a veggie burger." Farrah sipped from her refillable bottle of water, recapped it, and kept it in her fists protected by her curled up body.

"You obviously want to talk about something. Mute the TV."

"It feels like there's a lot to talk about. How's Frank? What did he want?"

"He didn't want anything really. I think he felt like he needed to unload on someone and since Jack is there all the time, he wanted a fresh ear to bend."

"Why you?"

"Because." June kept her promise to Frank, but still found a way to inform Farrah that she and her ex were the subjects of the conversation. Naturally she did so while going into nearly pornographic detail about the mountain of mashed potatoes she ate.

Inside her heart, Farrah knew that it wasn't her place to tell June that striking up a friendship with her ex-husband was a bad idea. Although, as best friends, there was freedom to express opinions as long as they were done nicely. She allowed their conversation to have pauses while she thought before speaking, not something she was used to.

"People don't need to hate their exes, but that's not the same as being friends. I'm not saying don't talk to Frank, but I will say that I worry about you and your heart and want you to be cautious."

"Oh, don't worry about my heart. There's nothing left between us there. I loved having a family with him. I loved that his kids were older and I didn't have to raise them while having miserable custody battles and all that crap. We never had to do the weekend swaps in public places because he and their mother couldn't be civil. It was basically the opposite. The kids had lives of their own. His first wife wasn't an issue. He did well providing for them and himself. My income was for upgrades. Getting better cable or taking vacations. I was able to sack a lot away which I used to buy the condo. It was a blessing."

"I'm envious. I don't know if Jack and I will even be able to be in the same room together without a fight breaking out."

"You will eventually. It's fresh. You're both hurt. But you have a daughter together who will always need you regardless of how independent she is."

"It's bizarre and seems wrong of me to feel it, but I resent how independent Nova is." Farrah's eyes left the polite direction of June's and focused on the intricate weave of the blanket wrapped around her.

June pulled her feet off the faux Persian rug and tucked them underneath her. "It's not that strange. You want to feel loved and the two people you thought would always give you that aren't here for you.

They're mad at you. But I'm here. Remember that. I know it's not the same, but I am here for you."

She was right. The problem was that June's philosophy wasn't curing Farrah's depression. Anything that made her feel better was temporary.

"There's something I don't think I ever told you. I thought I got over it and even during our drunkest moments with my guard down, I don't think I ever let it out."

"You can tell me anything. I mean, at this point, we've been through more together than some married couples." June picked at a thread that she mistook for a loose piece of lint, but it was still attached to her shirt. She pulled on it and snapped it, wrapping it around her finger. A small hole left at its source.

The delicacy of Lenore Lexington's pregnancy hadn't been evident. It lurked there, hidden within symptoms that her medical providers told her were common symptoms like morning sickness. Farrah didn't beat herself up over missing the seriousness of it; she was only the woman's massage therapist for a few days. She did however wonder if the doctors, nurses, and ultrasound technicians had done their jobs thoroughly and adequately. And her boyfriend, Dr. Joel DeSantos, seemed to be a reputable ob-gyn, but was he really?

"Science has obviously advanced a lot in twenty years, but I thought fetal mortality rates would have improved more than they have."

June sat and listened to Farrah's brief lesson on obstetrics. The conversation being steered back to Lenore wasn't too surprising since the news was only hours old.

Farrah knew she could trust June with anything. June Cho had been her best friend for over a decade, nearly two. They met not long after Farrah and Jackson had their first rough patch as a married couple.

"After having Janice — she was Janice back then as my little baby — money was tight for us. Jackson had hellish student loans from grad school. I was barely making anything, something that didn't change much with inflation. Anyway everything seemed overwhelming."

It was the most difficult conversation she ever had with June when she admitted she had been pregnant a second time. She wanted the child, but didn't think it was a good time with their struggling situation. Jackson made her feel like getting pregnant was all her fault as if he didn't have an important contribution to it. They had discussed options including abortion.

"But I never needed to go through with it because I miscarried. The guilt was unbearable. I felt like I prayed away my child."

CHAPTER TWELVE

"SHE suffered seizures which weren't necessarily the cause of the miscarriage, but it was like a perfect storm of symptoms that hit her." This was the first time Farrah got to talk to Dr. Joel DeSantos and the subject was the furthest thing from pleasant introductions.

"Thank you for filling me in, Dr. DeSantos. Can I go see her?"

"She's just waking up. As soon as the nurse comes out, you can go in. But, please, keep it brief. She's been through a lot."

"Of course."

Inside Farrah's bag, she carried two small books for reference about aromatherapy oils and the energy based bodywork, Jin Shin Jyutsu, which she planned to use on Lenore if there were no objections. The ob-gyn said it was fine with him and he didn't see any allergy concerns with the ingredients of the oils especially since it would be only a few drops used on Farrah's hands before touching Lenore's skin. She prepped before going to the hospital and put sticky tabs on the pages she wanted to use.

The amber glass vials held only a milliliter of the herbal extracts. Farrah carried them in small amounts so that if she left them in the car and they dried out, she wouldn't lose entire bottles of expensive essentials. Some oils were noted specifically as not to use on pregnant women because they had history or lore of being abortifacients; though Farrah realized that was a situation that no longer posed a risk. From the sound of Dr. DeSantos and the nurse's opinions, what Lenore needed more than anything was rest, serenity, and time to process her feelings.

"Thank you for coming." Lenore's coloring was an improvement on how she looked last time Farrah saw her. "They said I can probably be discharged by the end of the day."

"So soon? That sounds fast. Sorry, I shouldn't question your doctors." Farrah knew any comments made about Lenore's care would also mean she judged Lenore's boyfriend and that put her in the conundrum of acting as her practitioner and a friend.

"Well, it's insurance, ya know. They never cover more than a day or two unless you're dying. I guess they think I'm out of the high risk category now that…"

Farrah didn't need her to finish what she was going to say. She asked some basic questions to get more direct answers from the patient that the doctor may not have wanted to say. She asked if she had slept, if she was in pain or discomfort, and if she wanted the energy work done on her. Lenore nodded in affirmation. She wanted to smell the beautiful fragrances of the essentials to mask the nauseating smell of the hospital.

"I can leave you one or two of these bottles when I'm done. All you have to do is open the cap and waft it under your nose. Sometimes that's all you need. Don't drink them though. They aren't for consumption."

Farrah spent time working on energy points on Lenore's arms and hands, occasionally reaching for other points on her head and the inside of the knees with the gentle touch. She set out a vial of a blend containing sandalwood, lavender, frankincense, valerian, and several other ingredients formulated for overcoming traumatic experiences.

"I'm so sorry you lost the baby. I don't know what else to say."

"I'm sorry too. I'm really glad you're here. Star said she'll come by when she can."

"If you don't want to talk about any of it, you can tell me it's none of my business. How did Joel take it?"

"It's hard to say. I've been so out of it. They had me knocked out for so long. I know he was here and I remember his voice, but we haven't had the chance for a real conversation yet."

"Hmm. I guess doctors can't easily take a day off or even a few hours off."

"No, they can't. I love him so much and he's the only part of my life that hasn't been about working at either of the stores. And I love my jobs, but I guess, I wanted him to be more present."

"Are you sure you don't have any family or anyone else close to you that you want me to call for you? I don't think you should go home to an empty apartment."

She shook her head no. When Farrah took hold of her hand, her fingers, though relaxed, wrapped gently around her caring practitioner's.

"I'm not much for talking on the phone. I'll tell them. Probably email them. I doubt they'll care though. They'll called me irresponsible for being unmarried and getting knocked up. So old fashioned."

Farrah apologized again not that she had any reason to. She wasn't responsible for difficult parent/child relationships except her own.

The phone on Lenore's bedside table vibrated. She asked Farrah if she could hand it to her. One look at the number and she swiped the screen to ignore it.

"Ugh. Another unfamiliar number."

"Honestly, the only reason I kept a house line is to fill out forms. So far, it's been pretty good at keeping my cell number off telemarketing lists."

Lenore kept the phone in her limp hand and rested it on her thigh while Farrah continued to apply gentle touch to points on her calf and toe.

"I don't think it's telemarketers. A few times, I've answered and there's no one there. Then they hang up. Wrong numbers, I guess."

Farrah didn't buy that so easily.

"Have you gotten text messages from strange numbers too?"

"Yeah, I have. They've been weird."

"How so?"

"There are a bunch of different numbers. They started out like pretending they knew me. It seemed genuine enough just like any wrong number. Then it started to get worse."

"Threatening?"

"Yes."

"Do you have any idea who it is? Have you looked up the numbers online?"

"All they say is the wireless carrier and the city."

"Did you keep the messages? Can I can see them?"

Lenore hadn't kept all of them believing that they were mistakes. She didn't have them screen captured either. The ones she hadn't deleted yet she showed to Farrah.

I KNOW WHERE U R

I KNOW UR ALONE

SLUT

WHORES LIKE U ARE ONLY GOOD
FOR ONE THING

After Farrah's personal experience with online harassment, she took all methods of threatening as seriously as possible. She and Jackson had to deal with reporters knowing their home address and strangers having their work and home phone numbers. Farrah was torn up on social media more than once.

Lenore was already in a tricky situation having an affair and getting pregnant. She was a perfect target for slut shaming by both men and women.

"I have to ask, could this be from Joel's wife?"

"Of course, that's the first thing I thought. But I showed him the phone numbers and he said they're not hers."

"That doesn't matter. She could have easily gotten another phone." Farrah didn't want to upset the poor patient who was still groggy from her body being piped full of medications. "Look, when you get out of here, I think you need to show these to the police or maybe a lawyer — someone in law enforcement."

Farrah rested one hand on the top of Lenore's head and the other on her chest with her fingers applying soft pressure on a clavicle. She breathed along with Lenore silently for a few rounds then put the caps back on the bottles of oil, leaving them on the stand.

"How's your social media? Is that filled with hate comments too?"

"I haven't looked. They said people aren't supposed to use cell phones in here, but I've been texting."

"That's probably to keep people from talking loudly and being disruptive. But anyway, you need to focus on rest so you should probably keep off those sites anyway until you get home."

Underneath the thermal blanket, Lenore's feet wiggled as she stared at them as if the lumps weren't even part of her own body. She didn't look up at Farrah when she said she didn't want to go home.

"I was beginning to set up a nursery area. My apartment is tiny, but it would have been fine for at least the baby's first year. A lot of people start off cramped. It was supposed to be until Joel and I moved in together. He would've gotten us a proper place to live."

"And you don't want to go home to see all the stuff?"

"Yeah."

"How about if you give me your key so I can box things up before you get there?"

"Would you really?"

"Sure." She explained that if Lenore had been her own daughter, she'd want to know someone was able to be there for her to help her through the most difficult time of her life.

It was time to open up. She couldn't swoop in and save this girl from her problems when her own life was a disaster.

"My daughter hates me right now and my husband moved out. I told you all that in the tarot reading. So, I would not mind if the house wasn't so empty. I'd love to invite you to stay in the spare room for at least tonight or whenever they release you. I don't think it's smart if you're alone after this kind of surgery. It'll be hard for you to move around and do some basic things. Come stay with us for a few days."

Lenore said she appreciated the offer, but that she felt she should run it by Joel first. Was his say in the decision the final one? Would he be answering as the father of their deceased child or as her doctor? Farrah kept her concern to herself for that moment.

Regardless of whether Lenore agreed to spend the night at chez Wethers, Farrah's offer to box up the baby things still stood. Lenore told her to get her keys from the coat that was in a large plastic bag with all her other possessions. Her keychain was a star inside a circle and held two keys for the apartment and two for her jobs. She didn't own a car. The rest of the bundle was a mass of reward points tags stores used to give discounts. Farrah saw the similarities to her own keys which were now smaller without having Jackson's spare car key on it.

CHAPTER THIRTEEN

THE open floor plan studio apartment was cleverly divided up through Lenore's use of tall hutches, bookcases, and a folding Japanese screen. The double bed was surrounded by curtains and fairy lights much like the tarot reading nook at Star's Blessings. It was obvious that there weren't a lot of guests or entertaining done there. One threadbare couch sat against the longest wall. A relatively new TV facing it — probably a gift from Joel who wanted to enjoy some amenities when he wasn't actively screwing his mistress (or during, to each their own, Farrah thought).

Behind the Japanese folding screen was a rocking chair and piles of baby clothes and blankets. She had already begun to nest. There was a box with a changing table not yet assembled. No crib yet. Farrah looked around to see if there were other areas that would need to be packed up. She found an unopened bottle sterilizer on the counter in the kitchenette and a couple unopened three-packs of bottles with labels claiming they were shaped to be more natural.

Sadness sprouted in Farrah. She felt it move from her head down her whole body. Her hand unconsciously paused flat against her belly roll where she carried two children but only birthed one.

She had brought along flattened boxes, tape, a marker, and box cutter along with a few oversized tote bags. Once she got to work, her thoughts continued down the "what if" line where she formed fantasies of what raising a second child could have been like. She hadn't been far enough along to know the biology. She wanted a boy though, if only it had happened a couple of years later.

Lenore hadn't made a decision with what to do with the baby supplies. She mentioned that she would probably donate them, but since she truly believed that Joel would start an honest relationship with her and possibly have kids in the future, she knew all the stuff could come in handy later on. Farrah's words of wisdom had been that it was okay to donate the items this time and, later on, they should consider planning their family more carefully once they have a place to live; then of course, Joel's salary could easily provide for a brand new pregnancy.

"You're probably right," Lenore had said back in the hospital room. "I'd love the chance to go out shopping as a couple and not have to be upset that I'm alone because we can't be seen together. It'll feel better next time." She wasn't giving up on Joel so easily.

The boxes and bags were stacked neatly around the rocker and hidden by the screen. Farrah found a big plaid blanket that she used to cover the pile. It didn't help too much. It still looked like an unkempt dumping ground of boxes and bags. She pulled the screen around to make more of a corner shape which unfortunately made the bedroom area feel even smaller, but it did give a better sense of the storage being separated from the actual living space.

She didn't dig through all Lenore's personal things per se, but Farrah walked around the place and looked at as much as possible. She got a new perspective in how dedicated Lenore was to her religion. The furnishings, even mismatched, presented warmth and comfort showing off the personality of the resident. The bedspread and the silk decorative pillows looked like antiques that could have been thrift store finds or passed down through the family. Farrah concocted a theory that Lenore maybe inherited possessions of a grandmother or great-grandmother before she became estranged.

There were clean dishes in the drying rack next to the small sink. Farrah loved having a deep double sink. It had been a long time since she saw the micro scale of studio apartment living. The sink looked barely any larger than one a dentist makes patients spit into.

A small shelf unit screwed to the backsplash contained cooking spices neatly organized alphabetically. Without even knowing why she did it, Farrah opened a couple cabinets. She discovered Lenore's collection of loose herbs and tea in clear jars. There were a few store-bought ones that were commonly found in supermarkets, but it seemed obvious to Farrah that Lenore liked a personal approach to her tea infusions. She reached up and spun one of the jars around. It was labeled "serenity mix" written on a piece of torn paper and taped to the side of the jar. Lenore had listed the ingredients she used: valerian root, German chamomile, ginger, and lavender.

It seemed to Farrah that it would be the courteous thing to do to bring the tea back to her house so that Lenore could enjoy it. She opened up the refrigerator and checked all the expiration dates in case anything needed to be cleaned out. It was shocking to see a single woman's home without any sign of takeout containers. In the crisper drawers, Farrah did find some fruit that she packed into a tote with the tea jar; no sense in things going to waste. They weren't moldy so if Lenore's appetite returned, she could have food she was used to. Farrah pulled out some apples and found a hunk of ginger root hiding in the back next to a bundle of green onions.

She moved on from the kitchenette. On a small round table, some candles of various colors were halfway burned. There was a wood plaque with a pentacle painted on it at the top of the table arrangement. In the center was a tarot card, "The Empress," it had labeled underneath the image of a beautiful woman with a round belly. In the circular arrangement, there was also a silver bell, a small dagger, and an empty chalice. Farrah didn't touch anything. She wondered if Lenore would be open to explaining the altar to her sometime after she was in a better frame of mind.

The final thing Farrah had to do was retrieve specific personal items for her guest. Even though she had permission for perusing the dresser and bathroom, it felt a tad invasive. She perhaps over-packed, but made sure to take comfortable loose-fitting clothes, clean underwear for several days, and bathroom items. Farrah's house wasn't terribly far so if she forgot anything, Lenore could send her back to fetch whatever was missing.

*****

Once back at home, she made sure there were clean sheets on Nova's bed now that June was officially moved into the other room with her own possessions. She left the overnight bag there and then went to make sure the bathroom was clean. If the stairs were too difficult, they would have her set up on the couch or recliner.

"Hello?" Farrah quickly pulled the phone from her back pocket. It was Lenore confirming that the hospital was definitely discharging her. "I'll come get you around five-thirty if that's okay with you."

"Oh, don't worry. Joel said he'll bring me to your house. He said he'd like to meet you and June on a more personal level. Will she be home by six?"

"Uh, yeah, I think so. Pretty sure she's given up on that kickboxing class." Joel, the man who never wanted to be seen in public with his mistress, was going to personally drop her off at a stranger's house. Farrah was intrigued.

She had enough time to make a salad and get a quick vegetable soup on the stove. They'd need something more to go along with it to be sure that Lenore had plenty of calories. Even when she was pregnant, her figure was still waifish with only a small belly bump. Grilled cheese or soy cheese sandwiches on whole wheat would be good enough to round out the dinner. She was relieved that June got home before their guests arrived.

"I can't believe he's driving her here. What was he like?"

"He was professional when we talked at the hospital. It wasn't a long conversation. Maybe a minute. Two at most."

"Can we grill him?" June could show restraint if she had to, but she didn't like to.

"No. We're supposed to help Lenore relax. Doing anything to upset her would not be good. She already lost the baby which, I have to say, she was really looking forward to having, even under these circumstances."

The tires crunched over some leftover grit in the gutter from the sand and salt spread by the public works department during the winter.

The black Acura SUV looked like it would have been a safe ride for the whole family. June peered out the front living room windows to scour for any details about who this man really was. The car's windows were tinted too dark to see anything.

"Should we do something? I feel like we should be doing something?" Farrah's urge to gawk was suddenly derailed into anxiety about looking like they were spying.

"Like what? You already have dinner made. Do you want some music on?" Since the TV was almost always on for background noise, June reached for the remote and navigated to a special channel of the cable selections where there was streaming music but not music videos. There weren't a lot of choices, but she found one for jazz hits. It wasn't ideal and not even June's taste, but she figured it was the most neutral of the options.

Farrah went to the front door, a sign of visitors because regular guests knew to use the side door in the dining room that lead to the driveway. Lenore was bundled up in her large coat, scarf and hat and wearing the same clothes she wore when admitted. Behind her was Joel with a guiding hand on the small of her back. The car alarm chirped when he clicked the remote lock button on his key fob. Farrah wasn't an expert on the finer things in life, but she saw a strong contrast in what looked like his wool and cashmere compared to his girlfriend's outdated polyester blend.

"Ah, Ms. Wethers. It's nice to see you again." He reached out to shake her hand.

Farrah opened the door wide and ushered them through to the small foyer where she offered to take their coats as they stood on the threshold of the living room.

"This is my roommate, June. June, this is Dr. DeSantos."

He offered the same cordial greeting to her as he did to Farrah. Lenore didn't look around at her new surroundings at all. She only looked at June and Farrah. Joel's hand had moved up to her shoulder with a light grip — enough for her to know how close he was.

"Come on in! We're excited to have another roomie for a few days. Farrah made us a small dinner just in case they didn't feed you anything edible at the hospital."

"Where are my manners? Would you like some water or maybe a hot tea?"

The guests stood in the middle of the living room. Lenore put her hand on his and she moved it off her shoulder, keeping hold of it.

"Do you have to go?" She craned her neck and looked at him.

"Yes, I do. But I wanted to make sure that you had some place comfortable." He let go of her hand. Hand holding, it seemed, was far too intimate to show in front of strangers, yet a dominating hand on her back was supposed to be his concerned physician behavior. Farrah and June both noticed and eyed each other.

"Um, well, sure. I have the spare bedroom all set up. It's upstairs. But just in case you can't handle stairs, we can make you cozy right here. And we'll be around to wait on you, hand and foot."

"Actually, it'll be good for Lenore to get more active. Keep walking a little bit more each day."

"Hope you got some good pain killers." June tried to lighten the mood, but failed.

Lenore's granola-crunching earthy lifestyle could have presented either way: casual to heavy drug use or nothing deemed too chemical in her body. They didn't know her well enough to wager a guess.

"All I have is Tylenol with codeine to sleep and some anti-anxiety medicine Joel figured I would need to process the grief." She had no issues calling him by his first name in front of them, but he didn't seem to appreciate it based on the squinty side-eye glance he showed.

"Yes. That's right. It's doctor's orders to get as much restful sleep as possible. And start working on getting back to that light physical activity we talked about. I'd keep her off the caffeine a while longer though. It's not good for anxiety and she's been doing fine without it."

"No problem. I picked up some herbal teas for you. Why don't you sit down?"

Lenore turned to face him as closely as he would allow. She looked like a puppy pleading not to be left alone.

"I'm sorry, ladies. You have a wonderful, quiet dinner. I have so much to do." He put another hand on her shoulder and looked down from his towering height. "Now, you promise me you won't overdo it and that you'll eat something. You have my personal number to call me if you need anything, but I'll be sure to check on you in the morning if I can. If not, Rosemary will call you for me."

"Sure. But please try to make the time. I'd rather talk to you."

He had a sly smile and said he'd do his best.

*****

Lenore and Joel walked back to the illusion of privacy in the foyer so she could say goodbye while he put his coat back on. Farrah and June shuffled over near the dining room, trying to remain within earshot, but to give the impression they were fetching plates from a cupboard.

"Please try to call me personally. You know it's important. I don't want to talk to your nurse."

The parting was far from a squishy lovefest of hugs and kisses that a couple in love and in mourning would normally be expected to show. Joel departed in his shiny SUV and Lenore walked back towards the dining room where she found her temporary roommates.

"I hope you don't mind a simple menu for tonight. We haven't been living large exactly," Farrah said.

They went into the kitchen where she asked everyone's cheese preference for the sandwiches. Coupled with everything else she put together, it was welcoming and familial. Lenore didn't have much appetite. She ate half a grilled cheese with gooey yellow American slices, the soup, and she plucked out only the cucumbers of the salad avoiding the leafy lettuce and cherry tomatoes.

"You think I'm a bad person, don't you?"

Farrah and June exchanged looks before either could respond sincerely.

"Heck no!" June tried to add some comfort that they've all made their share of mistakes. "I might not be able to understand what you're going through, but I'm not judging you."

"Not at all," Farrah said at the same time. "You just got your timing off with the relationship and the pregnancy. If we didn't like you, you wouldn't have been invited to stay here."

"The important thing is that you're not alone and that you can heal with people around you who care." Sometimes June could take on the big sister or aunt role just fine. She didn't often get the opportunity to practice.

The older women tried their best, but there was no way to console Lenore. Time would be the best thing for her. She needed to grieve.

Part of the concern was that Farrah wasn't sure if it was only the miscarriage or if Lenore was also dealing with a breakup. It's a sad reality that most couples don't rebound after the loss of a child they've grown to love for years, but miscarriages might not be the same. She and Jackson stayed together. They raised a daughter successfully. Having a miscarriage wasn't the inciting event that broke them up, but Farrah, for the first time wondered if she had been affected all along and never acknowledged her feelings. Maybe she was distant after it happened. It was too late to ask.

She let her mind question every significant memory while she laid in bed unable to relax. Her imagination brought up the most ludicrous things. That time Jack needed to stay late every night for two weeks in 2007, was he really out having an affair? He didn't get overtime pay so there was no way for her know. Was he only going through motions for a couple years or had it been a lot longer? When he joined a gym and took up racquetball, was that because he didn't want to spend time with her?

Was there always writing on the wall predicting something as big as a divorce? Farrah knew there must have been. Hindsight and all that. They might not have been zealous and goofy like young couples in love, but she wanted to believe that they did have love. Decades of it.

As it turned out, Lenore was able to climb the stairs and felt comfortable enough in the spare room. Farrah heard footsteps walk down the stairs. At first, she wondered if it could've been Lenore, but knew it probably wasn't. She could tell it was June just from the sound of her gait. When she didn't hear footsteps come up after a couple minutes, Farrah got up to see what was wrong.

"Did I wake you? I tried to be quiet, but the stairs are creaky."

"No. I couldn't settle down either." Farrah saw June's mug in her hand with the teabag string over the side. "Caffeine this late?"

"Trying that herbal stuff you bought for Lenore." June stood at the counter and opened a drawer to retrieve a paring knife. She sliced a lemon she plucked from a red ceramic bowl on the counter. She took another sip to taste it and said it still wouldn't do. She fetched a bottle of Irish whiskey from the dining room liquor cabinet.

"Partaking so late on a work night?"

"You finally have someone else in this house to mother. Don't judge me."

Farrah explained that she wasn't picking a fight, only asking a simple question. When people are tired and cranky though, there's no such thing as a simple question. She kept her honest feelings to herself. Until June moved in, Farrah didn't know if it was normal behavior for her to have alcohol every night. She may have had the habit a long time.

"Do you need anything to help you sleep? Want me to massage your shoulders or something?"

"I'd never say no to that, but if you start here, I'll slump over right on the table. Don't worry about it. I'll be fine."

The light over the stove kept the room in an ambient glow. The loud clattering of ice cubes in the freezer being dumped into the hopper for the door dispenser interrupted the refrigerator's hum. The sound planted the idea in Farrah that she needed a glass of water. She pushed the cup against the handle of the fridge door and took only enough for a big gulp. She knew she'd be awake twice during the night to pee. Then remembered bedtime used to be more exciting.

CHAPTER FOURTEEN

THE new dawn didn't refresh Farrah's mental state the way she hoped. She had concerns for both her house guest and for her best friend. If there was status in worrying, she could have a PhD. in it.

June only spent ten minutes downstairs to pack up some lunch and a travel mug of coffee before running out the door to work.

"Veggie burgers for dinner okay?"

"Sounds great," was the last thing June said before she darted out the side door.

Lenore showed no sign of coming out of the bedroom. She had sedatives and anti-anxiety pills so Farrah wasn't sure whether to be intrusive and check on her or if giving her space to rest was the best thing.

She was deep in thought when the phone's alert chime interrupted her brainstorming. She saw that she had an appointment that day to give someone a hot stone massage. She loved that they were appointments with higher rates so she made more from them, but they were longer sessions and physically even more demanding than the already tiring Swedish method. It also meant that she'd have to leave Lenore alone for a few hours.

Steam rose in a thick white billowing cloud from the tea kettle that boiled on the stove. She poured the hot water over the ginger teabag, not that Lenore had morning sickness anymore, but Farrah's selection of herbal teas were limited and Dr. Joel Douchebag said caffeine was still off-limits.

"Come in," Lenore said when Farrah quietly knocked on the bedroom door.

"I brought you some tea and toast. I didn't know if you'd be hungry. You should keep your strength up even if the medicine makes you forget about eating."

She felt stupid asking if anything was wrong. Of course there was. There was a ton wrong in Lenore's life. Asking seemed like the simplest way to open up conversation.

"I've been awake for a while. I'm sorry I didn't come down and spend time with you guys."

"You don't have to apologize for that. You're entitled to privacy and personal space while you're here. We understand you're not here for a slumber party."

Her back was propped up by two pillows, long ago flat and worn, but Nova had taken the better ones with her to school. The big shirts Lenore wore weren't maternity shirts specifically. Farrah guessed they could've been thrift store finds she wore for comfort or Joel's shirts that he may have been willing to part with. Her legs stayed covered by the layers of blankets, bent at the knees, and curled tightly close to her body.

"Thanks for the tea." She took two sips and held the mug to warm up her thin fingers. Her fingers touched the teabag's paper label where it said "ginger" in a swirly script. "It was a rough night. Not that the bed wasn't comfortable or anything like that."

Farrah assured her that what she was feeling was normal. The anxiety, the sadness, wanting to be somewhere else with someone else while not sounding ungrateful for the hospitality. She noticed the girl staring at the tea label. Right there in her face was the baby name she had chosen.

"I'm sorry. I didn't know if you preferred another flavor."

Lenore shook her head slightly and said it was fine. A tear escaped.

"I got more texts overnight from those three different numbers, but this time I didn't delete them." She reached for the phone on the nightstand and handed it to Farrah. "Joel got me this nice upgrade and sometimes I wonder if I wasn't better off as a Luddite."

She scrolled through the messages to see plenty of "whore" and "slut" and, of course, "homewrecker" accusations. The worst one was so appalling. The cowardly, anonymous sender typed in all caps that they wished Lenore and her baby would die.

"You should probably show these to the police."

Before handing the phone back to Lenore, Farrah closed the screens filled with threats and looked at the home screen's icons. Some were familiar, but not all of them.

"Yeah, but I talked to Star about it before when it first started, but I didn't tell her how bad they were. She's the one who did the reverse look up searches with me. They didn't come back with anything useful."

"I'm sure the police could do more. Maybe they can see if a credit card is linked to them or something. I know a decent cop. He's a local detective. And even though he once accused me of murder, he's actually a nice guy." Farrah was embarrassed that she had to confess how she knew Detective Morrison.

"If you think it'll help, I don't have anything else to lose. I've already lost everything that mattered."

It seemed like she wasn't only referring to the baby.

"Do you want to talk? I have all morning. I don't have to leave until the afternoon."

Lenore looked more at the tea than anywhere else. She began to pour her heart out. She spoke about all the promises Joel made. They were supposed to start a life together. He would care for their family and she would only work her jobs if she really wanted to be away from their child and the home. She felt like she betrayed feminism for not wanting to be a die-hard career centric woman. She wanted to work at Star's Blessings and quit her bookstore job and spend the bulk of her time at their perfect home raising their perfect baby. She daydreamed of it often.

"What's going on with you two? You should be grieving together."

"He said he needs time alone to process all of it. I kind of think he's full of shit to be honest."

"So when he dropped you off last night, it was really supposed to be 'goodbye,' for a while anyway?"

"Yep. That's what he said he needed. Meanwhile, I'm all alone. No offense. But he gets to keep his nice comfortable lifestyle and not even take a day off work. My body has been destroyed. I hurt everywhere from the surgery and the seizures and the crying. I don't think he cares about me or the miscarriage at all." Lenore's body couldn't be burrowed into the bed and wall much more than it was. Tears changed the color of her face. Her breath stayed shallow only reaching the top of her chest.

"Be honest with me, do you think he ever intended on divorcing his wife and marrying you?"

"I don't know anymore. I thought he would. I guess I was just a stupid young girl that made him feel more virile or something. I'm probably not his first piece of ass on the side. God! I'm so stupid!"

"Everyone wants to be loved and feel special. You're not stupid."

As much as Farrah wanted to promise Lenore that the pain would go away eventually because even the worst heartbreak subsides, she knew that the woman had heard enough empty promises. She even knew that it never completely leaves a person. Days or months or years could go by, but at any given moment, the brain will send a signal to the heart reminding about that thing that was lost forever — that person, that chance, all the memories together and false memories of all the things someone once dreamed. Loss is always haunting. Lenore didn't need to know that yet.

They talked for an hour until Lenore wanted to close her eyes for a bit. After a short nap, she forced herself down the stairs. Farrah assisted in getting her comfortable in the living room. She made sure some amenities were nearby: the remote controls, a glass of water, a box of multigrain crackers, her medications, and of course the cell phone she carried with her. She'd be able to heave herself up from the recliner whenever Star arrived.

"I'm sorry I have to leave you alone for a while. I'm not in a position to turn away any appointments." Farrah pulled on her old winter coat and wrapped her neck in a pink scarf that clashed.

"It's fine. Honestly, I'm okay. I guess it's time to tell Star everything. And I'm doing better than before. Plus, I have those tranquilizers if I need them, but I feel like it's good to have my feelings and cry when I have to."

"It definitely is. You know how to text me if something comes up. If you need me to grab anything on my way home, just let me know."

Lenore's attempts to reassure her that she would be fine and not to worry because Star was on her way didn't convince Farrah. She was worried. Plus, she felt like she had a daughter in the house again. It was a trap she feared. She developed attachments quickly and this was someone she barely knew.

The dismal sky loomed above and the air felt like another snow was on the way. She could feel it in her knees. She pulled the car to the end of the driveway and paused as she turned in front of the house. Miles sat in the front window keeping watch on the neighborhood for anything a cat would find suspicious.

The maroon cotton scrubs weren't enough to warm Farrah up in the frigid temperature. She planned to put the bottle of massage oil into the roaster pan with the smooth river stones just in case the trip in the car made it too cold to touch someone's skin. Seven traffic lights later, she pulled into Peregrine Corporate Park and arrived at the Riverside Wellness Spa.

She punched in the code for the back door and walked through to the reception area. Inside, she was greeted by the warmth of the earth-toned oasis. Lights dimly glowed and the ambient music created an ethereal lull, signs that someone was working. The computer showed that Farrah's colleague, Diane Phelps, was in Room Five with a one-hour appointment. The opening of the front door surprised her. Her own client wasn't due for another thirty minutes and she needed time to set up and get the stones in the roaster.

Samantha Waterston charged into the foyer in her usual bustling way, arms full while talking on her earpiece. She plopped down a heavy canvas tote bag on the reception counter along with the other half of her loot which looked like a portfolio for a small computer device, her wallet on a wrist strap, and her phone. She tapped the device in her ear and greeted Farrah.

"I really liked your idea the other night about expanding the practice instead of scaling back. We were in this town first. We can show those franchises we're in charge around here."

"Oh. That's great. I was serious about wanting to make that happen in a more financially stable job role."

"Sure. Sure. We'll get to that. But that was Maggie on the line. We're going to meet with the country club to work out a plan that we can present formally to the bank when we ask for a loan. You're in Room One today."

"Okay. Great."

Typical Sam. Not a lot of time for catching up when her mind was focused on business. Farrah hung up her coat and scarf on a hanger by the front door then carried her basket of supplies to the first room on the left.

CHAPTER FIFTEEN

THE cat jumped down from the bedroom window and scurried to the kitchen when Farrah pulled her car into the driveway. She heard the sounds of the afternoon news coming from the living room television. Otherwise, the house seemed too quiet.

"Lenore?" Farrah called out not too loudly in case her guest was asleep. "I'm home. Are you upstairs?" She walked through the living room and paused at the bottom of the stairs in the front foyer. "Lenore?"

Still nothing.

The stairs beneath her groaned with each step. She stood at the closed door and tapped with her knuckles. When there was still no answer or sound from inside the bedroom, Farrah let herself in.

She found Lenore unconscious on the bed, an arm hanging lifelessly over the side. Farrah did the quickest examination she could. There was no vomit, no blood, no signs of the medication missing. She gently slapped Lenore's cheek until finally, there was a sign of life.

"What happened? Did you take too many pills? Are you hurt?" Farrah didn't know where to begin. Her mind raced with theories from suicide to accidental overdose to a bad reaction.

"I was just sleeping." Her words were slurred. She definitely hadn't been simply sleeping.

"I'm getting you to the ER immediately."

Farrah was about to press the last "1" when Lenore knocked the phone clear from her hands. Her voice was a little stronger each time she spoke.

"I'm fine. I was sleeping. I didn't OD. Jeez."

"Maybe not intentionally, but you were deeply out of it. It's probably a bad side effect or something. You need a doctor."

She had a little bit of fight in her, but not much. Farrah insisted on making the call. The paramedics arrived and she lead them up to the room. Vitals were taken and questions were answered. After the fifteen minute wait for them to get there and another ten for a preliminary exam, they asked Lenore whether she needed to go to the ER.

"You're asking her? She's the patient. She doesn't know what she needs." Farrah was guided firmly out of the room by a medic slightly taller than her and with much better hair.

"Ma'am, we did a thorough checkup. Her eyes look fine. Her speech improved. I am recommending that she go to the ER, but she isn't incapacitated. Whatever was wrong seems to have been temporary."

"Just take her. She has gone through a miscarriage and seizures in the past few days. She needs... I don't know! Something! An MRI? An ultrasound? Don't tell her she's fine."

Lenore was able to stand and said she felt weak though without any sign of dizziness. The medics insisted on assisting her down the stairs to the ambulance. It was a slight struggle for them to round the corner at the end of the hallway, but they skillfully maneuvered.

Farrah decided to follow in her car. On the way, she used the dreadful speaker on her phone to call June.

"I'm almost home. Should I swing around and meet you at the hospital?"

"If you want, but I don't know what good it'll do other than keep me company."

June agreed to wait for more information rather than rush out with another car to park in the always full hospital lot. Farrah had to zig zag up and down the rows of the parking lot until she found what may have been a space along the further edge. If it wasn't, tough. She parked behind another car that was half on the grass.

Behind a curtain, Farrah found Lenore reclined on an ER bed. She had been changed into a patient gown and covered with a thermal blanket.

"Has a doctor been in yet to see you?"

"A nurse was. She took my temperature and blood pressure again."

They talked while waiting. It was another fifteen minutes before a different nurse came over. She asked the same questions as the previous one: name, date of birth, address, why are you here? It was to double-check that the wrist identification bracelet she was about to put on Lenore was going on the correct patient. That's when Farrah realized the old one had never been cut off so the nurse removed it to avoid any confusion.

As soon as they were alone again, Lenore filled her in on the activities of her afternoon before the unconscious episode.

"After Star left, Joel showed up. I hope you don't mind. He did message me first to see if I was up for a visit."

"Oh? That's great. How did that go?" Farrah internally questioned if he had an ulterior motive or if the man did harbor some genuine concern for his mistress. With any luck, Lenore wouldn't have detected the snark in her tone.

Finally, a doctor came with some advice. He wasn't a gynecologist though and said that he would send Lenore for some tests. They took blood there in the ER before leading her away.

Before she left, Farrah asked if Joel was notified since he was the patient's ob-gyn.

"What department are you with?"

"I'm n— what? Oh, the scrubs! I'm her pre-natal massage therapist."

"Oh. Well I'm not sure if they called her ob-gyn, but I'll see if they can get a hold of him. You can wait at the other waiting room in radiology."

Cocooned by the curtain and surrounded by sounds of running feet beyond, the doctor left them waiting for someone else to transport her. His exit was like a stage magician disappearing through theater drapes. Farrah caught a glimpse of the bustling people in scrubs. The ER lighting reflected off the aqua fabric of their uniforms making everyone's skin look a sickish green. Her maroon uniform stood out and looked more like the staff at the women's health wing.

Farrah ended up seated in a row of beige hard plastic chairs mounted together at the arms. Dr. Douchebag shocked her when he walked across the hideous burnt orange speckled carpet of the waiting area to approach her.

"Ms. Wethers, I appreciate you looking after Lenore since she doesn't seem to have any family."

She was curious. Where was he going with this?

"I'm sure you've looked out for her wellbeing too, Dr. DeSantos. She tells me what a caring doctor you are. You even personally delivered her to my house for recuperation."

"Yes. Well..." he left his thought unfinished.

"What's wrong with her now? Will she be okay?"

"I believe it was another seizure. It was fortunate she was already lying in bed trying to rest. She doesn't show any signs of injury as can happen especially when someone going through the episode is alone. Her body is still sore and tender. These kinds of patients can flail against furniture and walls and hurt themselves considerably. She seems fine in that regard."

Farrah felt like his recap inferred something more. "But she's not in another regard?"

"I don't know how well you know Lenore. Has she ever discussed her mental health?"

"No. She always seems perfectly fine. I was in her apartment. There's no signs of anything troublesome. No signs of drug use either except what the hospital gave her. She's responsible and polite. Although her spirituality might be misunderstood, but nothing else comes to mind."

"Since you are on her contact list, I'll tell you. She's actually quite unstable. I'm surprised she manages to hold down two jobs. She's experienced delusions. And quite frankly, I don't believe she should ever be living alone. She needs supervision and proper medication."

That was certainly news to Farrah. It also felt completely unwarranted. The Lenore she knew, albeit briefly, was stable and composed, perhaps more so than other women in her predicament.

He looked around the mostly empty waiting area. There was one other person there reading an outdated magazine about the Prince and Princess of Wales.

"Look, Ms. Wethers. May I be totally honest?"

"Sure. As long as you're not violating any patient confidentiality of course."

"You're one of her healthcare providers and an emergency contact." He sat beside her and put his heavy thuggish hand on her shoulder. "Lenore is so out of touch with reality that she believed she was in love with me. I was in the process of referring her to another doctor. Her delusion was so grand and fantastical that she believed I was the father of her baby."

"You're saying you weren't? She did tell me in confidence that you were. That the two of you were a couple. That you'd be getting divorced and moving her to a more family-friendly place."

His smile was unsettling not comforting. He relished the thought of being the center of someone's delusion.

"Oh my. No. No. She's simply unhinged." The way he drew out the word unhinged made Farrah's skin crawl. She also didn't believe a word he was saying.

"When can I take her home?"

"She should be done with all her tests in about an hour."

"Fine. I'll wait right here."

CHAPTER SIXTEEN

THE message in June's inbox nearly made her choke on the grape in her mouth. She was sitting at the kitchen table when her phone vibrated alerting her to an email.

"Hey, I got something," she said.

"What's that?" Farrah was preparing soup and toast for Lenore.

"It's a hit from someone on Global Registry." It felt like it took her an eternity to read through the text, truly only a few seconds, before she filled Farrah in on the gist of it. "She says she might be my sister."

"What? For real?" Farrah grabbed the nearly burning toast by the edges and kerplunked it on a plate for buttering. "Ow! Dammit."

"I mean, I don't really know who she is or if it's for real, but she's the first person to contact me."

"Let me run this upstairs and we can talk about it when I get back down."

Farrah delivered the bland dinner to the recovering young woman in bed. She was met with a sad body that was practically lifeless and without much color. Lenore's expression was one of an old person right before they welcome death. Her hair was a stringy, oily mop.

"We have to do something for her," Farrah said to June back in the kitchen. "I think I'll be able to convince her to take a bath. I'm not sure she has the strength to stand in a shower."

"Oh my god. That poor girl."

June slid the laptop over so Farrah could read the email from the genealogy site herself. She read that the sender was a woman from New York who was raised by a single mother but had been denied contact to the rest of her biological family. Without knowing what age she would be, they missed a possible filter to weed out unlikely siblings.

"What are you going to do next?"

"I want to reply right away of course. New York isn't that far. I could go out there to meet her if she wants. But I definitely want a DNA test."

"Maybe you should call your lawyer. You need to follow up with them anyway about the suit against Caressa Lamour endangering your life."

"Our lives. And yes, I think I'll give them call and see if anyone there is experienced in family law that's more extensive than divorce and custody cases."

June was prepared for a big win against the international cosmetics company that didn't properly provide a safe environment at the retreat where she worked as Farrah's administrative assistant. Farrah was a natural doubter and didn't expect she would come into any financial windfall since it was June who was drowned. Farrah's near-assault by a Caressa Lamour employee didn't bring her to the brink of death (only to the realize she had terrible judgment). She wasn't used to having luck on her side. If June did get a handsome settlement, she'd likely have people coming out of the woodwork claiming to be her long lost relatives. They had had their fill of the nosy press already.

"So you know how Hellen thinks you and I are lesbians?"

"Like everyone else? Yeah, you've mentioned it." Farrah sighed. She was quite over the assumptions that women couldn't be friends without it being something physically intimate.

"She keeps insisting I go out there and stay with her and Jae for a couple weeks. I think they want to pray over me or something."

"You're not going to go, are you?" Farrah's eyebrows furrowed.

"I told her that I couldn't take the time off work, but that she was welcome to come out here — in a hotel — and visit." June picked a paring knife out of the drawer and began peeling and slicing an apple. She cut off a piece and put it up to her mouth with the sharp blade dangerously close to her lips.

Farrah had been through all she wanted regarding defending June's sexual orientation. Jackson had never been supportive because he was so threatened by it. She would have to find the strength to make nice with Hellen and Jae for June's sake.

"When are they coming?"

"Friday."

"In two days?"

"Hey, maybe they won't stay long. Probably just the weekend. I don't think they'll be comfortable out here in the suburbs. My mother won't know what to do with herself if she has to have Jae drive her everywhere."

Farrah said she would keep her distance since Hellen already seemed to have plenty of reasons to get upset.

"What are you going to do? Is there really any place out here they'd want to see?"

"No. But I figure if I take them out to Pennsylvania for some gambling, it'll keep them content for a while. I can drop them off at the Sands and leave them there for days. They probably wouldn't even notice when I'm gone."

"Oh stop. I think Jae loves spending time with you. You used to play cards and games all the time."

"That was a long time ago, Farrah. Now they think I'm this warped, uncontrollable, confused daughter that's specifically alive to embarrass them. My mother anyway. Jae, not so much. They'll be lucky if I don't show up my Xena costume."

June's mother was definitely a force that Farrah had no interest in reckoning with. The Cho family was ruled by the matriarchy. Jae had always been a decent man and seemed to have a will that was strong in his own convictions, but he was quiet about it; whereas, Hellen made her opinions known loud and clear.

"Do you think Lenore will still be staying here by the weekend?"

Farrah shrugged. She wanted to know that their new friend would be healthy and safe before letting her out of their care. "She's not a hostage. She can leave whenever she wants. I don't think it's a good idea though. She needs a support system now more than ever. I don't think Star has the room to take her in."

"Maybe I should offer to take her out. If someone else is around, it'll be a buffer with my parents."

"Don't use her that way, you goofball. But I would get behind us all going out for something fun — taking a girls' night and going to the movies if you can swing it."

"Hmmm. I'd definitely love that a whole lot more than being lectured about all the mistakes I've made and how I shouldn't be searching for a sister I've never heard of until recently."

Even though the plans weren't likely to come to fruition, Farrah found herself clicking around on her phone's screen. She opened up the movie ticket app and scrolled through to see what would be playing that weekend.

"Action, rom com, or kids movie?"

"Nothing with a dramatic death. Can't even safely pick a kids movie these days. I was traumatized by *The Bridge to Terabithia*." June shuddered with her arms hugging her torso. "I thought it would be so cute. Good Lord."

"Yeah it seems they've really been adding a full range of emotion to kids' movies. You and Frank were still together when that came out. Wow — it's like forever ago." Farrah pulled her legs up and crisscrossed them on the chair.

"If we can ever take Lenore to the movies, it'll be tough to figure out which one. Action might be the best. Maybe she likes horror."

"No horror!"

"We can't take her to something about relationships falling apart or sick kids or anything like that. She'll need a lot of explosions or some unbelievably stupid frat boy comedy."

"I'm going to go check on her again before bed. You staying up?"

"Yeah, I'm wired. I want to do some more digging. I'll see if I can get this woman's name to give me any details if she's real and has any social media presence."

"Happy snooping."

Farrah left June alone in the glow of a laptop. At the top of the stairs, she craned her neck to see if there was any light coming through the crack under Lenore's door. It was dark. She tapped quietly and waited for any sound. With no reply, she decided it was best to let Lenore sleep. She ate the toast and soup instead.

Miles was already sound asleep hogging the bed when she entered her room. She picked up the wrong remote trying to turn the TV on. Finally, she found the right one of the four and the screen came alive as the late news wrapped up.

A small lined pad of paper was always kept on her nightstand. She propped up her pillows, grabbed the little yellow pad and a pen, and began brainstorming more thoughts about Riverside Spa's potential for expansion at the country club. Even though it sounded like all the business partners were in their own beginning stages of seeing what would be possible, Farrah wanted to prove that she could bring something to the table. It was her idea and if there was going to be a second location, she wanted to be the manager with that stable paycheck and more predictable hours.

CHAPTER SEVENTEEN

THE new day brought new worry. Farrah and Lenore sat in the kitchen having oatmeal and cups of coffee and tea respectively.

"Have you ever liked coffee?" Farrah remembered that her first sip of coffee was unpleasant because her mother took it black. But in college, when she tasted the decadent-barely-coffee-anymore cups with tons of milk and four sugars, her addiction began. Since then, she's enjoyed a more toned down approach valuing better beans sweetened with agave and using her guilty pleasure, vanilla almond milk.

"Not really. I hate the aftertaste. I don't eat much dairy so adding a lot of milk doesn't help. Herbal teas have a lot of variety and I feel like when I pick one out to drink, there's some kind of purpose behind the flavor or blend." The small indication of pleasure was something that Lenore hadn't shown since her miscarriage. Farrah appreciated that someone could find a reason to smile in the smallest of things like choosing a cup of tea.

"I know you want to go to the shop and visit with Star today. How about I take you so you don't have walk?"

"Thank you. I feel like I've taken over your life. I don't want you to miss out on appointments or anything because of me."

Farrah wanted to reach out and hug her, but she didn't know if that would be too familiar and weird. "You're not interrupting anything. If I had an appointment, I wouldn't have offered. Or, I would've dropped you off on the way. It's fine."

"I miss working. I miss all the people." She sputtered on her sip of tea. "Oh, I mean, not that I don't like hanging out here with you and June. You guys are fun and very sweet to me."

"I didn't think anything of it. You have a couple of interesting jobs where you meet all kinds of people in a bigger, more public way than my job. I meet people, but it's still got a bubble of isolation about it most of the time. The exception is when I do those large events for ten-minute sessions, which after my last experience, I never want to do again."

It was awkward, but Farrah filled Lenore in on all the gory details about the Caressa Lamour retreat and how it began with her trying to rescue their CEO, but turned into a horror with June being nearly killed and then a seductive man trying to assault Farrah herself. And between all those horrible things, she was giving massages to overworked people.

"So, if you hear June mentioning a lawsuit, that's what we're talking about. It was traumatic. It nearly drove me off the internet completely. Trolls came after us. People tracked down my home address. They pestered my husband at work. My bank accounts were being attacked so we didn't have access to our money. It's really something how people can destroy you from anywhere in the world nowadays."

"Oh my god. But look at you now. You got through it. I hope I can be that resilient."

They washed up their dishes and relaxed for a couple hours before heading out. Farrah spent the time typing up her notes from the yellow pad in case she needed to print or email them in the future.

*****

The incense wafted from Star's Blessings as someone exited the shop. Farrah heard the bells over the door jingle. The man held the door seeing that Farrah and Lenore were close. She said thank you absently, not really looking at him at all, but detected a hint of stale pot coming off his coat. The entry way had a corkboard covered in flyers about local musical events, random business cards, and a lost cat flyer that was so crumpled and worn the poor critter probably hadn't had a good outcome.

The nag champa aroma greeted Farrah's welcoming nostrils. She felt a wave of peace cascade over her. She knew the power of aromatherapy well, but it had been quite some time since she felt the effects this immediate and strong.

"Baby girl! You're here! Oh, I've missed you!" Star's outstretched umber arms swam around in her loose cotton tunic. It was evident who Lenore looked to for style inspiration.

The woman's flawless skin looked decades younger than Farrah despite being about a dozen years older. There was barely a hint of her Georgia accent when she spoke, though it was emphasized with certain words and phrases.

"Farrah, you remember my boss Star Turner?"

"Of course. It's nice to see you again, Star. I love this shop. There's so much in here that I don't even know where to begin looking."

"Ah, last time you were in for readings and you were pretty nervous if I recall." She held her arms around Lenore like a protective mother.

"Yep. That's an understatement."

"Well now you're back and Lenore can show you around properly. I just need to grab that ringing phone. It's just another annoying telemarketing call, but I can't exactly ignore them or I might miss something important."

Lenore began a slow tour for Farrah. She started with the front display case of crystal balls, black mirrors, and tumbled stones in every conceivable color. The next case had unsharpened blades of various sizes; the pièce de résistance at the bottom of the case taking up a shelf by itself was a full length sword in a sheath that Lenore said is used in the highest form of ceremonies usually by people of European descent.

There was a case dedicated to figures and statues of South American and African loas or deities. A horned god caught Farrah's attention. It stood behind a tented piece of paper labeled *Ikenga, God of Fortune and Industry (Igbo)*. She wondered why her boring Christian upbringing didn't have gods with specific purposes and rituals of worship. She felt a longing that she needed divine intervention from someone like Ikenga in order not to go bankrupt.

They perused the bottles of oils on the top of the case and then the jewelry in the next two cases including mala beads used in meditating and Yorubaland hip beads. Along the wall behind the counter were shelves lined with jars of dried herbs. The opposite wall had shelves of statues; incense in sticks, cones, or small bags; and the rest was the biggest selection of candles that Farrah had ever seen. They were every color, mostly small votives, but there were varieties in shapes Farrah wondered about. She didn't know if it was rude to ask why someone would want a red vulva or red penis candle to burn.

"Baby Girl, how are you feeling after burning that Saint Philomena candle?"

"It hasn't been good. Today is the first day that I finally feel more human. I'm not myself. I feel so different. Like I'm just this different, other person. I don't know how to explain it." Lenore's hands rubbed her belly before she wrapped her arms around herself, gave a squeeze, then let them drop to her sides.

There were some helpful labels in front of the black cat candles explaining they were to be burned when needing a reversal of bad luck. Farrah felt the sensation inside her to be spontaneous and irresponsible. Retail therapy. She knew it would be fleeting, but for a little while, it would feel so good. Star must have noticed her biting her lower lip in contemplation.

"Do you need some help with that?"

"Me? Oh. I don't know. I could definitely use some good luck."

"Do you want to tell me what parts of your life you're looking for help with?"

Her expression said it all. She needed help with everything. Her life was in ruins and turmoil. Her job was on the line. Her husband was seeking a divorce. Her daughter wouldn't talk to her.

"First thing is my family. My husband and I split up and now my daughter won't speak to me. And this might sound strange since she's just a kid in her twenties, but you remind me of her. She wears her hair natural like that now. She didn't used to."

"Oh, I see. What's your daughter's name?"

The bells over the door jingled and Lenore volunteered to help out the potential customer while Star talked with Farrah.

"Well that's harder to answer than you might realize. Her name was Janice Margaret Wethers. Margaret was after her grandmother. But she changed it. Legally, I mean. She didn't even ask her father or me about it. She came home from college one day and announced that she legally changed her name to Nova Harper Wethers."

"And this upset you?"

"It was only the beginning. We used to be so close. Now she's grown up. I'm so proud that she's her own person, really. But she hates me. I can't stand it."

"Your daughter is black, I take it? If she wears her hair like mine?"

"Yes."

The black cat candle was returned to its place on the shelf. Star's fingers and wrists were covered in jewelry of all different colors, metals, and beads. She moved a few feet over to a shelf of tall candles in glass jars. They had printed labels over the glass so one could still see the color of the wax inside. Star took down one that was blue with white lettering.

"The first thing you're going to do is burn a candle for a peaceful home a little every day for seven days." She told Farrah to set the candle in front of a picture of her daughter.

"Okay, those are instructions I can manage to follow."

"Now, let me explain something. I don't know what kind of African blood your husband's family has, but in mine, we take our names very seriously."

The hair on Farrah's neck and arms stood up. She was petrified that she offended her. Then her lightning fast thoughts made her wonder if she offended her own daughter.

Star continued, "We have pretty long names by American standards. Back in Liberia and Ghana, children can be given names connected to their family members like you said your daughter had her grandmother's name. But then they add in the city where they are from. And then the family has a special nickname that only they use for the child. And it's not over then. Sometimes the people of the community come up with their own name for the child too."

"I didn't know that."

"Identity is critical to who we are. At certain milestones in our lives, a lot of people make the decision to choose their own new name. Other folks have to respect that."

"I wonder if that's why she did it. She never said it had to do with her connection to roots. I thought she was being impulsive because she loves acting and entertainment. Like a stage name. I feel terrible."

"You should."

The bluntness felt like Farrah was being hit while she was already down. She loved her daughter. And it's not that she would never have supported such an important decision, but as her mother, she was never consulted. It was a surprise to the family. The family would have supported her and would've paid for it somehow.

"She asked strangers and friends for the money to do it. She never even came to us. She never talked to us."

"This was about Nova. Not you. Now tell me what else has you worried?"

Farrah turned away as her eyes teared up and burned. She felt like a complete jerk and needed to compose herself to continue. When she could, she told Star a bit about the instability in her career and how she wanted to be given a chance to become manager. By the end of the discussion, Star rang up over seventy dollars of supplies in candles, anointing oil, a pewter charm of Saint Rita of Cascia, a small tied up bundle of white sage to cleanse the house, and a tumbled piece of aventurine, which Star said was to overcome naiveté and ignorance.

Okay, I deserve that, Farrah thought. Then a voice in the back of her head reprimanded her since there's no way she would be able to pay her credit card.

After Lenore had helped the one customer, she sat on a stool to pet the long haired Calico cat perched on the counter. She said goodbye to Star with a huge hug. She walked slowly, leading Farrah out the front door and said she couldn't wait to show her how to smudge her house with the sage.

Before they got to the car, a series of three chiming notifications sounded from Lenore's phone. She looked at the screen, turned off the power, and slipped it back into her bag.

CHAPTER EIGHTEEN

THE trip back to the house was short and eerily silent. Farrah had her own suspicions about what the texts to Lenore said or at least whom they were from. She didn't feel it was appropriate to bring the subject up at that moment.

Once inside the house, Lenore perked up more, but not fully as she was in Star's Blessings. She took the shopping bag Farrah had placed on the dining room table and unpacked it.

"I'll leave the peaceful home candle ritual to you. It's not hard. Just remember what Star said to do." Lenore moved into the kitchen and, as if she were right at home, began going through the cabinets. She found a small pottery dish that would be suitable for use as an ashtray for the sage smudge stick. A long lighter was easily accessible on top of the kitchen counter in a pottery jar filled with wooden spoons and spatulas.

"I'll be right back." Farrah went upstairs to her bedroom. She opened a door on what looked like a miniature version of a clothing wardrobe. It was a jewelry box. Necklaces hung inside on the small double doors. There were shelves full of boxes and three small drawers. After their struggling early years together, Jackson had begun buying her "real jewelry," he called it. Not that it was worn in any way different, but genuine stones and pearls that weren't made from plastic. That's when he decided she needed a proper place to house the treasures.

Once Farrah had begun her journey to better her inner self, she had also become aware of the destruction of the planet. She had since banned herself from buying conflict jewelry and tried to stick with using her old pieces or on rare occasion treating herself to something shiny from an estate sale. She felt a lot less guilt if the piece was recycled to a new owner and had some history behind it.

She took out a silver necklace that had a relatively cheap dolphin charm on it from one of their family vacations to the Baltimore Aquarium. The charm was swapped for the Saint Rita of Cascia medallion Star chose for her. She wasn't religious, especially not Catholic. Any little bit of comfort was necessary even if it was hokum, as Jack would have said. She didn't have the answers and in a way, she didn't want them. She only wanted help.

The necklace that she wore daily was a white gold herringbone and on it were her wedding rings. She couldn't wear rings while massaging anyone so it became her habit not to have them on her hand but still have them on her. She unhooked the chain and hung it on one of the pegs of the wooden door. Her hand automatically went up to her chest where she felt the missing weight. It was time to replace her past with the new medallion and hopefully, a brighter future for her family no matter what configuration it became.

"What do you think?" Farrah asked Lenore when she returned to the kitchen.

"I like it. I hope it brings your family some peace or at least patience with one another." Lenore's smile was sweet and innocent. Her pain was visible when Farrah looked close enough for the signs.

"So... how do we smudge? I've sort of got an understanding. I've seen pictures of it and I think characters on TV have done it, but I don't know what I'm actually doing here."

"It's simple — one of the easiest ways to practice incorporating ritual in your life. It's also nondenominational."

"I remember the priests with the incense going up the aisles at my friend's wedding. It smelled nice. Wasn't sure what it was for exactly."

"A lot of religions use incense for purification and meditation or prayer. That's why I didn't mind recommending this to you, although, you seem open-minded anyway."

Lenore lit one end of the bulky sage bundle that was tied up with string. The ends burned into embers and she blew out any flames.

"I don't have my wafting feathers with me. They're back at my place. But we can use our hands or some paper. Whatever's lying around will work fine." She held the dish under the smudge stick in case any ashes dropped. The smoke filled the kitchen quickly so they began waving their hands around.

Lenore suggested covering as much of the house as possible so they began in the utility room with the laundry machines and Miles' litterbox. She held the dish up high into the corners then repeated close to the floor while Farrah kept wafting the smoke. They went through the kitchen and then covered the rest of the first floor. Lenore took the lead to go up the stairs and then they repeated the steps in each bedroom and the bathroom on the second floor.

"Do you have an attic?"

"Yes. Is that necessary?"

"We should be as thorough as possible."

126

Farrah showed her the way through a door and up more stairs. Lenore's smaller stature kept her from having to hunch over as much as Farrah. It was an awkward maze where they had to climb over boxes and trunks of dusty possessions.

"At least Jackson took all the things he thought were important, but he still left a lot up here." One of the boxes was thin but large and wrapped in plastic. It was her wedding dress which had been professionally preserved for storage by the dry cleaner. She didn't think there was any chance her daughter would want it now.

When they were finished covering the house's interior, Lenore had to convince her to make a round of the outside of the house and the yard.

"Plus we can do your car too. I mean, as long as we have it burning, we might as well cover everything."

Farrah grew fearful of what her neighbors would think if they saw a couple women walking around a house waving smoke at everything. If she had any luck, they wouldn't be home yet, but Farrah had not felt lucky in ages. She went through with it and indulged Lenore in her quest to rid the house of something, Farrah wasn't quite sure what to call it other than bad energy vibes.

When they were finished, they sat in the living room for a while so Lenore could mindlessly watch TV and Farrah could reply to some emails. She made the mistake of looking at social media for just a minute which turned into an hour passing and she didn't realize it until she heard June come in the side door through the dining room.

"Hey, honies! I'm home!"

"Well, what's got you in a good mood?" Farrah closed all the browser tabs and plopped the laptop onto the coffee table.

"It's my calm before the storm. My parents are coming tomorrow. And get this, it's weird." She took off her coat, hat, and scarf and left them slumped over a dining room chair. She dropped her lunch bag and purse on the floor.

"What's weird?" Lenore asked.

"I told you guys that I have been speaking politely to Frank again, right?" They confirmed. "I made the huge mistake of telling my mother. Now she wants Frank to come to dinner with us Friday night. What am I going to do?"

"You're not dating him. Just don't bring him." Farrah made it sound easy.

"Wait, did you tell Frank that your parents want to see him? If he doesn't know then you can get away with it, but if he does..." Lenore said.

June made a loud grumbling half-roar at herself for her slip of the tongue — or more accurately thumb — for texting him that bit of news.

"Yeah, did you tell him? What did he say? This is still weird to me that you're talking, just FYI."

June kicked off her shoes. She took the throw pillow from the chair, sat down with it, and then buried her face in it.

"I only mentioned to him that they were coming. He wanted me to say hello from him and that's where all this erupted from. I really should go back to kickboxing class and work this out."

Without any doubts, they agreed that if Frank casually dined with his ex-in-laws, there would be false hope of not only reconciliation, but Hellen's prayer for a heteronormative daughter to be answered. Like a lot of people, she wrote off June's female romantic partners as phases since she married a man and would still occasionally date men.

"Why the hell does it smell like Lilith Fair in here?"

Farrah was embarrassed, but Lenore was used to the question. "It's only sage. We cleansed the whole house, inside and out, and even Farrah's car and the property."

"It's making me hungry. Hungrier. Is sage supposed to do that?"

"Everything makes you hungry," Farrah said.

"It's not that unusual. Your olfactory sense is probably connecting sage to some great meals like Thanksgiving dinner or something," Lenore said.

"This is why aromatherapy can be effective. I'm so glad I don't have to defend myself in that regard to Jack anymore. Who cares what he thinks?"

June snapped her hand at the wrist. "Oh screw him. You and Lenore know what works for some people and some conditions, especially if they're emotional. I know my mood instantly changes once I smell things that remind me of autumn and Halloween."

Farrah knew how important Halloween was to June and Frank while they were married. Now it was important to Frank and Jackson. Frank's competitiveness about Halloween had left June bitter about the holiday for several years.

"Do you think those associations will be more pleasant now that you guys are friends again?"

"I don't know. I guess so. Make me a pumpkin pie and I'll tell you." June pulled her phone out and scrolled through some screens. She got quiet when she typed.

"You two are really plugged in, aren't you?" Lenore said.

"Not me. After that Caressa Lamour trolling, I try to keep myself restrained and my time limited. I only check my email and do the bare minimum I have to for business. I see June every day. My daughter used to text me. I have no real reason to keep checking my phone. But that one… she's a different story."

June confirmed it. Her phone was practically an appendage. She said she was surprised someone as young as Lenore wasn't as addicted.

"Joel only bought me the fancy upgrade recently. I had the pay-as-you-go phone and only used free Wi-Fi which wasn't great in my apartment. He didn't put his name on my bills or anything, but he used his credit cards to upgrade my cable package too."

Farrah and June exchanged curious looks. If Joel was careless enough to pay for anything on his credit cards, his wife had to know what was going on, unless he had a secret card his wife didn't know about.

CHAPTER NINETEEN

BY Friday, Lenore was feeling better physically, but still followed orders to rest as much as possible without returning to her busy jobs. Farrah was uneasy about the advice coming from Joel, especially after the bombshell he dropped in Farrah's lap about Lenore having mental issues. It was tempting for her to tell Lenore what he said, but no good would come of it until she had regained more strength.

"I know I'm not supposed to go to work, but is it all right with you if Star drops off some things for me package?"

Farrah was in the middle of smashing up hardboiled eggs for egg salad. Adding a hint of dry mustard was her secret ingredient to make them taste like deviled eggs the way her mother used to make them.

"I don't mind. I'm happy you're feeling more comfortable here. If you wanted to return to your apartment though, I would understand. You know June and I were worried about your immediate recovery, but it's great to see you bouncing back."

Lenore smiled. "June and I talked after you went to bed last night. She said she's going to take her parents up the casino and spent a night there so as long as you aren't kicking me out, I'd love to stay. We can keep each other company. Not like Joel is coming to visit me ever again." Miles was in Lenore's arms, his eyes squinted closed while she scratched under his chin.

"Can I be blunt?"

"Sure."

"Are you afraid to leave? To be alone, I mean."

Lenore moved one of the kitchen chairs with her foot to pull it out. She sat down without disturbing the happily spoiled orange cat.

"Not really. I mean, I know I shouldn't be."

"But those messages are getting to you, aren't they? Trust me, please. I know kind of what you're going through. I received all kind of horrific comments and threats. People looked up where I lived and worked. They made my life a nightmare. And those people, sweetie, were total strangers. You're in a very complicated situation here with Joel. There's no way it's a secret. And there are likely to be people, more specifically one person, hating your guts."

"I know. I don't think Nikki is dumb enough not to realize we were seeing each other or rather that he was seeing someone. I don't know how she'd know it's me. I'm not sure if she knows about his promises to me to leave her. And I doubt if she knows about the baby."

Her youthful face sagged again as it did whenever melancholy overcame her. Farrah saw the discoloration under her eyes from not sleeping enough. At least it seemed like Lenore's pallor had improved somewhat after several days of healthier meals. One cannot live on toast and tea no matter how delicious it is or Farrah would have tried.

Lenore gave the cat more kisses. "I would like to go back to my place though just to swap out clothes and pick up a few things that I miss having around me."

"I can take you whenever you're ready."

While Lenore went upstairs to shower and get changed, Farrah decided to do a little research. She and June already snooped into the reputation of Dr. Joel DeSantos. What had her curiosity piqued now was how much of a role stress could play in miscarriages ruled to be caused by eclampsia.

What she read was more informative that anything covered in her pre-natal massage training. The unfortunate news was that Farrah's internet research explained the symptoms, but all the sites said there was no medically identified source for pre-eclampsia or eclampsia. Symptoms included uncontrollable high blood pressure, headaches, vomiting or nausea, proteinuria, anxiety, shortness of breath, and several other symptoms that could have easily been mistaken for other conditions or possibly neglected in a pregnant woman being told by her own doctor she had severe morning sickness and wasn't taking care of herself.

Lenore flowed through the room in a yellow crêpe skirt and matching blouse cinched at the waist by a braided belt. She looked like sunshine on chilly forty-degree day. Luckily she had on another layer with a second skirt underneath and under that thick woolly tights with tall vintage flat-heeled brown leather boots.

The gutters were filled with black water from the dirty melting snow. There was a small parking lot for tenants about a block away from Lenore's building. Lenore never used it since she gave up owning a car a few years prior. Her license was still valid and she told Farrah that Joel planned on getting her something used but reliable and safe in order to make chores like food shopping and getting to appointments easier once they started their family. Farrah heard the guilt and regret in her voice as she spoke past tense.

"It's not like you'll never have another chance at starting a family. But maybe it shouldn't be with Joel. It's hard for most couples to actually make it after something tragic happens." Farrah patted Lenore's back as they walked.

"I've cried so much. I didn't think it was possible for anyone to cry like this." Lenore choked back the tears and attempted to rein in her emotions all together.

The sidewalks of Clinton Avenue were not a town priority. They were cracked and in dire need of repair which was how they had been for a number of years. It was the street of lower income apartments above businesses like the check cashing place and the low income medical clinic. At one time, one of the offices at street level was the headquarters for the district's only Hispanic politician. He never got re-elected for a second term. Lenore lived in the only stand-alone apartment building sandwiched on the second floor of the three-story walkup.

"I guess it made sense for you to consider moving out of here. I can't imagine trying to lug a stroller or carrier up and down these stairs, no less trying to haul groceries at the same time." At what point was it insensitive for Farrah to talk about baby things, she didn't know. It was the real world life of her friend and pretending there were no baby related things in the world wasn't necessarily a great approach.

"There's a service elevator but it's pretty smelly. These units are small so there's not a lot of families in it anyway. Studios and one-bedroom mostly with only a couple of two-bedrooms."

"And I'm guessing no one in a wheelchair."

"Not that I've seen, no."

Lenore's scream as she rounded the top of the stairs sent Farrah backwards as she stumbled down a couple steps grabbing for the railing.

The ugly dark brown doors of apartments 301, 302, and 303 were almost identical except for the last names of the tenants labeled under the peep holes. Lenore's door, however, had a brand new feature, a ghastly unwanted one.

Farrah was quickly by her side with her arm around her. Her purse's strap fell to the crook of her other arm and she just about tripped again when her leg knocked into it.

Hanging from a miniature noose was a naked baby doll covered in filth and (hopefully fake) blood. The eyes were scribbled over with black marker. The body of it was cut open from what appeared to be several stabs with a knife. The legs were bound together with black electrical tape. Wrapped around an ankle was red yarn and tied to the end of that was a scroll of paper.

"YOU DESERVE IT!" The note said in cut out magazine letters like an old fashioned ransom note.

"Okay this is going too far! I'm calling Detective Morrison and telling him we can't wait for him to find a convenient time to talk anymore. He's got to send people over here right now." Farrah had the number saved in her phone. She had called him so much in the past that she even changed the generic head silhouette avatar on the contacts page to a cute cartoon cop with a bushy mustache much like his.

Farrah kept one arm wrapped around Lenore while she spoke to the police detective on the phone. He agreed to send over one of the patrol cars immediately and he'd meet them there. He advised her not to enter the apartment in the off chance that someone was inside.

It wasn't a long wait and they were grateful for the expediency. Officer Jeremy Groff was a hulking man in his early thirties. He asked them basic questions to make sure they were unharmed physically and whether they saw anyone coming or going from the building. He drew his Glock and since Lenore was there with her keys, he entered as quietly as possible without a dramatic break in. Groff only needed a minute to cover the studio. There weren't too many options for a person to hide. Closets, under the bed, the ledge outside the windows. All clear.

Detective Morrison arrived and before talking to anyone, he used his phone to take photos of the bloodied baby doll in the noose still on the door. He checked the lock to make sure there was no tampering, but from what he observed, whoever did it didn't need to break in. There were no security cameras on the floors either. He only saw one pointed at the front entrance.

"I've never needed to think about security cameras before," Lenore said to him when he mentioned it. "It's not the nicest building, sure, but it's hardly a high crime area. I think our biggest problem is packages being stolen."

Morrison took the doll off the door and placed it inside a clear plastic evidence bag. There was barely enough room for all of them inside the designated living room area.

"Groff, take a look around the rest of the building. Canvas the neighbors and see if anyone saw anything."

"Yes, sir. Do you want me to call Rosie over to assist?"

"Yeah. And call the county too. I want the dog over here." Riverside didn't have its own K-9 unit and like a lot of services, resources were often regional acquisitions and shared or owned by the county to be loaned out. The sheriff's department wasn't terribly busy with anything other than transporting prisoners and guarding the courthouse. Somehow, they had bigger budgets each year compared to the smaller municipal departments.

Farrah had a modicum of familiarity with Lenore's apartment so she offered to make tea. She served Lenore a cup of something that was labeled "healthy mommy blend" similar to the one labeled "serenity mix" that Farrah retrieved before. The mommy blend also looked like a variety of herbs that Lenore mixed together for herself. The only ingredient Farrah recognized was the aroma of ginger root.

"Leave the jar out, Farrah. I want to take that back to your house."

"Of course."

"Are you going to spend the night at the Wethers' house then?" Morrison held a small notebook and a pen, but didn't seem to hear anything compelling enough to jot down yet.

"Yes. I've been staying there for several days. Tonight was going to be my last night there, but…"

"Don't worry about it," Farrah said. "You can stay as long as you want. I told you that. I don't know if you're safe here and I couldn't possibly let you come back here until I know the person behind this is stopped."

"Speaking of," Morrison said, "Ms. Wethers told me about the text messages you've been getting. Do you have any idea who wants to scare you or make these threats?"

"It's okay. Just tell him the whole story."

CHAPTER TWENTY

FARRAH asked Detective Morrison to escort them back to her house. Even though he wanted to begin his investigation immediately and planned to send Officer Rosie Alvarez with them, she insisted since they had a certain level of a casual relationship already.

"Plus, I have coffee and I know you love my coffee."

She caught him trying not to smile, but it was there and it made her smile too. Under the distressful set of circumstances they faced, she appreciated any opportunity to experience a little joy.

It was Lenore's first time back at her apartment since Farrah had tried gathering and unsuccessfully hiding all the baby accoutrements. She packed a couple canvas tote bags that were normally for her grocery shopping. She put clothes in one and magickal tools and her jar of tea in the other. Farrah wasn't sure when or how Lenore planned to use a tarot deck, a silver pentacle that she called a peyton, the black dagger she called an athame, or any of the other various objects Farrah noticed before on the altar space.

"I don't know if I'll use any of it, but I just want my things near me."

"It's fine. You can make yourself comfortable at the house. If that means having all these things, then so be it. The place has been a lot emptier without Nova's and Jackson's things anyway. June didn't move in with very much at all."

Lenore carried the lighter bag of clothes while Farrah bore the burden of a heavier one without any problem.

Morrison was practically right behind them. He parked his unmarked sedan on the street rather than block Farrah's car in the driveway despite having enough room. His driver side door had a barely noticeable variation in the paint from being replaced after a deer ran into it. In New Jersey, it's awfully common. They can't be avoided. Police departments hated the embarrassment, but it wasn't uncommon for cars to get bodywork done after run-ins with wildlife. Another time, a Canada goose broke a windshield of a Riverside patrol car. It happens.

Farrah began by grinding some coffee beans that June bought at the health food store. The aroma immediately filled the dining room where there was still a residue of the white sage smell. The expensive beans were meant for special occasions, and this had to qualify albeit an unpleasant situation. Treating the police officer well was something Farrah used to do out of nervousness, but after a few times, she decided she actually liked him.

"Ms. Lexington?" Morrison leaned forward in his seat at the table as he tried to spot Lenore bustling around.

"Lenore." She came in from the kitchen with a fresh cup of hot tea for herself.

"Lenore. I'll see what I can find out from your phone carrier, but nowadays people are tricky about using burner phones. What I'll try to do is match the timestamp of the texts to anything else significant that you can you think of." He accepted the cup of coffee from Farrah who took the seat at the head of the table next to him.

"Okay. Honestly, I don't have much of a life. I work and I'm home. Until this hospitalization, I never did much else."

"Well, that's not the complete picture," Farrah interrupted. "You come in for massages and you have... had... doctor's appointments. So you did leave the house sometimes."

"Yeah, I'm not a hermit. I mean that I'm not particularly social outside of work. I see the most people at my jobs. I only see my boyfriend, if that's what he still is, after hours at my place."

Since they had filled Morrison in on the awkward and ethically questionable details back at Lenore's apartment, there wasn't much more for Lenore to say about who could want to threaten her.

"Have you noticed anyone following you or taking a particular interest in you at any of these locations? The doctor's office? The book shop or the new age shop?" Morrison wasn't too graceful glugging down a third of the coffee as soon as he had the chance.

"Oh, I don't know. It's sounds ridiculous. I'm nobody really. When I think someone is looking at me, I wonder why. But now that you mention it," she stopped and didn't continue until he urged her. "There's an ultrasound technician at Joel's office. I thought she just had terrible bedside manner. She's cold and surly. When she does smile it's more like a forced, snarky smirk like her face is actually sarcastic. I didn't know a whole face could be, but that's how I feel when I have to see her."

Farrah was surprised Lenore hadn't mentioned this woman before considering all the conversations they'd had about her pregnancy and medical care.

"Do you know her name?" Morrison reached into his pocket for his small notebook and pen.

"Marlena. I'm not sure what her last name is. I think she's in her forties maybe. Tan skin, black hair, speaks Spanish. I don't know anything about her really except that she makes me uncomfortable."

"I'll check her out. And I'm telling you now, I'm going to be digging deep into Dr. DeSantos. I know you don't want that and wish it could be different, but he's the closest to this situation. It's usually the boyfriend or an ex-boyfriend or angered wife. I'll be looking at her too."

"Her name is Nikki." Lenore grew visibly anxious.

Farrah noticed the signs of panic attack. "Do you need something? Maybe some food. You don't look so good right now. Detective, maybe we can take a break. She's been through a lot."

"I don't know what's wrong. I was never the type to have anxiety or depression. But I keep falling apart." Lenore's hands trembled and her face became flushed.

Farrah leapt up and moved over to the empty seat on the other side of her to hug her. Morrison made some notations and closed his notebook. He finished his coffee, but Farrah could tell he wasn't in a hurry to leave now that he had gotten Lenore talking.

"I feel like I'm going to be sick." She pushed out from the table and ran to the utility room off the kitchen where there was a toilet next to the laundry machines.

Farrah took some paper towels and ran them under cold water. She held Lenore's hair out of the way and put the cold towels on the back of her neck until the heaving was over.

"Look, I know I'm not a doctor, but I'm ordering you to bed right now. Call it maternal instinct orders."

Morrison hadn't budged from the dining room table as if he wasn't going to let the interview end that easily. Dry heaving or not, he needed Lenore to answer as much as possible.

The women walked back in his direction, but Lenore didn't stop. She continued through to the living room and foyer then up the stairs.

"Detective, she's in no condition to talk anymore. I promise you can come back tomorrow if you have to or call me later and I'll see how she is."

"Farrah, you know that if I'm going to figure out who's terrorizing that poor girl, I'm going to have to dig into her life no matter how scandalous or upsetting it is." He stood and handed the empty mug to her.

"Phil, I like you and I'm going to forget that you're being a jerk at this very moment. She needs rest and I'm not letting you near her right now."

"Thanks for your time." He took his coat off the back of the chair and pulled out his knitted winter cap from one pocket and gloves from the other. "Call me later. You have my number."

"I will. I promise." Leaving behind the dirty mugs on the dining room table, she showed him to the door before heading up to Lenore's temporary bedroom.

The bedroom door wasn't closed. Inside, Farrah saw Lenore sitting and curled up on the bed with a small wastebasket clutched in her arms. Her hair was now pulled back in a sloppy half-bun half-ponytail nest with a scrunchie.

"Has anything come up?" Farrah hated to ask.

"Bile and spit."

"Morrison is gone. I agreed to call him later, but that doesn't mean you have to talk to him tonight." She sat at the end of the bed and thoughtfully patted Lenore's foot.

"I thought I was doing better. I really was. I know as well as anyone that healing takes time, but I didn't expect to slide backwards."

"I'm not sure what's going on exactly with your body. I thought eclampsia symptoms would end after the miscarriage. And honestly, I think you should see a doctor, but not Joel. There's absolutely no way he's impartial. You're very sick. You need to be able to eat and function."

Lenore placed the wastebasket on the floor next to the bed. She grabbed a tissue from the box that was always on the nightstand and nearly empty from her days of crying.

"I guess I could go to the ER, but it seems extreme and I just got out of the hospital. I don't want to go back. I was fine yesterday and was fine up until seeing that thing on my door."

"The human body is pretty complex. I wish I could help you better." Farrah's phone was inside her pants pocket and vibrated against her. "Damn. That's June. She's out of work and meeting her parents for dinner and then leading them over here. You do not have to leave this bed and meet them. You need rest. I'll bring up some toast and ginger ale."

"Thanks. I don't know what I'd do if I wasn't here with you. You're a great mom."

Farrah's eyes instantly grew tears. A great mom? She's the mom who has a daughter that hates her. Taking in Lenore like a stray kitten hardly made up for the fact that she felt like an utter failure in the mom department.

She sniffed up the wetness forming in her nose. "Any mom would be lucky to have you." She had to keep herself from saying that Lenore would be a great mom herself someday because that ambiguous someday would be far too traumatic for her to hear.

CHAPTER TWENTY-ONE

HELLEN and Jae were exactly as June had described them to Farrah minus the demon wings and flaming eyes her own imagination added to the acerbic matriarch. It wasn't until this past year that June talked much about her parents and when she did, Farrah realized how unloved her best friend felt. She never had her own children and Frank's kids weren't part of her life anymore. As far as people to call family, Farrah was all that June had on a reliable basis.

"Let me take your coats," she said greeting them at the side door. "I'll go hang these in the foyer."

When Farrah made her exit from the dining room, she heard Hellen comment on the "mess" not being cleaned up. Three recently used mugs that she didn't have time to move into the dishwasher was Hellen's idea of a mess. Farrah expected her to be a hard nut to crack, but hadn't prepared herself for personal criticism.

"Mom, it's not a mess." June picked up the mugs and they were gone within seconds. "Can I get you anything? We have excellent coffee."

They asked for water which June delivered with a small plate of sugar cookies. They sat around the dining room table in an awkward

145

silence as Hellen examined everything within her eyeline, even the construction of the table itself.

"Mrs. Cho, I hear you've been volunteering at your church a lot. Tell me what things you get to do there." Farrah mostly wanted them to leave for their hotel over the river in Pennsylvania, but she promised to be polite.

"I am in charge of the food pantry now. Young Sun had it in complete disarray. It's much better now."

"Oh wow. That sounds like a huge project. You must have a lot of help."

Breaking Hellen's icy demeanor seemed to be working. She was happy to talk about her accomplishments in her retired years after many decades of software engineering.

"Mom, maybe Farrah can give you suggestions about your wrist pain?"

"I have to take so many pills. There's the inflammation, high blood pressure, cholesterol, allergies." She ended with a dramatic sigh.

Jae reached over and held his wife's wrinkled hand in his own.

"You take them so I can keep you around longer." His words were sweet and genuine. His fingers rubbed against her wedding band, unable to spin it around easily because her fingers were swollen from arthritis.

Hellen reached out with her other hand and pulled the clear glass jar of Lenore's healthy mommy tea herbs towards her.

"What's this? Healthy mommy mix? June, are you pregnant?" Hellen was momentarily excited, possibly happy.

"What? No! Mom, that's Lenore's. I told you we had a guest staying here to recover after her hospitalization."

146

"Lenore makes her own blends of herbal tea. She came up with that one to try and ease morning sickness before she lost…" Farrah trailed off. She didn't know if it was decent to speak about Lenore's personal medical problems. As a general rule of her massage business, she was used to talking openly about such private matters with her coworkers. She briefly forgot that she was not around other healthcare workers.

"Oh? That's a shame." It wasn't hard for Hellen to fill in the missing words. "Being a mother changes your life."

"Yes, it does." Farrah wasn't even trying to relate to her anymore, but since Lenore came into her life, she's thought about her own miscarriage a lot. Coupling that with her dysfunctional relationship with Nova, every mention of motherhood punched her in the gut.

Hellen removed her hand from Jae's gentle grasp and opened the jar of tea. She looked closely at it and took a big whiff.

"You can probably smell the peppermint in that one," Farrah said.

She continued to sniff the herbs, jostled them around, and sniffed again like a sommelier. "She should label this. Some herbs can be dangerous. You wouldn't want people drinking a tea from these if they shouldn't."

"You're overreacting. It's just infused herbs." June was a bit too quick to brush off her mother's concern.

"Just herbs? Cyanide is made from plants too. Doesn't mean people should eat it."

"Your mother is right, June. Plus, herbs are absorbed differently depending on whether they're raw plants, cooked, seeds, or essential oils. Medicine has the same consideration. That's why injectables are different doses than pills."

Hellen closed the jar and put it about a foot in front of June. She pointed emphatically at it.

"I can tell you that your friend should not have been drinking tea from that if she was pregnant."

Everyone was stunned by Hellen's proclamation. All eyes were on her.

"What do you mean, Mom?"

"There's ma hwang in that. I can tell."

Farrah saw the look in Hellen's eyes and the crinkled up brows and knew that she had lived a life being doubted.

"That's serious. It's even banned in some places. How can you tell?" Farrah picked up the jar and smelled the contents for herself.

"You think only Chinese people know about herbs? That's racist." Hellen wasn't going to educate Farrah so easily on her Korean remedies.

"What? No!"

"Mom!"

Jae took the jar from Farrah. He peered inside and added his own thoughts. "Your mother used to take it for bladder problems."

"It's supposed to be banned here now," Hellen explained. "But somehow it's still being sold everywhere as a weight loss herb."

"What do you know about this, Farrah?" There were various pill bottles in the bathroom and kitchen that June knew were Farrah's feeble attempts at sticking to supplement regimens.

"I don't understand all the variations, but the FDA has terrible labeling practices. I've seen ephedra everywhere, even health food shops. Their definition of healthy is something I question."

"Okay, so why is it so dangerous?" June asked.

"I had to stop taking it because of my high blood pressure," Hellen said.

"Increased heart rate is a common effect. It's sold as something that boosts energy and burns fat. The bladder remedies are barely marketed now." Farrah reached for the water pitcher and refilled the glasses on the table even though they were hardly touched by the Cho parents.

June didn't seem convinced of her mother's expertise. "So, Mom, you can smell the ma hwang?"

"Yes, June. It's in there. If I had to guess, I'd say it was liquid and mixed in with all those other things."

"Do you think this could be what's making Lenore so sick?" Farrah sat right next to Hellen and hoped for solid answers.

"It could be. I'm no doctor." Hellen ate up the attention. "But, if I were you, I would not let her drink anymore of this. Stupid girl. She's probably been poisoning herself."

June was on the other side of Farrah. She put a hand on her shoulder and leaned in to speak lower, but not intentionally to keep her parents from hearing her. She did it more or less to keep Lenore from hearing even though she was on the second floor.

"Could this have caused her miscarriage?"

"I don't know." Farrah turned back toward Hellen who had heard the question. "What do you think?"

"It's not my place to guess. You have the internet. Look it up. Then have her ask her doctor." Hellen finally took one of the cookies from the plate they had been ignoring. "Could I have coffee now, please?"

"Sure." June quickly popped up and tended to the request. "As far as asking her doctor anything, that's kind of a tricky situation. It's personal. We can't really explain."

Hellen's offense wasn't hidden. She clearly expected quid pro quo.

"She definitely was excited about that baby. There's no way she would have taken something on purpose to lose it." June chose to use the already ground coffee from the supermarket. She and Farrah had a tendency to hoard the expensive whole beans from the health food store.

"We still have to tell her. She can't drink anymore of this. She lost the baby and she's still getting sick." Farrah picked up the jar from where it was left on the table and made sure the lid was clasped tightly closed.

June carried over two mugs of hot coffee assuming her father would want it too. Finally, the ice was broken. They snacked and enjoyed the drink. Farrah excused herself. The new information about the herbal supplement in Lenore's homemade blend piqued her curiosity stronger than the urge to stay with June's parents. She was also interested in making an exit while it seemed as though they liked her. She didn't want another mishap like when she accidentally sounded racist.

"I'm just going to take my laptop, find the cat, and head up to bed. I can still catch the late night news." She said polite goodbyes and escaped. The laptop was on her makeshift desk by the stairs. She grabbed it and headed for her sanctuary on the second floor. Miles was already there hogging the bed. He never showed any indication of missing Jackson in the bed.

She texted June to keep her thoughts away from Hellen's attention. She suggested they leave Lenore undisturbed for the night. Since June was taking her parents to Pennsylvania, Farrah agreed she would talk to Lenore in the morning about the possibly dangerous substance in her herbal tea. She had to find out if Lenore was merely ignorant of the serious side effects or if there was more at play. June wrote back when she was in the kitchen cleaning the coffee mugs. Texting back and forth, they agreed that Lenore probably didn't know the ephedra was in the tea in the first place and that someone else, most likely Joel, put it there.

Somehow they were going to figure out how to open her eyes to his mistreatment. The tea, the harassing texts, the negligent and unethical ob-gyn care, and then the terrifying baby doll in a noose left on her door. There were a lot of signs that pointed to Dr. DeSantos as a psychopath.

CHAPTER TWENTY-TWO

IT was late, but with June out of the house and Lenore asleep, Farrah had a couple of ideas to occupy her time. First, she opened her laptop and researched ephedra which she learned was sometimes called *ma huang* with variable spelling *ma hwang*. According to the internet, the herb was indeed banned from the United States, so how the hell was it being sold everywhere? The only thing she could assume was that the controversial alkaloids in ma hwang were the banned substance, not the herb itself. Farrah never pretended to be an expert at the U.S. regulations. They had always been confusing and misleading with labeling practices.

Some information, Farrah already knew. Ephedra was a stimulant which what made it so popular for people seeking weight loss. They easily misunderstood the energy from it as effective fat burning. The issues with supplements was that they weren't meeting any standards as far as safe doses or even chemical breakdown.

She double-checked the warnings: irregular heartbeats, fainting, shortness of breath, stroke, heart attack, and even death. It was not recommended for people with heart disease, insomnia, eating disorders, asthma, other mental health issues like anxiety, seizures, and a host of other maladies. Basically, if a person wasn't already in tip-top shape, they should avoid it. The Mayo Clinic site specifically recommended pregnant and breastfeeding women avoid the supplement.

Among the over fifty adverse reactions listed, several jumped out at Farrah despite her sleepy eyes. First of all, they could easily be confused with other conditions. Most importantly, she thought about Lenore's pregnancy and her behavior in correlation with effects that were listed: delirium, hallucinations, euphoria, rapid heartbeat, vomiting, tiredness, depression, and headaches.

Poor Lenore was being told by her unethical ob-gyn that she was going through normal pregnancy hormone changes and that she had brought on the anxiety herself. The man was a first rate fraud and Farrah's anger grew steadily thinking about him. Any of the mental effects listed were things that could have been contributing to Lenore's stress and anxiety about the pregnancy and the miscarriage. No matter how hard Lenore tried to maintain her true desire to be calm, she had unwittingly sabotaged herself by drinking that tea.

"Hey, I'm sorry to call you so late, but I did promise I'd fill you in." Farrah couldn't distinguish between Morrison's normal husky vocals or half-asleep timbre. She momentarily thought about being near him while he was sleepy rather than curmudgeonly. The warmth of that thought took her by surprise. She jostled her head and got back to business.

"I'm not asleep yet. How's Ms. Lexington doing?"

She could hear the background noise from his end go silent. *Probably some cop show on TV*, she thought.

"She's sleeping, but I think I've figured out why she miscarried. It's unpleasant and there's a lot I have to tell you. The thing is, I once promised her that I wouldn't pursue this path about the father of her baby. I just don't see any way to avoid it now."

"You're being mysterious. Just tell me what you found out."

She appreciated his no-nonsense personality most of the time. In her limited interactions with him, she felt that he had some compassion, but didn't get to show it. Maybe it was because of the job. Maybe something else like his divorce or whatever other unpleasantness was in his background.

"Well, maybe I can give you some details, but leave the rest until tomorrow — after I've had the chance to talk to her. It's not like anyone is going anywhere."

He wasn't thrilled by her pussyfooting around, but she felt waiting until morning was the best option.

"Lenore's baby daddy has had access to her apartment and I believe he added something to the jar of herbs she frequently brews into tea. June's mother Hellen said it was ma hwang."

"Ephedra?"

"You're familiar with it?"

"I've never taken it, but I've seen it in the weight loss aisle of the vitamin and health food store. I take it pregnant women should avoid it?"

"Yes. Among a lot of other people. The way that Lenore was getting sick, it's no wonder she thought it was extreme morning sickness. She presented with some of the usual symptoms, but they are known to be caused to be caused by this supplement too."

"How come she never noticed it in her tea?"

Farrah reminded him of the jar of dried herbs that Lenore wanted from her apartment when all the police were there. She explained Hellen's theory that liquid ephedra was added to the jar so it wouldn't have been visually noticeable.

"That's hard to believe Hellen would be able to smell something added to the herbs if Lenore couldn't even tell and she drank it almost every day."

"Not really. When I was pregnant, my sense of smell went off on the fritz. I couldn't taste anything without salting the crap out of my food. Plus, Lenore does keep herself around a lot of incense and candles. Maybe she just couldn't pick out a scent that subtle." Farrah closed the laptop and moved it to the empty side of the bed. Miles had already turned around a few times and was nestled against her legs.

"It's an interesting theory. Do you have the tea? Can you keep her from drinking it?"

"Yes and yes. I was hoping you could maybe have it tested?" She scrunched up her face like it was asking him to break rules and be the biggest favor possible. He assured her that, based on the harassment investigation, he would be able to consider anything as evidence that someone was continuing to put Lenore's life at risk.

"Ya know, there's a lot going on in the courts about fetuses. I don't know what her chances are of proving fault if that's the way she wants to go. Civilly, she probably stands a chance. Criminally, that's something for the prosecutor's office to determine. All I can do is collect the evidence and file the reports. Ya understand that, right?"

"Yes. And really, I appreciate it. I'm just glad you're willing to listen and not write me off as a lunatic crying wolf."

"Hey, I saw those texts and what was done to her apartment. I know you and Lenore are not crying wolf. Now get some sleep if you can. We'll talk tomorrow."

The conversation went far better than Farrah could've hoped. She owed Morrison more than a great cup of coffee. Maybe some cookies or dinner. Then she scolded herself because she felt unworthy of a happy moment especially with a new man. She fucked up so horribly last time.

Morrison made her think about politics and the great debates of the female body. Lenore tried to exercise her choice in having the baby. Farrah didn't look at her as an incubator, but she knew that Lenore was excited. The little bit she knew about Joel colored her theories on how he had been feeling about the situation. Would a biological father regret their unplanned addition so much as to cause mother and child harm? Would a doctor who spent years caring for women and their pregnancies be able to cross that line? It sounded so unlikely in Farrah's head, but how many other possibilities were there? The darkest thought came to her: if this was true, was it his first time?

Then there's the wife. Nikki DeSantos certainly had every reason to hate Joel, Lenore, and their off-spring. She would be not only scorned, but very likely humiliated by the circumstances. A younger, beautiful woman stole her husband. Even if Lenore hadn't planned on it, that's what happened. Then before any legal action, the new girl got pregnant.

That was enough to make any woman snap and breakdown. Not every woman would be driven into action though, especially the kind of action causing so much danger. Sure, she could make lewd and inappropriate social media remarks. That's a big leap to nailing a mutilated baby doll to a door.

Farrah had faith in Detective Morrison. She also wanted to give him the best chance at wrapping up the investigation. It was an easy decision for her to express her theories.

CHAPTER TWENTY-THREE

IN the morning, she sat down with Lenore and laid it all out.

"My tea was poisoned?" Lenore's fingers toyed with the string and label of the store bought tea that Farrah served.

"We're not a hundred percent sure, but the police will check it out. Detective Morrison will come over today to pick it up and have it tested. So under no circumstances are you allowed to eat or drink anything that came from your apartment."

"I would never take ma hwang. I'm already thin and I was pregnant. I was looking forward to gaining baby weight."

That must be an interesting way to live, Farrah thought. Being around Lenore and June made her feel like the only person to ever be concerned about clothes not fitting and counting carbs. She never resented baby weight because she was overjoyed to be a mother, but she greatly resented her middle-aged figure and the lack of fashion over a size ten whenever she went shopping.

Lenore didn't take another sip of the tea even though it was safe. She opted to stroke the handle and loop the string around her finger. "I better get dressed before the detective arrives."

Farrah noticed that Lenore still put her hand over her belly whenever she got up from a chair or if she was nervous while talking.

"Me too. I think he's seen me at my worst, but I may as well make an effort."

Two hours later the sun tried to poke through the overcast skies just as Detective Morrison arrived at Farrah's home. With him, he had a paper shopping bag that he used to collect any edible items from Lenore's apartment. There wasn't much. She had two glass jars of her herbal tea blends, some frozen bagels, vegan cookies that were still sealed in their individual wrappers, and a bottle of açai berry juice.

Morrison took a seat at the kitchen table without Farrah even offering. The sac of food stuffs was next to his leg. Miles came over to stick his head in it for a proper feline inspection and made sure he approved of the items leaving his house. He even approved of Morrison by rubbing up against his ankle. The familiar little notebook and pen came out of Morrison's pocket to proceed with the questioning.

"Ms. Lexington, I was wondering if you've had any other thoughts since we last talked about who would want to threaten or harm you."

"No. Like I said before, I know Joel's wife hates whoever would be sleeping with him, and I don't blame her, but their marriage was over a long time before I stepped into the picture. They sleep separately. They never do anything together. All that was holding him back was dividing up all their money and funds and the house. It was going to be a huge effort for him and his lawyer. I wasn't even sure if she knew who I was."

"He still should've made that effort before asking you out." Farrah felt their friendship had reached a point where she could be honest even if it hurt her feelings.

"I know."

"And now let's address your apartment and everything that happened there." Morrison wouldn't let the interview lapse into a Joel-hating tirade. "Was your tea jar always kept there or did you take it places, say to work or something?"

Lenore's fingers tapped her bottom lip. "Now that you mention it, I have carried it places. Sometimes I had long days with the two jobs and the ob-gyn appointments. But I don't think any of my customers would have been so angered at me that they'd want to poison me!"

His expression said it all: you never know.

"I think the more obvious suspects are a better path to pursue unless you have actually had customers show earlier signs of violence. I understand you're a fortune teller or something? Any possibility that someone took your advice and it was the wrong decision?"

"I'm not a fortune teller, detective." Lenore laughed it off. "I read tarot cards and runes among other divination techniques. And per the law, we have a sign up that says readings are for entertainment purposes only. A woman in Hoboken was arrested this month for swindling forty thousand dollars from a client. Trust me, we don't do that."

Farrah interrupted. "I'm a customer of hers if that gives you any pause."

"Not really."

At least he was honest.

"What I mean is, it's like praying. You want to believe in good news or you want to believe that things will work out in the end of a really bad run of luck, but you know it's not a chess game."

"I understand religion, ladies."

He stood up and buttoned his long coat. Instead of a suit, he wore a sweater that looked fit for a sea captain and more tactical police issue pants with cargo pockets. Farrah figured it was his choice from a list of approved options that weren't patrol uniforms and definitely better during winter weather than worrying about shiny dress shoes and slacks.

"Just so you know, I'm going to be asking some questions at your doctor's office. I know it's a sensitive issue and there are privacy laws. I'm not out to subpoena anything yet. I want to see what kind of people work there since you mentioned that ultrasound technician." He flipped through his notebook searching for the name. "What was it? I wrote it down from their staff page online. Marlena Ramirez? And I'm going to poke around and see how the employees feel about their boss, Dr. DeSantos."

"Oh, I wish you didn't have to."

"He has to, Lenore. He has to find out if Joel was a liked person and kind to his employees." Farrah nodded as if doing so would hypnotize Lenore into agreeing.

Farrah walked him to the front door and asked him to call her later with any updates.

"Ya know I don't have to do that, right?"

"Yes, I know. But please?"

He agreed to call, but wouldn't promise to give her the nosy details she wanted.

CHAPTER TWENTY-FOUR

LENORE was ready to return to her work at Star's Blessings which was less physically demanding than the bookshop. Farrah offered to chauffeur her back and forth to work since no one felt it was safe for her to return to her apartment downtown yet. That left Farrah alone for several hours.

The empty house welcomed Farrah. More specifically, Miles did. He was sitting on the dining room table when she walked in the side door. Instead of a reprimand, she gave him some petting and chin scratching.

What Farrah hadn't been able to figure out was how she had such a busy life with only a fraction of the work that she had with a full-time job. She picked up Miles and put him on the floor before heading over to her desk and computer.

Her email inbox was filled with responses between Samantha and Maggie talking over the expansion possibilities. While Farrah wanted to be included, it wasn't her money or investment. She didn't have much to add to the conversation or decisions other than the initial ideas and plead for a management position.

The inbox was also filled with bills from the utility companies, her car insurance notice reminding her that the premium was due in three weeks, and her membership dues for the professional massage and bodyworkers network was about to expire; basically a ton of places looking for money that she didn't have.

Another message surprised her. It was from the law firm that was representing her and June in their cases against Caressa Lamour. The discovery part of the process seemed to take forever. The only good news was that it was making some kind of progress with talks of a settlement.

A settlement. It wasn't winning the lottery, but since the mere glance at her bills to be paid caused her to cry, any amount would help. What were the attempts on their lives worth though? Surely the lawyers would advocate for that, she hoped. A middle-aged, barely employed mother of a college student with a divorce looming — what was she worth?

June had been drowned by a different person than the one who threatened and tried to assault Farrah. Farrah hoped, for her friend's sake, that she'd be given a bigger payout for the added trauma. Regardless of what was offered, the fact that the companies involved wanted to settle gave her a modicum of relief knowing they bared some fault.

"Mom?"

The emails had had her so consumed with feelings from despair to hope that Farrah hadn't even heard the side door open.

"Honey, I didn't know you were stopping by."

"We need to talk. I hope that's okay."

Farrah assured her it was more than okay. It was longed for. She wanted her baby to come to her and not push away. Seeing her daughter as an adult didn't make her feel any less hurt by her pain. That bond was not going to be so easily broken. Not if Farrah had any say in it.

"Let me go first."

They moved to the living room couch where Farrah's plaid shirt clashed with the decor. She took one of her child's youthful brown hands in both of hers and pulled it up to her face for a kiss.

"I'm sorry, baby. I'm sorry, Nova." It wasn't easy. She knew she still needed time to get used to saying her daughter's new chosen name, but it was a start. As the woman who named her Janice and called her that for two decades, the past year of trying to call her Nova hadn't been a priority.

They had a great talk with hugs and tears. It was one step — one thing where failure wasn't an option and Farrah wanted to fight for their relationship harder than she ever fought for anything else.

"The owner of Star's Blessings explained some things to me. I had no idea how important it was for you to choose your own name."

"I didn't know you and Star Turner knew each other that well. In fact, I didn't know you had even been there before."

"Lenore works there. That's where she is right now. Star seems like a great person. She spent a lot of time talking to me when she could have been helping other people. Not to say I got away easy. She sold me a ton of stuff. Candles and whatnot."

The strength of Nova's personality shot out of her eyes. Farrah didn't know what she said to bring out that kind of expression.

"What? What'd I do now?"

"Nothing. I guess it's none of my business." Nova leaned back and created more distance between them on the couch.

"Spill it."

"It's this Lenore girl. Why is she here? Why has she taken over my room? Who is this person, Mom? First it was June. Now it's her."

The flood gates were opened and it was only fair for her questions to be answered. Farrah let it all out: from Lenore's miscarriage all the way up to the point of the vandalism at her apartment. She didn't get into the details about the possibility of poisoned herbal tea.

Nova calmed down and saw that it was out of kindness that Lenore had practically moved in. She agreed it wasn't smart to let her be alone in an apartment with an angry, jealous person after her.

"Thank you for understanding. I wasn't trying to replace you. I could never replace you." Farrah wanted to drill her maternal passion into her daughter's brain. "She's only here until it's safe for her to go back to her own place. Though, to be honest, I've enjoyed having the house full again."

"But?"

"But, nothing. June and I are doing the right thing. Lenore doesn't have any family that's she's close to. Sometimes friends are all you have. Besides Star, now she can count on us too."

"You mean you. I don't see June anywhere." Nova gestured around the empty space.

"Well, no, not right now. She took her parents away for the weekend. They have a lot of things to work out too." Farrah knew she raised a headstrong child, but didn't have to face that side of her often.

"Look, Mom, I came here to collect more of my stuff too. Frank said I could keep things there even though he's basically out of space because of Dad. But I don't know how else to handle it. You have to sell this place, right?"

"That's the plan. June and I could scrape by. There's hopefully going to be some progress on the work front for me, but for all I know that could take a year or more to happen. That would mean she'd have to be able to pay to support both of us in this big house which is terribly unfair. She managed in her little condo fine."

Farrah admitted that she didn't have any of her nest egg left. It was the first time she opened up to her daughter about finances. She wanted to keep her from that ugliness and enjoy her time in college.

"I don't want it to get nasty between you and Dad."

"Trust me, neither do I. I think that ship has sailed though. Never thought I'd see the day that I'd need this many lawyers for this much crap in my life."

✳✳✳✳✳

Nova wasn't able to take any furniture, but packed up a few more boxes. She stacked them by the side door in the dining room where they were immediately inspected by the cat. They loaded up the rental car she needed for the weekend.

"I have to say, it does feel nice getting places faster than a bus or a train, but I don't know if taking care of a car is for me."

"It's necessary out here, but maybe you'll land somewhere you can walk easily."

"About that..." Nova didn't normally hesitate with her words and Farrah clenched her muscles at the pause. "I'm looking at a summer internship in New York."

"New York City? Good lord, no."

"Mom! It'll be fine. I won't be going alone either."

Farrah continued to brace herself. Turned out her daughter was madly in love. It was probably a great balance in her life as her parents were divorcing. The plan was for them to share a room together rented from a friend's family in eastern New Jersey. Nova swore everything was above board and safe. She romanticized the prospect of living on almost nothing in cramped quarters.

"At least Theo and I will be able to use the kitchen and have our own bathroom. It's sad circumstances, but it's perfect timing for us. Lou's grandmother was living with his family, but she went into hospice care and died a month ago. They've been putting her things into a storage unit hoping Lou would move back after graduation in a few months, but since he doesn't want to, he suggested Theo and I stay there."

"I wish I could afford to have you stay here. I feel like such a failure that I can't provide for you properly. This is your home." Farrah's tears couldn't be held in any longer. Nova took the box from Farrah's hands and put it on the ground so she could hug her.

"Mom. Don't. I'd be taking this offer anyway. It's close to mass transit. I can't afford a lot of rent, but we offered to chip in taking care of things around the house and yard so that Lou's family can focus on whatever they need to do. Plus they spend two weeks down the shore every year anyway and they feel better having someone in the house, taking in the mail and stuff like that. Speaking of dying, Gordon has been sick too."

"Shit. You father doesn't talk to me unless he has to. I guess I understand why he didn't bother telling me."

"He still thinks you hate the dog." Nova loaded the last box into the trunk and closed the hatch.

"I don't hate the dog. I never hated him, per se. I'm cat person. They're better. And he never consulted me about bringing him here."

They started to walk back to the house from the driveway.

"Jeez, does your father really think I wished harm on Gordon?"

"I don't know. I'm sure he doesn't think you would personally hurt him, only that you wouldn't care if he wasn't around anymore."

"That was kind of true for a while anyway. I'm not proud of it. Your father was spending a lot of time getting the town to turn a plot of land into a dog park. I was feeling neglected and jealous. It caused a lot of friction between us."

In the kitchen, Farrah poured two glasses of iced tea for them. Nova said her only plans for the day were to get back to Frank's to drop off the boxes and then head back to Pennsylvania.

Nova held the cold glass and walked from room to room. She took a close look at every new detail, the absence of the family that was and the new, different home it had become. She came to the sideboard Farrah used to store linens and bottles of booze that she didn't use on a regular basis. On top of the honey colored maple, Nova ran her fingers on the texture of the woven runner. That hadn't changed. It was given to Farrah by her grandmother a long time ago. The only time the sideboard had a different fabric on it was during fall and Christmas. The rest of the time for as long as Nova had been alive, that one piece of blue, grey, red, and white fabric with one tassel missing was a constant in their home. The rest of the decor wasn't completely familiar though.

"What's this?"

She found the candle for a peaceful home with her photo next to it.

"You caught me. That's one of the things Star sold me. It's supposed to bring our family peace and comfort."

"I guess it worked. Between us anyway."

"Hey, how would you like to go down there? I have to pick Lenore up in a couple hours. We could go and have coffee then head over to Star's shop. Since neither of us knew we both liked it, we can finally go together."

"That sounds good. Would you mind if I took the run over to Frank's first? I'll come back and we can take your car into town."

It was Saturday and Jackson would be there.

"Actually, since you said Gordon is sick, would you mind if I went along? I'll say goodbye to the big fella."

"Are you sure that's a good idea? Mom, I don't think you're heartless if that's what you're worried about."

"It'll only be a few minutes. I promise I won't start anything with your father."

Nova agreed under a further condition: that Farrah would wait outside by the car and she would bring Gordon out to her. Whether or not Jackson talked to her would be up to him. Farrah agreed to the terms and felt guilty that her daughter was adamant about being a referee between two adults. She attempted to point out that fact, but Nova showed she could be pertinacious when she wanted.

Frank Morelli's bachelor pad was a large Victorian home currently occupied by the exes of June and Farrah plus a young coworker of Frank's from his day job. Not much of it was used for living space. Frank had a workshop for making special effects. It kept Frank and Jackson busy and distracted from family problems when they had rough patches.

"Hey, Farrah."

"Hey, Frank. I'm just here to see the dog. I heard he probably doesn't have much longer."

"Yeah. Jack's been spending a lot of time with him. June isn't with you?"

"Uh, no. She's with her parents in Pennsylvania for the weekend. She said she told you."

She wasn't sure how much of June's private life was being shared with her ex-husband. Just because they've had dinner and drinks a couple times didn't mean he needed to know her every move. Farrah always had a feeling Frank didn't want the divorce. He was swept up in work and his hobbies. He had his own grown kids too. June wanted some freedom.

She had told Farrah how different their divorces were. On more than one occasion she said she and Frank didn't fight and that it made the situation sadder. If they fought for each other, they would have at least known there was something between them. Now they were trying to be friends. How close and specifically whether that friendship came with extra benefits, Farrah didn't know. She had unfortunately, not paid much attention to June's relationships except for healing things with her parents. Plus, Lenore had her pretty distracted.

Frank took out the heaviest box from the trunk and walked away. Jackson was there on the stoop holding the door open for him. He turned his head away from Farrah's eyes and said something she couldn't hear. The slow form of Gordon the bloodhound lumbered out the door.

The dog stopped and looked up. Farrah could tell Jackson was telling him it was okay to go down the stairs. It seemed like Gordon wanted help not permission when he thumped to the ground.

"Hey there, big guy. How you doin'?"

Jack kept his distance until Farrah asked him what the prognosis was.

"He's got a week at most. They told me I could bring him home. No point having him miserable in a cage when he can be miserable around his people and things."

"What is it?"

"Cancer."

"I'm so sorry."

She meant it for both of them. She didn't want either to suffer more than they have. Jack had been through enough, mostly because of her. The dog was the thing in his life every day that gave him joy and she didn't want to see that taken from him. They were good for each other. Gordon didn't have too much spring in his step when they adopted him, but he improved for a while. Then age and illness began to show. She watched as Jack's eyes turned watery and red.

"Thanks. It's probably going to come down to me taking him in so he doesn't suffer too much longer." The words didn't come out easily.

"I'm sure the answer is no, but if you want me to go with you, to drive or just be there, I will."

Maybe he was confused or simply couldn't bear to think about it. He didn't say no or thank you or anything. He turned to hide his face even though she had seen him cry before during all their years together.

Farrah scratched behind Gordon's ears and for once didn't care that he slobbered on her. He was easy to hug at his size. She knew he'd be even more spoiled if possible.

"Is he eating okay?"

"Not great. They said that's how I'll know. He'll stop eating and probably have trouble going to the bathroom."

Nova bounced out of the house and down the short flight of stairs. Her puffy curls bounced in time with the rest of her perky posture.

"Ready?"

Farrah let go of Gordon and stood close to him, keeping one hand on his large head like she needed an outside force to let go. She realized her time with him was up and that Jackson was unlikely to take her up on her offer. She bent down to give big lug one more squeeze and kiss goodbye knowing it was the last time.

"Okay. Let's go."

"See you in a bit, Dad. I'll swing by before I head back to school." Nova kissed her father on his cheek and tried to hug the sadness out of him.

*****

In the car, Farrah and Nova talked about what a good dog Gordon had been for their family. On Farrah's part, it was mostly romanticizing the situation since she never wanted to keep him. They drove back to the house for Farrah's car. She felt a bit guilty about wasting the gas and driving two cars to the shopping district, but Nova wanted to go back to see her father afterwards rather than the house she used to know with a strange new addition. At least she was able to openly talk about those feelings.

They ordered coffees and found two empty seats flanking a small table. The cafe was busy along with the rest of the town. The temperature finally reached above forty-five and felt like spring in the northeast. People were out in only sweatshirts, some silly enough to wear shorts while being half bundled.

Farrah caught sight of a woman in pink scrubs and a woolly brown hat over short black hair. The long sleeves covering her arms were forest green. Not a fashion maven. Probably too tired to care about matching her work uniform. Then Farrah noticed the embroidered logo on the breast: J.D. Women's Health Center.

"Mom, what are you staring at? You look like a creep."

"What? Oh, sorry. Just that nurse. I think she's from the ob-gyn office that Lenore has been going to." The ceramic mug warmed Farrah's hands nicely so she didn't let go of it even when she rested it on the table.

"Aight, well, you might not want to ogle her."

"I am not ogling." Farrah was firm yet quiet in her tone, but that didn't stop her eyebrows from furrowing. "You know internships aren't going to pay you enough to drink macchiatos in New York or Hoboken."

"Give it up. I'm going. And I'll drink black coffee all summer if I have to."

The woman in the scrubs stopped looking at her phone when the barista called out, "Marlena!" at the far end of the counter. She took her to-go paper cup without saying thank you, slid her phone into a pocket of the shirt, and headed for the back door.

"How do you know she's not a doctor?"

Farrah was knocked out of her staring again by the conversation. "Huh?"

"The woman. You said she's a nurse and I asked how you know she's not a doctor. Women can be doctors now, ya know?"

"Smart ass. I know. I wear scrubs sometimes too. I was only guessing because Lenore made it sound like the other staff in Dr. DeSantos' office were women. He might be the only rooster in the proverbial hen house. My mistake to assume she's a nurse. Plus, now I have a strong feeling that she's the ultrasound technician Lenore said had no bedside manner. She mentioned the name Marlena."

While she spent days hoping her daughter would speak to her again, Farrah considered how much to disclose about Lenore's situation. She thought she found a comfort zone in stopping at the poison tea and the suspicions about Dr. Douchebag and his possible abuse. She was used to gossiping with June freely. When it came to Nova, she didn't want to burden her with more worry. The girl was dealing with enough. On the other hand, a fresh perspective on the situation might not be a bad thing.

"Before we pick up Lenore, there's something I want to tell you about why June and I are so concerned about her."

It wasn't an easy conversation, but it was important. Lenore and Nova were close in age. Even though Nova was in love for the first time and it was someone her own age, chances are she could fall for a controlling asshole like Lenore had.

Farrah explained about how Lenore was sheltered and how she believed every promise Joel ever made to her — about how much she relied on him because of her poor finances and the dreams of stepping up from near poverty to upper middle class. And how Lenore never once believed that his constant surveillance of her whereabouts, like showing up at her jobs without asking, was truly stalking and not visiting.

"What you do you know about an app called something like 'You-Heart-Me'? They write it less than three on the icon."

"I don't use it, but I've heard about those kinds of apps. They're for couples to text each other."

"What's wrong with regular texting?" Farrah knew she sounded like a dolt, but if she couldn't ask her darling daughter tech questions, then she couldn't safely ask anyone without embarrassment. At least kids expected it.

"Nothing. Those apps do more that's all. They have shared calendars and To-Do lists. It's all stuff that can be done other ways, but it's cute."

Farrah took her phone and click on the app store button, cursing herself for not investigating it sooner. She was surprised at the number of apps that existed for couples to communicate with phones. She didn't know why they needed more ways to have misunderstandings and fight about who forgot to walk the dog or pick up eggs.

"Hunh. This... this is odd. It says here in the privacy notes that each user would grant access to the partnered user to things like their photos and their GPS location."

Farrah's mind quickly thought about the implications. Knowledge of where your partner is at every given moment could be great for convenience or safety. It could also be dangerous and is a major invasion of privacy. She realized how the knowledge could have angered or calmed her suspicions of where Jackson used to spend his evenings. Had they had an app like this back then, things would have been even more volatile.

"That's probably just generic cover-your-ass language for the terms of service. I'm pretty sure you have the options of turning off the GPS. The photos and other stuff are just like every social media app. It means that if you attach a picture to your text, you're allowing that other user to see that picture. Why are you asking anyway?"

"I saw this app on Lenore's phone when she showed me the scary text messages. She said he bought the phone so I have a feeling he suggested this kind of app to keep track of her."

"Maybe it was her idea. Girls like feeling connected to their boyfriends and girlfriends too." Nova's phone was on the table within quick reach. Without the thought registering, she had checked it about every two minutes.

"I suppose so. I think it's creepy, especially knowing how Dr. Douchebag comes across like a manipulative asshole. I hope you'd think twice before using something like that."

"God. You keep calling him that! It's funny hearing it out of your mouth. Mom, I'm not letting some guy install apps on my phone without my knowledge. Besides, no one says it has to be a romantic couple. Best friends or roommates could use those apps so they know the other one is somewhere safe when they go out. Even parents and kids."

"You say that now, but I'm sure if the right twinkling eyes and smile came along, you'll hand over your PIN because you don't think you have anything to hide." Farrah craved a coffee refill, but knew better. She indulged in enough caffeine and sugar for one day.

"There's a line between not trusting someone and feeling like your privacy is invaded. I'm not sure what Lenore got herself into, but I assure you, my dating history has not been like that." Nova dunked her biscotti into the remaining half of her macchiato. "Speaking of spying on people and being creepy, get back to why you were staring at that woman in the scrubs."

Farrah admitted she was being nosy. It wasn't an apology though. Detective Morrison didn't owe her anything in terms of his discoveries throughout the investigation. Logically, Farrah also knew that the spouse of the cheating husband was the best suspect, but that didn't mean she was the only one. A philanderer like DeSantos could have had a history of cheating on Nikki not only with patients, but also his staff. Suppose he got tired of one mistress and moved on to a new one, there could be another angry woman in his life. Maybe more than one.

"Lenore mentioned that not all of the staff were friendly over there. She wrote it off as people having bad days or lacking in bedside manner because that's how Lenore thinks."

"And you think there's something else?"

"It makes me wonder, yes. Let's just say I have a difficult time believing Lenore is the first Other Woman his wife has had to deal with."

Nova asked if there was any legal way Farrah planned to get more information. She suggested friending Nikki online, but after Farrah's personal experience with trolls, she took her various friends lists seriously and tried to use the utmost caution with what she posted publicly.

The deep, unspoken truth of the matter was that Farrah intended to pry what she could from Morrison. Talking about a case that was connected directly to her gave her a reason to call him. He may have once been more of a frenemy, but the common ground that evolved was something she enjoyed. Having a friendly relationship with him wasn't something she was ready to discuss with her daughter yet. The sheer thought of ever having a date after that brief affair terrified her. She would continue with the coffee meetings. Those weren't dates, she convinced herself. They discussed his investigations and theories. Besides her tangents on what constitutes good coffee, they hadn't shared too much.

"Phil told me he'll look into the ob-gyn staff."

"Phil huh? First name basis?" Nova played up razzing her mother with the old sitting in a tree song.

Farrah hoped that meant she was forgiven, at least on some partial level, for breaking up the family. She realized it felt good to laugh and blush again.

"Does this mean I'll be getting a baby brother or sister?" She kept laughing.

Despite the mortifying thought of being pregnant by someone she barely knew and over forty, Farrah loved the sound of her daughter's joy.

"You bite your tongue! No more babies for me. Or you, yet!"

They finished their coffees and walked to Star's Blessings enjoying another rare day of sun at the tail end of winter. Sunny or not, Farrah still had to wrap her scarf around a couple of times and kept her mouth and nose buried in it until they arrived.

CHAPTER TWENTY-FIVE

AFTER picking up Lenore, Farrah took her straight back to the house. It had been a full day of stress, worry, and even some fun. Her body wore the fatigue like an old burlap sack. She had a feeling Lenore was in need of a quiet night too.

What she didn't expect was getting to her house and finding a stranger knocking on the front door. She slowed down her approach and watched. The stranger gave up on the front door and walked to the side. He knocked more and then leaned over to peer through the window of the dining room presumably looking for signs of anyone home.

"Who's that?" Lenore asked.

"I have no idea."

After the nightmare of the previous year, Farrah didn't welcome strangers to her door. She swung the car into the driveway which alerted the visitor. He carried a large envelope and clipboard in his hands covered by fingerless knitted gloves.

"Mrs. Wethers?"

"Yes."

"I need your signature. Right here." He tapped near an empty line on the log of scribbled names.

He handed over the envelope, tucked the clipboard into his armpit, and walked in the direction of an old sedan parked in front of her neighbor's house.

"What is it?" Lenore asked.

Farrah didn't have an answer. She couldn't wait for one either. Standing in the cold, she tore open the envelope to find a letter from an attorney representing Jackson. Attached with a paper clip were the papers of his motion to divorce.

"Let's get inside. I need to sit down."

Farrah sat at the dining room table and dropped the paper stack in front of her. She peeled off her gloves and worked the buttons on her coat, stripping from the layers of warmth piece by piece.

"Can I get you something?" Lenore could try everything possible to repay the kindness she'd been shown, but nothing could ease Farrah's pain.

"A scotch and soda would be nice." She was half joking, but then relieved when Lenore fetched the bottle of Glenfiddich 18 from the shelf. It was the stuff she and June saved for special occasions. This had to count, she thought.

The cover letter's thick paper stock with fancy linen weave made Farrah feel like the Queen had sent her a memo. She wished. Anything but what it was. The words on all the pages didn't register or make much sense. It was black font on white paper. She knew she hadn't entirely lost her ability to read, but she had lost her ability to move her eyes line by line, left to right, and comprehend what the hell all of it meant.

"Do you want to talk about it?"

"Hang on. Let me text June just to let her know you and I are both fine and that this arrived. I hope she's okay alone with her parents." She pulled out her phone and tapped out what she hoped made sentences or a semblance of text speak. She had to backspace a lot with her shaking hands, misspelling every other word.

"Take your time. I'm going to hang up our coats and get myself some water." Lenore pulled at the neckline of Farrah's coat a couple times to get her to life her butt off the rest of it. Her arms were full when she walked away to the front foyer.

June's text came through right away. All she said about her own situation was that everything was fine, the usual. Farrah interpreted that to mean that June was fielding an endless series of backhanded compliments and nosy questions from her parents. Farrah replied that she wasn't fine but wasn't wallowing yet.

Lenore returned to the table with her glass of water. Farrah already had half of her drink gone.

"What are you feeling right now?" The young woman had her own heartbreak and catastrophes to deal with, but the distraction gave her a moment's reprieve from all that.

"I'm pissed off. I'm angry. I'm sad. I feel like a complete failure. I feel guilty. It's the same shit I've been trying to process for months."

"You knew this was coming, right? Or had you hoped there was still a chance?"

"A chance? At reconciliation?" Farrah hated to admit it, but that often entered her mind. She thought about it a lot even though they were different people than twenty years ago, they had to still love each other. "I guess all the emotions can best be described as confusing."

"Right now, for tonight I mean, all you need to do is accept this letter and if you want, take the time to start finding a divorce lawyer."

Farrah knew Lenore was right. There was no reason to delay. She and June already knew they had to find another place to live and get the house on the market. Jack was moving on and enjoying his new life except for his dog dying. He was keeping busy and so was she.

"I guess I could ask for the contact information of the lawyer June used. I'd rather get a personal referral than pick someone from an internet search." She picked up the tumbler and admired the mixing skills of someone who never seemed to drink alcohol. Not too much club soda. The right amount of ice. Her favorite scotch. "Where the hell am I going to find money for a retainer?"

"Can June loan you any?"

Farrah snorted. "You have no idea how much I already owe her. She helped cover me the last two times I've needed legal counsel. At least one of them will hopefully be paying off soon and I can give it back to her. Which reminds me…"

Lenore's face turned quizzical as she watched Farrah fidget around in her chair. "Reminds you of…?"

"You know that lawsuit that June and I are part of because of the threats against us at that retreat center?"

"Yes, you mentioned it a few times."

"They want to settle. I haven't had the chance to sit down with June or those lawyers to talk about it. But I would love to settle! But…"

Lenore waited a few beats and had to encourage the rest out of her. "But what?"

"Let's say I get some money. Now I have no idea what kind of payout they're talking about, but let's assume that even a low figure would be more than I ever made in a year at my old day job. Since all that crap happened while Jack and I were married and still living under the same roof, would he be entitled to half of what I get?"

"Oh, I don't have the slightest idea. That's why you need a lawyer right away. Maybe you can have a lawyer put in some kind of clause that since a settlement is above and beyond your family income, that he shouldn't get any? I have no idea how that works."

"Goddamnit. Damn it!"

"Well, hang on now. If this money or rather imaginary possible money, isn't something you have and let's say the worst case scenario is that you only get half, that's still a lot more money than you have this second. It's still a good thing. And you still have something positive to look forward to."

Farrah loved Lenore's philosophies, but her own brain argued against the logic. Half of the imaginary sum should still be better than no imaginary sum. She wanted to see it that way too. Sometimes she felt spiteful towards Jackson for not owning up to his side of why they split up, but she wasn't the type to screw him out of anything. The guilt was too strong for that.

"And there's something else you should be thinking about right now," Lenore teased.

"Oh god, what else?"

"A certain sexy, mature detective who loves to find reasons to talk to you." She sounded like a teenager, but it was delightful.

Farrah couldn't control the smile that broke out across her tense jawline. She didn't think anything could lift her spirits, but about five pounds of the ton of emotional baggage had levitated off her at that moment. It was a start.

She wasn't about to confess that she had dreams about the man. It stunned her when it happened before they were even on friendly terms. He dropped into her life unwanted, yet something about him made her stir.

"I would like to get to know Phil better, as something other than the detective I know I can call anytime of the day or night."

"See! Now look at that stack of papers one more time. That's your permission slip to do just that. I'm not saying it'll be easy after such a long marriage, but maybe it's the right time for something new."

"How did you get so wise for someone so young?" Farrah chuckled as she brushed away a tear that snaked its way down her cheek.

"Oh, all the credit goes to Star. She imbues all her wisdom on me as often as possible. She's been the best mother-aunt-godmother figure I've ever had. Now I can add you and June to that too." She put down her water glass and stood up, taking Farrah's free hand in hers. "Come on. Leave that stuff where it is."

Farrah kept her drink and allowed Lenore to lead her into the living room. She was told to sit while Lenore retrieved something from upstairs. She returned with small blue votive candle, a glass holder, her athame, and a lighter.

"What's that for? Can you summon my sanity because I don't know where the hell it is?"

"Here, take this and this." Lenore thrust the athame, handle side out to Farrah with one hand the votive with the other. "You're going to carve the name of your ex in that candle and then write other words or symbols that represent what you want to achieve through all this mess."

"Should I tell you what I'm thinking?"

"Sure. It's not a secret. Plus it's like we're working the magick together like how Star and I and the other people at the shop do."

"Okay. Well, first off, I don't want to hurt him anymore. I mean that. I'm angry and bitter, but he's hurt already." Lenore guided her to continue with her thoughts out loud. "I want the house to sell for a good price quickly so we don't have to worry about that and June and I can get a place. And..."

"And?"

Her hands holding the blade and the candle dropped to her lap almost as if she felt defeated.

"And I want enough to start over and to pay him back for covering the years after I got laid off and have tried to be a massage therapist, failing the whole time."

Her chin dropped to her chest as fresh tears fell. Instead of reaching for a tissue, Lenore used her fingers to wipe the tears and then took the candle from her. She anointed it with the tears, rubbing them into the pillar of blue wax the way she normally would have done with essential oils. Then she took the blade back as well and did the carvings for her.

Lenore took a seat next to her on the couch and wrapped one arm around her shoulders. She put the candle in the glass holder on the coffee table and picked up the lighter. Once the wick glowed with bright fire, Farrah calmed down. She kept her gaze on the flame just to watch it flutter in space.

"Does this make us a coven now?" Farrah's face still retained the tension. Her teeth barely unclenched to speak.

Lenore smiled. "Not yet."

They held each other and mourned their respective losses. Not realizing the time that passed, Farrah came out of her trance.

"I know what I should do!"

"What?"

"I'm going to ask Jack to join my lawsuit against the cosmetics company and the retreat center. He was harassed a lot too. People tracked him down and called his office and staked out on our lawn all because they hated me. If he joins me in the suit, then that will have more weight to it and he'll get half of a higher amount or basically, his own share. I hope. I don't really know how this stuff works."

"That's a great idea. What the hell happened anyway?"

"I tried to save the life of the Caressa Lamour CEO, but because it was then outed that the company was testing on animals despite all their labeling to the contrary, animal rights activists came after me for keeping him alive. Which, by the way, was only briefly because he ended up dying anyway."

"That's messed up."

"People suck, Lenore. That's my wisdom to imbue on you. It's not as eloquent as what Star tells you, but it's the damn truth."

CHAPTER TWENTY-SIX

AFTER June's parents left, the house regained its vibrant energy as one more stressor went out the door. Farrah had felt the change another time, after Jack left and June moved in. Lenore's addition brought them fresh vigor. Farrah was puzzled by how her own problems seemed less catastrophic while she was caring for Lenore who suffered terribly. She missed being needed and useful. She heard somewhere that it's not a competition to see who is more depressed, who is more ill, or who is more in need. It was a lesson that finally made sense to her.

Lenore's petite frame practically floated like a ghost when she descended the stairs and moved from room to room. Her wardrobe of long skirts added to the effect. Her bony hand was odd without a cup of tea in it. Unfortunately, it was shaking holding her phone.

She stopped at the threshold of the kitchen where June and Farrah were having their Sunday morning coffee and breakfast wraps of eggs, soy cheese, avocado, tomato, and onions; they believed brunch was always healing.

"Honey, what's wrong?" June got up immediately and went over to her.

Farrah stood up but didn't want to crowd her. Lenore looked like she had been crying so hard that she ran out of tears. Something Farrah knew all too well.

"It's Joel."

"Did something happen to him?" Farrah honestly didn't think that was case, but hoped it allowed a cushion against a harsh conversation about to happen.

June guided her over to the empty third chair at the round wooden table. Miles realized his particular feline expertise was needed and began weaving through Lenore's legs once she was seated.

"Nothing happened to him. I haven't heard from him in days. I figured he had written me off, ya know? But today, out of nowhere, I get these messages from him."

June and Farrah exchanged glances. June gave the stereotypical New Jersey mime of a chin nod telling Farrah to take the lead. It was body language that meant a variety of things, but in context, she got it.

"What did they say? Were they threatening like the others?"

"No. Not at all." She spoke between stuffy nose sniffs. "He wants to see me tomorrow in his office."

June chimed in, "For an appointment?"

"Yes. He said he's too concerned about me to not follow up."

"That's odd, isn't it? To phrase it that way?" Farrah said. She recalled Dr. Douchebag telling her that he was helping Lenore find a new doctor because of her delusional attachment to him.

"I don't know." Lenore gripped harder on the phone as if her very life depended on not letting go of it. "I mean, if he cares so much, where the hell has he been? Why hasn't he checked in on me?"

"Maybe he means as your doctor exclusively not personally. I mean, if you have texts like that to show the police, there's the evidence that he's crossed the line into a personal relationship. Right?" June stood close to her and rubbed her back, not that it helped. Lenore was hysterical like she had been right after the miscarriage and the vandalism at her apartment.

Farrah sat back down and scooted closer. "If you want my honest opinion — and I can't speak for June, but I have feeling she'd agree — you definitely do need follow up appointments, but not with him. He's not the right doctor for you. We'll get you into Planned Parenthood. There's one in Washington, not too far from here."

"I want to see Joel!" Her head collapsed onto the back of her crisscrossed arms. There was a muttering of slobbering girl speech from under all her hair, but June and Farrah deciphered it: she wanted Joel back.

Nothing could have made the conversation less difficult short of Lenore's fantasy coming true that Joel would march through the door, announce his divorce, and then propose to her. The reality was that she had agreed to go into his office the next day for an appointment. Since Farrah didn't have any massage clients scheduled, she offered to go with her.

Later on that afternoon, Farrah sucked up her own anxiety and called Jackson. She presented him with the idea about joining the lawsuit. Fortunately, she got the result she hoped for. First of all, he was pleasant to her on the phone. Then he listened and agreed that it was smart action to take. The companies were already chomping at the bit to settle so with any luck, the two of them wouldn't have to worry much longer about whether the mortgage and utilities could be paid.

"Speaking of the house, I was wondering if you wanted to buy me out, ya know, if all this money does come through for you and June?" he asked.

"Oh. Uh. I hadn't thought of that as a possibility. My head was so focused on the idea that I'd have to move that I never even considered staying." She realized how fantastic it would be not to pack up all her possessions and move. On the other hand, with all the new beginnings she had been talking about with June, Lenore, and Nova, a different home could make a huge difference on her emotions. Her mind flip-flopped faster than a politician on the campaign trail. As a couple, they were in love there. They raised Nova there. They had so many years of memories in that two-story Colonial.

"Since we're talking, you know how you said you felt bad about Gordon?"

"Yes."

"I'm going to call the vet tomorrow and make the appointment. Do you still want to be there?"

Shit! She wanted to be there for Lenore, but the dog dying was important too. She wanted to keep her word to him.

"Oh, yeah. I mean, I meant it that I'd be there for you and for him. The thing is, I'm helping someone out on Monday. Is there any chance he can hang on until late afternoon or Tuesday first thing in the morning?"

"Jesus, Farrah. It's not like death cares about your schedule. I'm taking tomorrow off. I already put in a message at the office. I don't even know what time the vet will have an opening, but when I had him there, they said anytime. They'll fit it in."

"Okay. Okay! I want to be there for him. But please, can you wait until I call you back tomorrow? Lenore is supposed to go in for a follow-up appointment after losing her baby." She fully intended on the drama to weaken Jackson's hackles. He was stressed, but so was everyone else.

"Fine. Call me as soon as you know. I'm going to take advantage of the next twenty-four hours and sit with him."

"I'm sorry, Jack. I really am. And thank you. I'll call as soon as I know when I'm free."

*****

Morning arrived and along with it came another two inches of snow overnight. June cleaned off Farrah's car after she did her own which was warming up for her commute through the hills to the county seat. She was a dynamo and quickly swept the fluffy powder snow off the walkways in about five minutes.

Farrah found a note on the kitchen counter from her: "Text me when you get up." June needed another thirty-five minutes or so to drive, so Farrah waited to follow through with her instructions. Lenore hadn't made a peep, but they had to be ready in case the ob-gyn office could fit her in right away.

She grabbed a large three-ring binder from her cookbook shelf and flipped to a plastic covered page. She bustled around the kitchen to make hot apple and cinnamon muffins. It was the perfect treat for a snowy day as winter made its last ditch effort to be remembered. Two cups of cinnamon laced coffee were the perfect companion to her indulgence.

She was halfway through her breakfast when Lenore finally came downstairs. Farrah asked how she slept or rather if she slept at all and how she was feeling.

"I guess I'm fine. I'm nervous and scared."

"Scared?"

"Well not scared-scared. I mean like scared about things not turning out how I want them to. I have to get through this and I'm exhausted from worrying all the time."

"Do you need to let them know that you're coming in? I wasn't sure if you still made appointments like regular patients given your relationship with Joel."

Lenore smelled the cooling rack of muffins and delicately picked one up in her fingers. Instead of her usual layers of billowy gauze skirts and leggings, she was bundled up in a cute flannel pajama set with the thickest socks Farrah had ever seen.

"These are delicious." She swallowed her first bite before answering Farrah's question. "Yeah I do call for appointments. Since we are — were — whatever, trying to keep things private until his divorce was announced, I would at least call to say that he asked me to come at a particular time. Basically it was whenever I could borrow Star's car. She's been great about that since it's been so freezing cold. She didn't want me to walk the mile from the shop to his building near the hospital."

"Aww, that's sweet. Those sidewalks get pretty icy and they refreeze overnight anyway. This town at least seems to handle it better than some others I drive to."

"Yeah," Lenore mindlessly replied.

Luck was finally on their side. The receptionist answered the phone at 8:30 and scheduled Lenore for 10:15. Farrah texted the update to Jackson and said she hoped they wouldn't be long, but added, "You know how doctors are." Even if the patients got backed up for a couple hours, Farrah could still drop off Lenore at home or the shop, wherever she wanted to be, and then have enough time to zip over to the veterinarian to meet Jackson and Gordon.

The magazine selection at the ob-gyn was typical and unimpressive. Farrah wasn't in the mood for articles on teething and whether or not to let babies cry or to pick them up when they wouldn't go to sleep. The television in the corner was tuned to an annoying cable channel showing a marathon of hipsters buying tiny homes at exorbitant prices that were neither smart purchases nor reasonable living quarters. Farrah spent the time texting June while Lenore kept busy reading social network posts.

A nurse opened the door to the waiting room and called out, "Lenore?"

"I know this is weird, but do you want me to go in with you?" Farrah asked quietly in Lenore's ear.

"No, I'll be fine."

With the door held open to the exam room area, Farrah caught a glimpse of the woman she saw at the cafe. Marlena, she believed her name was. She watched Lenore get led away and the door close behind her. The signs taped up near the receptionist behind a closed sliding glass window were aggressively worded warnings about payments being expected immediately and that they were not held responsible for billing rejections for being out of network providers. Hardly the presentation of a warm and nurturing office that was supposed to be about caring parents planning their families.

Farrah bit her cuticles during the forty minutes she waited. She looked at the door every time she heard the metal clicks of the knob turn. Finally, Lenore was escorted through the door. Marlena pushed Lenore in a manual wheelchair.

"What happened?" Farrah asked as she ran over to assist.

A nurse behind them walked around to Farrah. "This is just a precaution. She can support her weight, but she's still dopey. She got rather excitable so Dr. DeSantos gave her a sedative that's a bit stronger than her previous prescription. She has new orders to have it filled. Will you be the one to help her get them and get her home safely?"

"Yes. Absolutely." Farrah had no intention of drugging Lenore more any time soon.

The nurse stayed behind while the tech pushed the wheelchair. They got her into the passenger seat and buckled her seatbelt. Marlena handed Lenore's purse to Farrah along with the small slip of blue paper for the prescription.

"Make sure she takes these exactly as the instructions say."

"I'll take care of it after my roommate gets home."

"Do it right away. We almost called the police."

Farrah had no idea what could have caused that reaction from the staff. Where did they get off sedating a patient to a catatonic, practically drooling state? She was in there to have her baby parts checked. She didn't want the details from Marlena. All she could think of in her spinning mind was getting the hell out of there as quickly as possible. She closed Lenore's door and walked to the driver's side while Marlena watched from the sidewalk. Her arms were crossed and the expression on her face told Farrah to watch out.

A bottle of water poked out of Lenore's purse. Farrah took it out and asked if she wanted any, but the despondent girl declined. Farrah opened the purse to put the bottle in secure enough that it wouldn't roll out. That's when she discovered something shiny inside.

She put the bottle back in her lap and moved the wallet and cell phone out of her way. There was a scalpel inside Lenore's purse! How did it get there? Did she steal it? Did someone else stash it there? And why?

Farrah left it there with plans to keep it away from Lenore. She piled everything back on top of it and tucked it behind the passenger seat. Lenore's head lolled to the side as she was nearly asleep.

Marlena didn't turn to head back inside until Farrah had the car reversed and was shifting into drive. Farrah immediately dialed Detective Morrison. She didn't want to put the call on speaker while Lenore was in earshot. Instead, she plead with him to meet at her house because she had to get Lenore into bed or at least on the couch. The detective was curious about the mystery item Farrah claimed to find and he agreed to meet her.

She clicked the red button to end the call and dumped the phone from her trembling hand into the cup holder.

"Don't worry. I've got you. I'll keep him away from you."

CHAPTER TWENTY-SEVEN

MORRISON had a short ride from the police station and was waiting for them when Farrah pulled into her driveway. Lenore didn't need to be carried so much as guided up the stoop and into the house. She stood still for Farrah to remove her coat, hat, gloves and scarf which Farrah had gotten her into like a child. Farrah had Lenore's purse slung over her midsection with her own messenger bag. She got Lenore settled on the couch and put an afghan over her legs. Before leaving the room, she turned on the TV without paying attention to the channel selection and placed the remote control on Lenore's lap.

The detective already had his coat and hat removed and draped over a dining room chair. Farrah left Lenore and showed him to the kitchen, far enough away that Lenore wouldn't necessarily hear, but close enough to check on her. She brought Lenore's purse to the table and gave a cursory glance back making sure she wasn't watching them.

"Look at this." She unpacked the water bottle and everything else from the purse. She held it open and held it for Phil to see inside.

"Did you touch it?"

She told him no and explained how she came to find it in there.

"There doesn't appear to be anything on it like blood." He asked Farrah for a zipper bag and a napkin. He gently lifted the blade from the purse and put it in the baggie.

"Be careful it doesn't stab you. There's no cover for it."

"Thanks." He put the baggie on the table and covered it with the napkin after examining it through the plastic. "There might be prints on it. But why would she have this? Do ob-gyn doctors normally leave these out in a room with a patient alone in there?"

"Not that I've ever seen. I honestly can't imagine why should she would pick it up and hide it."

"You don't know her that well."

Now he sounded like Nova, Farrah thought. "No, I don't, but I know her well enough to not be afraid of her and let her stay in my house. Have you found out anything about the doctor's staff or the vandalism or the threats? She's not doing this to herself for attention!"

"I agree with you there. We don't have much more to go on. It's not like TV where there are cameras everywhere that crimes take place."

When it came to following the trail of the burner phones that had been texting Lenore, Morrison said that he and the other officers watched a ridiculous amount of security footage from the closest retailers.

They were given lists of SKU product codes from the stores and records of daily purchases. Then they had to check to see which receipts had SKU codes for burner phones and find the time on the security footage of the checkout. They hadn't seen Dr. DeSantos, Nikki DeSantos, or Lenore on any of the footage yet. Farrah tried to tell him that looking for Lenore on the footage was a mistake. She didn't believe that Lenore had bought phones and sent herself threatening messages; nor did she vandalize her own apartment and poison herself on purpose.

They had more footage to sift through and if they didn't find anything, they'd consider expanding the radius to include other stores, but using that amount of hours on it was already getting a close eye from the chief.

"Doesn't the chief want the case solved?"

"The reality is that the vandalism is the only crime we have any chance at pursuing. The texting doesn't have much hope. I'm just trying to be honest with you."

She felt so defeated. There had to be a way to track down whoever was texting Lenore. They didn't have the FBI at their disposal. As he said, it's not like it is on her favorite crime dramas where a few keystrokes from a hacker genius would give them all the answers. Morrison was right. They had to face the reality of a dead end.

"As of right now," he said, "the only thing this scalpel is evidence of is a possible theft and that's only if it wasn't somehow already hers."

"That's absurd. Of course it's not hers."

"Look, I'm only pointing out what a prosecutor would. It's a sharp object in her purse. If none of the staff reported to the police that something was stolen from the exam room, there's nothing I can do except take it away from her since she is definitely on the unstable side."

"She's depressed, Phil. She's not unstable. They drugged her!" She kept her voice low but as firm as possible.

"You're starting to sound ridiculous now. Do you really believe there's a suburban doctor's office conspiring to make this one girl look insane?"

"I'm beginning to. There's no other explanation. I don't trust Dr. DeSantos one iota and I seriously question the integrity of his staff too."

Morrison almost forgot the one piece of information that was the closest thing to good news that he had.

"The tea was laced with ephedra."

"I sense a 'but' coming."

"But, the only fingerprints on the jar were Lenore's and there's no way to prove anyone else put it in there. One could easily argue that in her delicate frame of mind or being ignorant of the effects, she accidentally poisoned herself. That herbal stuff shouldn't be trifled with if you don't know what you're doing. The good news is that it was only the morning sickness tea not anything else we took out of her place."

"She does know how to mix herbs and which ones are safe, Phil. She wanted that baby more than anything. There's no way she would have put a dangerous substance in her own tea." Farrah twisted around in her chair to make sure that her elevated voice hadn't caught Lenore's attention.

He didn't let go of the possibility that Lenore was dissociated from reality and poisoning herself. But if it wasn't Lenore, who was it?

"You know, there's a chance it's not the boyfriend."

Farrah was surprised at Phil's openness. He didn't have to share any information with her just because she was acting as the caretaker of the victim. She recognized it and appreciated his willingness to let her in.

"I thought the police always looked at significant others first?"

"Oh, we do. But that doesn't mean it's always our perp. This case screams of a jealousy motive."

Farrah's hands pulled back the mop of sandy tendrils on her head and stretched backwards in her chair. She knew what he was saying. The evidence wasn't definitive. No one was the clear cut suspect.

"But I think it's Joel. The timing of his text to her yesterday? And then this? I guess it could be his wife who knows he's cheating and got someone else knocked up. It could be some other scorned ex-mistress. I think that Marlena could be one. She's rough around the edges and gives me the creeps. I didn't like the way she was looking at us."

He pulled back on her reins a little explaining that bitchy looks don't mean someone is violent or interested in threatening anyone. She could have had a long day or maybe wasn't feeling well.

"I know, but if it's not the most obvious suspects like Joel or Nikki, then we have to think broader."

"It doesn't matter. If we can't prove anything with the evidence, we would need a confession."

There was the lack of confidence Farrah feared. He might close the case unsolved.

"So what? You're just going to let someone continue to terrorize this poor girl?"

"I didn't say that. But if you want me to be perfectly honest, and I think you do, as long as she stays away from Dr. DeSantos, I think the threatening messages and the vandalism will stop. If he has a psycho wife or ex-girlfriend, it becomes his problem."

Farrah knew the detective wasn't a perfect man especially since he was once convinced she was a murderer. She did, however, think that he was the kind of cop to ferret out the truth and not give up so easily.

"Are you seriously one of those men that sees all women as crazy lunatics?" She huffed. "I thought you were different."

"Whoa-whoa-whoa. I don't think all women are crazy. I think women that get hurt by a philandering bastard are more likely to behave like they are losing control and want revenge. Is that better?"

"No." Her head tilted, brows furrowed, and one side of her mouth twisted up to say a barrage of things in her head that she refrained from blurting out.

"Look, Farrah, she can try to get a restraining order against him. I'm happy to process it and serve it myself. But that's about it. And it would most likely be only a temporary one until more details are presented to a judge and then it would probably get thrown out. There's nothing to point to him abusing her. From what I've seen and what you've told me, it doesn't sound like she wants to give him up no less have him legally barred from contacting her."

They came to an agreement that he and at least one other officer would spend another few days scouring security camera footage of the shops that sell burner phones as long as nothing else came across his desk that needed more immediate attention.

"It's a small town. We don't have a lot of resources. It just happens to be a time when I don't have much in the way of actual investigating to do that the patrol officers can't handle themselves."

"Yes, well, I appreciate you taking a break from busting teenagers selling pot, but this really is important. I don't know if you have a proper public relations person, but if you show that your department takes threats against women seriously, it'll look good for all of you."

She felt dirty when she said it. It shouldn't be a give and take. He shouldn't have been concerned with getting a gold star for doing his job. She knew that she couldn't lash out at him though. Catch more flies with honey and all that.

Farrah took the awkward pause in their conversation to check on Lenore who was still lethargic on the couch. She had slid down and made herself more comfortable with her head resting on a pile of small throw pillows. On the TV, a gardening show played, but Farrah couldn't tell if she was really watching it.

Morrison was already putting his coat and winter gear back on before Farrah left Lenore's side. "Thanks for the coffee. I'm going to head out and get back to subpoenas and requesting security camera feeds from three other stores in the area."

"Wait a sec." She quietly asked Lenore if she needed anything. She replied no with a silent nod. Farrah met the detective in the dining room so he could exit from the side door.

"I'll check in on you both later, okay?"

"Thank you. I'd appreciate that."

He lingered. He had more to say, but nothing else came out. He patted her on the shoulder. She didn't know if he was giving her an "atta boy" or if he meant to be comforting. It was weird. She would have rather had a more personal gesture.

"Hey, when this is over, would you like to come over for dinner? I mean with me and June and maybe Lenore will still be staying here. Nothing fancy. Just friends. Eating. Having a glass of wine."

"Oh. Um. Maybe? I guess we'll see if you think I'm a sexist asshole by the end of this case before making social commitments."

It was a fair dig. She called him on his crap and now she knew that he understood.

"Prove me wrong and we can be friends."

"Wasn't there a movie that said men and women can never be friends?"

"There was. You don't believe that, do you?" She remembered *When Harry Met Sally* verbatim. She had watched it a hundred times and usually once a year when it happened to pop up on cable.

He carefully put the zipper baggie with the scalpel into his overcoat. "I'll have to think about that. Meanwhile, I'm taking this, but unless there's a reason for it to be in evidence, I can't do much about it."

"Thanks for getting it out of here anyway."

CHAPTER TWENTY-EIGHT

IT took some time, but hours later Lenore came out of the drug-induced fog imposed on her. Farrah got her to eat some tomato soup and a muffin.

"I don't feel right."

"I don't remember what tranquilizer they said they gave you. I'm sure the hazy feeling is normal."

They sat on the couch under a blanket together with their feet on the coffee table, careful not to kick the empty plates and bowls.

"It's not that. It's an unsettling feeling. I don't feel like myself. I guess it's too hard to explain."

Farrah asked her if the harassment had stopped. Unfortunately it had gotten worse again. Lenore told her that she doesn't answer her phone unless she knows who was calling. She left the ringer switched to vibrate or completely off.

"I wasn't using social media much until Joel bought me that nice phone. I'm gonna stay offline. I'm not missing it to be honest. I know I have friends out there, but I need more time before I log in. And if people want to check on me, they can be patient and wait for me to look at it."

"Hey, do you want to change your phone number? All they have to do is register the SIM card to a new number."

"Does it cost money? I've only worked a couple of hours in the last two weeks."

"We could look into it."

Farrah would have suggested heading out right then to go to the nearest wireless store, but her own phone rang. It was Detective Morrison. Strange since she had seen him only a short while before.

"We might have a huge problem," he said.

Her jaw dropped when she heard what he had to say. Not only had someone from Dr. DeSantos' office called the police to say that the scalpel was missing, she also claimed that their patient, Lenore Lexington, showed signs of being a danger to herself and others.

"The call came from that woman Lenore mentioned, Marlena Ramirez. She acted like she was calling out of real concern for Lenore and that her call was merely a courtesy. I asked her why Ms. Lexington was allowed to leave their office if she was such a danger. It's protocol to send someone to the ER. Ms. Ramirez said she believed that Lenore would settle down from the medication and since she was under your care, she hoped everything would be fine. But then she discovered the scalpel missing."

"Is she trying to file theft charges? What's her end game?"

"Worse than that. She said she wanted the police to take Ms. Lexington to the nearest psychiatric facility for observation."

"Can she do that? She can just ask to have someone brought in?" Farrah put her hand on Lenore's thigh and gave it a squeeze. No one would take Lenore out of her house without a rational cause.

"No, don't worry about it. You're there with Lenore and I saw her earlier. Unless you were personally worried and called 9-1-1, then an emergency squad would show up and take her to the ER first and wait for a doctor's recommendation. A court order would have to be signed by a judge to hold her. That office lost their chance when they let her leave."

Lenore asked what was going on, but Farrah wouldn't say while she had Morrison on the phone. She shook her head slightly and gave a small smile. Don't worry, she wanted to convey.

Morrison assured her that Marlena was grasping at straws. The missing scalpel only meant it looked like a theft considering the lack of action taken by the staff at the time. He asked Farrah if she could bring Lenore to the police station to answer questions about it.

"But I don't think she even knows about it."

"Knows about what?" Lenore said. She grabbed the phone away from Farrah's ear and asked the cop directly. "What don't I know about?"

"Ms. Lexington, I need you to come to the station and answer some questions about an item that went missing from your doctor's office."

When she couldn't get an answer from him, Lenore asked Farrah, what specific item. Farrah didn't answer until they agreed to go over and talk to the police at the station. Once they hung up the phone, Farrah filled her in.

"A scalpel. There was one in the bottom of your purse. I found it when I was offering you water in the car. I was worried so I gave it to Phil — Detective Morrison. He said there wasn't anything alarming about it at first glance, so let's not freak out. I'm sure there's a logical explanation about how it ended up in your purse."

"I didn't take it! Why would I take that?"

She jumped up to her feet and shook her head. She kept saying she didn't do it. She had no reason to.

"Before we go over there…"

"I'm not going to the police! They think I'm crazy! You said they want to lock me up!"

"No, no. Listen to me. They don't think you're crazy. Marlena Ramirez is behind this. We need to prove it. Do you remember every single minute of being in that exam room? Do you have any gaps in your memory?"

Lenore thought hard about the day. It was filled with anxiety. She didn't want to be there to begin with, but it was the only opportunity for her to see Joel since he had been keeping his distance.

"I'm going to prove I didn't do this. I don't know how, but dammit! I did not steal anything! Someone is out to get me. I'm not paranoid!"

"I know. And I believe you. You have to trust me. I don't want you going through all this alone. I'm calling June and telling her to meet us over at the police station."

Before she could make the call though, Jackson texted her. He asked if she was going to go with him to have Gordon put to sleep.

"Dammit! This day!" Farrah had to keep her promises, but how? She knew Jack would be fine. He was sad, but he wasn't on the brink of being arrested or committed to an institution. He'd have to go to the vet without her. She called him right away to explain.

"Whatever, Farrah. I knew you wouldn't be there." He hung up on her.

Life was one disappointment or catastrophe after another. All she wanted was a break. One break. Whatever one the universe was willing to provide. Would it be that her monthly bills were paid? Or that her daughter's summer internship was safe and successful? Or that she didn't fail at her business? Or that Lenore got out of a toxic relationship and returned to her life? Any of those things, Farrah was willing to take. She couldn't bear one more minute of her entire life going to hell.

They arrived at the police station, some place Farrah thought she'd never have to see again. She and Lenore waited in her car for June to arrive. Luckily, she had plenty of vacation time to burn and left her office without any conflict. She pulled her SUV into the slot next to Farrah's sedan and slammed her door when she got out.

"What the holy hell is going on?" June demanded.

They filled her in. She hugged Lenore and promised her it would all be okay. June and Farrah swore they would do whatever they feasibly could to make all the trouble stop.

Farrah pushed the intercom button and announced who they were. The doors buzzed and unlocked so they could enter. It was the same boring color palette of beige, grey, and white as the rest of the building. Inside the main door was a directory with white pegged letters giving the departments, room numbers and phone extensions. A phone was mounted on the wall next to it.

Farrah knew her way around and led Lenore to the large office where the on-duty officers were, including Detective Phil Morrison. Everyone else had to share two desks between them, but Morrison and a sergeant had their own desks. They weren't privileged yet to get their own offices with walls. They could have had them, but instead chose to spend the capital budget on an upgraded interrogation room. Farrah considered herself unfortunate to be familiar with all the gadgetry in there: digital recording equipment, a camera affixed to the wall instead of a bulky unit on a tripod, and a microphone that came down from the ceiling.

"Is that asshole really going to arrest her over a scalpel that she doesn't even remember taking while someone drugged her?" June was furious and barely able to contain herself in the small sterile hallway.

"No, I'm not planning on arresting anyone, Ms. Cho." Morrison surprised them from behind as he exited a side corridor with a hot cup of terrible office coffee. "If you'll come with me, ladies." He walked around them and gestured to have them enter the office first.

"We didn't bring a lawyer," Farrah said. "I hope this really is just a courtesy for Lenore to clarify her side of things without needing to get all formal."

"Let's talk at the table." He lead them into the interview room where four chairs were around the table, two by two.

June and Lenore took one side while the detective and Farrah took the other.

"Is this being recorded?" June asked.

"No. Would you like it to be?"

She looked at Farrah and then up at the ceiling. June knew that the most accurate details of any interview were recordings rather than a human being's report. No matter how unbiased they were supposed to be, it was impossible to get the tone of an interview judgment-free when it came from someone's transcribed viewpoint.

"We'll be fine without a recording. For now," Farrah answered.

"I don't think you two need to be in here though," Morrison said to June and Farrah. "I know there will be details for Fa— Ms. Wethers to fill in from a certain point forward. I'll call you back in when I get there."

They weren't eager to leave the interview room, but complied anyway. He told them they could sit next to his desk; Farrah knew which one it was.

Lenore gave the details about her visit to J.D. Women's Health Center that morning. She explained that the doctor personally requested her for a follow-up appointment.

"Is it normal for your doctor to be that attentive and contact you off-hours?"

Lenore had been through enough and didn't have the strength nor will to continue hiding her affair with Joel from the public. She was used and hurt even though she continued to grasp at the last straw that they had any relationship to salvage. She gave up and spilled the truth unaware that he already knew it. But her account of it formally would then be on some public record typed up by the police. In the back of her mind, she heard the repeating voices of June and Farrah who wanted her to report the unethical relationship to the medical board.

Out in the office area, Farrah and June got caught up on everything going on. June's ex-husband had continued to text her and wanted to have dinner because he enjoyed talking to her. She hadn't given him an answer since dealing with her parents and the search for her half-sister occupied her time. Farrah confessed that she screwed over Jackson yet again by not being with him while Gordon was put to sleep. Together they questioned why they still wanted friendships with their exes. Were they hanging on instead of moving on?

"Do you trust him?" June asked.

"Jackson?"

"No. Morrison. She's in there without a lawyer or even a friend."

"She's not being charged with anything yet. It would be a minor offense anyway if he's forced to pursue the scalpel theft."

"That's not an answer to the question, girlfriend."

Farrah's head turned toward the wall with the one-way mirror and the door into the isolated interrogation room. She couldn't see them from her seated position, but looked anyway.

"Yeah. I think I trust him."

It didn't even take thirty minutes for Lenore to finish her interview. Phil led her out the door and asked Farrah to answer a final few questions. Even though she had less ground to cover with him, she was in there longer than Lenore.

"It seems to me that anyone, including Ms. Lexington, could have slipped that scalpel into her purse during the exam. There were times when she was alone, but times when other people like the ultrasound technician, the nurse, the doctor, were all in and out of there at one point or another." Morrison hated loose ends, but the blade didn't have any usable prints on it. When Farrah handled it, she barely touched the thin sides of the handle and Morrison had used a napkin.

Lenore's entire reputation was on the line and Farrah spoke up to defend her again. "It seems unlikely to me that a patient would grab some rubber gloves from the dispenser, rummage around, pick a scalpel — not drugs or something sought after — hide it, toss the gloves, and finally get back on the exam table."

"The staff members there have said that she has a history of odd behavior though. But I'm no doctor. However, I haven't witnessed anything that would compel me to have her taken against her will into the ER for evaluation either. Something is going on."

Since Farrah and the detective had already talked about theories and possibilities before, they didn't have new ground to cover. He told her she could go, thanked all of them for their time, and said he'd get back to the security footage and daily receipts regarding the burner phones.

"Will you be talking to the doctor and the staff again?" Farrah pulled on her gloves and dug for her car keys from her coat pocket.

"I'll have to. I'll tell them that they can have the scalpel back but that there's no clear proof Ms. Lexington stole anything on purpose. They probably won't like it."

"Well, it's Marlena Ramirez that won't like it. I still can't figure out what Dr. DeSantos' end game is. I'm not sure he wants Lenore to be arrested. He seems to enjoy having her around to toy with."

"Hey! I'm right here," Lenore said.

"Sorry, sweetie, but he's an asshole and it's time you realized it."

Farrah didn't regret the hard truth one bit. Plus, June backed her up. They couldn't stand to see Joel disappear only to resurface via text to see her then pretend that she's the one who's inventing their relationship and mentally ill.

Morrison didn't know her that well, but his gut told him she wasn't a knife-wielding patient who hopped off a table in a gown to threaten the man she claimed to love. "Look, Ms. Lexington, from what everyone has said, I have to agree. That guy is bad for you. He's controlling and screwing with you from the sound of it. I'm going to request that he come in and give a statement about the scalpel and — if it's all right with you — I'll ask him informally to stay away from you, that it's in his best interest."

Lenore thought about it. She wanted her fairy tale. Luckily, she had enough sense to listen to her friends and this authority figure. She was reluctant to believe that she was brainwashed by an older man. The more everyone talked about it, though, the clearer it became.

"He loves me. He did at one time anyway, maybe not anymore."

They let her believe that. No sense in crushing her completely while the pain was so raw.

CHAPTER TWENTY-NINE

JUNE offered to pay for a takeout dinner so they could be well fed and gorge in the comforts of home. She even asked Lenore to invite Star to make sure the support of friends from all parts of Lenore's life were there for her.

Business was so much slower in the winter that Star often closed early. On a Monday, it wasn't a big deal at all because one of her experts scheduled a Reiki workshop. Only people who signed up would be at the store. She closed out the register and agreed to meet up at the house.

Farrah excused herself while everyone else unpacked the takeout containers and set up plates and silverware in the dining room. She went upstairs for as much privacy as possible even though she didn't expect Jackson to answer when she called. He surprised her and picked up instead of tapping the ignore button. She apologized as best as she could and asked if there was anything she could do for him now that it's over. What can you do if you're not there to hold someone while they cry? She felt the offer came off shallow, but she wanted to at least let him know that she cared.

When they ended their call, Farrah sat on the edge of her bed — their former bed. Ghosts of Gordon and Jackson and Nova as a little girl fluttered around the room. She thought of the perfect way to honor Gordon and hoped Jackson would appreciate it.

At the bottom of stairs tucked into the foyer, Farrah sat at the makeshift desk. She opened up the laptop and sent off an email.

"Farrah! Get your butt over here or I'll eat all your fries!" June yelled.

The spread of appetizers, meat and non-meat burgers, regular fries and sweet potato fries covered the table. June had already poured glasses of wine. They toasted to friendship. Things seemed to be looking better and tension was finally dispersing. That is, until Farrah got a text from Detective Morrison.

"He wants to come over. Said he wanted to talk in person and didn't want to wait until tomorrow and ask us to come back to the police station."

"That's weird, isn't it?" Star asked.

The worry washed over Lenore's face. She stopped eating. Her shoulders slumped and she was about to burst into tears again. "I can't take anymore. What the hell does he want?"

Star left her seat and put her arms around her adoptive daughter. "Shhhh. Don't you worry about it. I'm sure everything is fine and the police just want to talk. We're not letting him take you away so don't you get that idea in your head again."

Lenore flinched when he knocked at the front door.

"I'll get it." Farrah darted through the living room with June in tow. They quietly asked him what the hell was going on before unleashing any more bad news on Lenore.

"It's weird. I didn't expect the case of a missing scalpel to send me down the rabbit hole, but sit down and I'll fill you in." He peeled off his coat and accessories hanging them up on a hook in the foyer with growing familiarity of the Wethers house.

Lenore and Star stood in the living room waiting for the next shoe to drop.

"Have a seat, please." Morrison would have normally stood to maintain his air of authority, but Lenore was already fragile and towering over her would scare her. He waited for all of them to sit, shook Star's hand and introduced himself; then he took the only remaining spot in a vintage caned chair which he wasn't sure could support his weight.

The news was not good. He didn't sugarcoat it either. Phil had talked to Dr. DeSantos and heard his side of the story about Lenore's latest visit. Like Ms. Ramirez, he reported that Lenore had often acted strange, but that he wasn't concerned for her safety until he found out about the missing scalpel.

"I know this is hard to hear, but I have to tell you. He said your claim that he's the father of your baby is completely false and denied knowing you on a personal level."

The shock and outcries from the ladies could not be contained except for Farrah who already heard this bombshell first hand from the doctor. That lying sack of shit! Lenore cried and swore that they had been seeing each other for almost a year. No matter many times she said that he bought her the things for her apartment and that he would drop by the places where she worked, the story was that he did that as acts of charity and because he felt so bad for her being young, alone, and pregnant.

"You don't believe him, do you, Phil?" Farrah looked straight into his eyes.

"No. I believe her. I think he's a scoundrel and a dirtbag. Don't care how much money he has. But the thing is, unless we can definitely prove he is somehow behind the harassment, the only thing I can suggest is that they stay far away from each other."

Star had Lenore safely in her arms, stroking her hair. The poor girl was terrified and distraught again. Her anguish seemed to never end. As soon as there was light at the end of the tunnel, it was snuffed.

"Does this mean that she can't report him to the medical board? Would they really need proof of an affair?" June asked.

"How? Submit bedroom photos?" Farrah jumped in.

Morrison didn't have the answers. The protocols of the state medical board weren't part of his line of work. He encouraged them to find out though.

"I don't have photos!" Lenore cried from Star's bosom.

"I'm just saying, it was a private relationship. There's no way to prove it was intimate now unless his text messages were scandalous." Farrah had a feeling that her out loud thinking was making everything worse. "Lenore? You said no one knew about your relationship except for those of us here in this room, right?"

"And I only found out recently that the snake was married," Star said.

"Yes, but I think his wife knew because I think she's the one texting me." Lenore lifted her head and gained some strength. Her shoulders finally shifted back showing that she had a little dignity and confidence left. Not much, but there was a spark there and sometimes that had to be enough.

The chair under Morrison's butt creaked as if to scream, *You shift your weight one more time and I'm giving up!* He looked embarrassed and tried not to move at all below his torso.

"I plan on asking Nikki DeSantos if there was an extra-marital relationship. I find that wives who are being cheated on don't hold back. If it gives her the chance to vent about him and Lenore, she'll probably take it."

"Did that ultrasound tech say anything to indicate she knew about an affair?" Farrah asked.

"No, I only talked to her about the theft incident. She emphasized that Lenore was acting mentally out of touch and it was progressively getting worse."

"Ask her or the other staff. I bet you'll find that employees love to gossip about their bosses."

Lenore's supporters were confounded by Joel's audacity to deny his part in all her trouble. The burden of keeping the secret was lifted. Farrah hoped she would stop feeling that it was eating her insides.

Morrison said his goodbyes. It had been a long Monday for him. Star left shortly after. Sleep was difficult for all of them.

At 11PM the buzz of her phone against her nightstand surprised Farrah lying in bed with the TV playing. She was relieved yet excited to see the text came from Detective Morrison. She thought she insulted him with her meddling theories and didn't expect their blossoming friendship to further grow.

Instead, he apologized that he didn't have better news and that he wasn't helping her friend as much as he wanted. He emphasized that he would continue to follow the leads on the harassment.

Maybe we need a special candle for that, Farrah thought. She wondered if they made candles for revealing a person that hangs bloody baby dolls on doors or texted threats. What they needed was a bonafide miracle and she was willing to expand her notions of faith and spirit if it meant justice for Lenore.

CHAPTER THIRTY

THE next day, June took the afternoon off from work again. She and Farrah had appointments with lawyers in their suit against Caressa Lamour. It also meant that Jackson would be there to be added as an additional plaintiff. In other words, they expected an afternoon of high anxiety and enough stress to kill an elephant.

Farrah dropped Lenore off in the charming downtown area to resume her work schedule at the bookstore and Star's new age shop. Lenore's first shift was at the bookstore which opened early since they had a small cafe counter and sold morning newspapers. With the fright still on her mind from the baby doll vandalism, Farrah waited to see that Lenore safely entered the shop before pulling away. Maybe it was paranoia, but with the people on the sidewalk or exiting their cars, she worried that any one of them could be their suspect.

The journey to Riverside Wellness Spa felt barely hopeful as the sun fought its way from behind the sullen expanse of clouds. Farrah had to meet with Maggie Llewellyn and Samantha Waterston about the possible changes for the business.

There weren't any massage appointments on the schedule between nine and eleven. A slow day for business. Even though that offered them the opportunity to meet at the spa instead of Sam's house, it meant that they were already feeling the loss of revenue from the franchise massage business that opened up a few minutes away.

Maggie stood at the reception counter. She pulled a USB drive from the pocket of her scrubs blouse. She plugged it into a laptop and tapped a few keystrokes. A moment later, she went around the reception desk to retrieve copies of reports from the printer.

"Farrah, can you see if there's a basket in the kitchen for the muffins?" Maggie said.

Farrah got up from her comfortable spot in the waiting area. The rattan sofa had plush cushions and exquisite accent pillows in spicy colors of a Moroccan marketplace. The interior decorating was Farrah's favorite thing about the spa. It was an oasis for anyone coming in with pains and stress, including the people who worked there.

As she walked down the hallway lined on each side with the work room doors, the lingering scents of verbena, lavender, and rosemary caught Farrah's senses. Someone must've been using aromatherapy the night before.

In the kitchen, some of the cabinets were used by the practitioners to store their supplies or reference books if they didn't have permanently assigned rooms. The cabinet to the right of the sink had mugs, glasses, a couple platters and various baskets. She chose one of the baskets in a dark brown color and found a green tea towel to line it with. As soon as she broke the tape of the muffin box and opened it, the triggering aroma made her want to eat all six of them.

Once Samantha and Maggie took seats in the waiting room, Farrah spoke up. "Who else are we expecting?"

"My husband is at his job, so as the primary owners of the company, I'll be speaking for him too. It's just us. Seemed easier to meet in person than all those emails." Sam didn't need the caffeine she consumed from her travel mug of coffee. Her tenacious energy was something that eluded Farrah. She reached into the basket, peeled some of the wrapper away from the bran muffin, and took half of it on a napkin.

Half? Really? Farrah worried that she looked like she couldn't control her eating whenever she ate in front of other people. *Who eats half of a womuffin? Maybe Sam was on Adderall.* She waited to see what Maggie would do before making her own decision, but Maggie didn't seem eager to eat leaving Farrah's attention distracted by muffins while trying to listen to what her bosses said.

The reports were sanitized to keep Farrah, a non-partner, out of the loop regarding their cash flow. The numbers of clients and types of sessions were visible. Even the lease payments and expenses on the office space were visible. Not the intake though, but it wouldn't have taken rocket science for Farrah to calculate it knowing the fee schedule. Farrah's previous job required her to make charts and design reports that dealt with figures in the millions. She felt a bit insulted that the spa wouldn't trust her with their small business details.

"I talked with some people at the country club and they are definitely interested in having massage and other spa services there. There's a catch though: we aren't estheticians, but there's no reason we couldn't bring someone on board. It would be great to expand our services not just in new locations, but also with what we can offer customers," Samantha said.

"What kind of equipment does that require?" Farrah still sat there muffinless, but wanted to get into the nitty gritty of business.

Maggie handed out another sheet with estimates on special reclining chairs, ideas for suites, and a basic supply list. It was costly. She explained they would also consider adding mani/pedi services too. All those options required people with different licenses than massage therapy.

The motivating news that Samantha explained was that the country club was willing to take on the construction costs for the space and then lease it out to the spa. Recently the club converted their old paper filing systems to scanned documents and sent the hard copies to an off-site records management facility. It freed up tons of space where the records room had been. Construction still required a lot of work including climate control, wiring, plumbing, not to mention turning a big ugly storage room into attractive usable suites and a reception area.

Distracted by hunger, it was time for a muffin. Farrah knew she would choke on the dry crumbs of the corn muffin if she didn't slather it in a ton of butter so she reached out and picked the chocolate chip muffin from the basket. *Screw it*. She was four sizes bigger than her coworkers and she required food. Unapologetically, she peeled the wrapper and began eating it.

"So the club will take care of the permits and stuff like that because it's their construction?" She asked once she mostly swallowed her first bite.

"Yes, but we need to really nail this down. We've drawn up a business plan and presented it to the bank we've been using." Samantha took off the lid of the travel mug and tried to get every last drop of coffee out of it.

"We should hear back in a few days," Maggie added. "But what we needed to talk to you about was the idea you had — about how you wanted to be the manager. We barely take salaries of our own. Mostly mine comes from my own appointments just like everyone else's."

"And mine is pittance whether you believe it or not."

"I believe you. Running a business in this economy is arduous." Farrah felt the time was right to get into some details about her idea. She told them she wasn't looking for much, but since appointments weren't paying her bills, all she wanted was a somewhat dependable hourly wage in exchange for running things day to day. It would probably be less than the average grocery store worker but in a business she enjoyed.

They said the numbers were calculated with different variables: twenty-hour week, thirty-hour week, and forty-hour week. Since the country club had hours that were specifically busy or practically dead during the winter, a flexible approach would be needed.

"Look, I don't expect a salary to be handed to me. I love our work. I love what we do. I want to be more vested in it and still be able to pay some bills. I don't know if I'll ever make what I did in an office and I suppose I could still pick up another job between working as practitioner and a manager. I'll do whatever I can handle."

"But the thing is," Maggie pussyfooted around things. "There won't be a manager job for quite some time."

"What Maggie is saying is that we know your situation for income is urgent because of your divorce. This construction? We're looking at maybe a year or more before opening the doors."

That was not the best news. Farrah had hopes and dreams. She wanted to believe anything was possible. She wanted to know that a single woman could support herself. It wasn't turning out that way.

"I understand you have a 'friend'. Is she helping you out for the time being?" Samantha didn't make air-quotes, but her voice may as well have.

"Roommate. June is my roommate." Farrah lost all patience with everyone assuming people couldn't live together Platonically. "But, yes, she's paying her fair share. And, not that it should matter in this situation, but my husband is still paying for things until the divorce is finalized."

The tension of the room strangled her. Farrah wanted to run out. Her reasons for needing more hours at a steady wage weren't any of their business. At some level, coworkers and even bosses are sort of like friends. You talk about your lives. You get to know each other's crap. But talking about personal money issues and her bills was not what Farrah wanted to do. She wanted to work out the business plan to see that they would add a new employee position for a manager and put her name at the top of the list instead of Christine who had been with them much longer. Christine had more clients, made more money, and had young children that required her time. Farrah knew she had more business experience and she was definitely available for the hours.

"Okay, well, looks like you have everything under control." She stood up and put her crumbled napkin with the muffin wrapper on the coffee table. She twisted around to pick up the strap of her purse.

"It's okay. You don't have to rush!"

Samantha sounded offended. Why should she get to be offended when she wasn't open about the revenue, but felt the need to poke her nose into Farrah's personal finances? Their business relationship had already been devastated twice before. She wondered why Maggie and Sam kept her on their books at all. At first, Samantha forced Farrah to take time off which was helpful, but did cause her to lose out on income. She worked tirelessly trying to get new clients who hadn't heard of her scandals. Always handing out her cards and telling people she ran into about her services. Instead of pulling her into their fold, Farrah felt like Maggie and Sam had her crushed at the bottom of a rugby pile. They had plenty of other MTs to assign their customers.

"Oh, don't worry about it." Farrah tried to ease the muscles of her face and hoped she didn't look too outraged. "I appreciate that you invited me at all. If it's going to take a year, then I guess I'll wait and see how the progress is... in a year."

"Come on, Farrah. You didn't honestly expect there to be a job overnight when there's nothing built yet, did you?" Sam stood and took an even stance. She kept the coffee table between them as a barrier.

Farrah took a breath to look away and find an appropriate thought. "No, of course not. I guess I was hoping for something more concrete in terms of the job itself. I know the construction will take time. I know there's a lot of work to do first. I guess what I wanted was an offer to start training before the grand opening."

Maggie closed the laptop and moved it to the coffee table. She rested her hands in her lap and looked up at Farrah. She was the less harsh one of the partners, but still never gave Farrah the warm and fuzzy feeling of someone she could count on.

"We're just not there yet. We're really sorry if you felt mislead."

"No-no. It's not your fault. It's my fault. I guess I have unreasonable expectations. Ya know — because of my situation." Farrah emphasized the end with some heavy snark.

These were women who had massive houses aptly called McMansions for the speed with which they were erected over former farmland. They might not have been rich, but they were well off. They didn't have to worry about how to pay for their kids' tuition or their mortgages. Of course, it never stopped them from many attempts to be relatable with *woe-is-me* talk every so often. Farrah kept her mouth shut every single time Samantha complained about the expense of her son's skiing equipment and trips to Vermont. Poor them. How challenging it must be to have to wait for the K2's to go on sale after Christmas when other people couldn't afford groceries or their winter heating bill?

"Honestly, guys, I'm fine. Now that we're actually on the same page, I look forward to the progress reports and seeing how it all comes together. It'll be great." She tried hard not to grit her teeth. She forced a smile while her hand had a death grip on her purse strap.

Once safely in her car, she texted June that the meeting had not gone as expected.

CHAPTER THIRTY-ONE

"I'M glad you could leave work even earlier so we could grab food." Farrah perused the menu board of the deli and saw so few non-meat options. It was basically egg salad or all the standard sandwich toppings with no cold cuts. "God, how hard is it to have veggies or hummus on a menu?"

June left her side and grabbed a couple bottles of water from the refrigerator case.

"It's on me anyway. I'm already celebrating."

"June, you don't even know what their settlement offer is. I think it's premature to celebrate on deli subs. Just get me a toasted wheat bagel with butter."

"You're impossible to cheer up. You know that?"

The bagel sat in Farrah's stomach, an immobile lump of mashed dough next to the muffin. She felt like she hadn't even chewed it when she realized there wasn't much left. It might have only been two dollars, but it was the kind of treat a perpetual dieter savors. There was something comforting in the way her teeth sank into the last two bites. Butter squished between her teeth and had that undeniable flavor that the fake stuff she normally used couldn't replicate. Real butter. It was the closest thing to an orgasm she had in months.

"Aren't you nervous?" she asked with the dough wedged into her cheek.

June was halfway through her New Jersey specialty: egg, cheese, and pork roll on a huge everything bagel.

"No." She shrugged one shoulder. "I have faith in our legal team."

Farrah had already spent months internally wrestling with whether this lawsuit was beneficial to anyone or if she filed it out of anger and rash decision making. Part of her felt that June pushed her into it. June's situation had been so much more dire that Farrah never considered that case frivolous. Filing a civil suit against companies wasn't Farrah's style, nor Jackson's for that matter.

"Have you talked to Frank lately?"

"Yeah. But I make him initiate it. Don't get me wrong. I love having him as a friend that lets me vent, but he's still my ex. It's still pretty weird."

"I wonder if Jackson and I will ever be friends. I keep mucking things up."

"Stop beating yourself up. You wanted to be there for him and the dog, but you couldn't. You're helping another friend and her problems are more serious."

"The dog dying was serious. He was part of the family."

"That's not what I'm saying. Gordon was old and very sick. He's at peace now. Lenore has been going through hell every single day. You shouldn't regret trying to help her out when she needed it." June picked off the edge of egg that stuck out from the bagel. It was fried to a crispy brown and tasted of salt and grease from the pork.

*****

The meeting with the lawyers stretched out to three hours, a good portion of that was waiting. It mentally exhausted Farrah.

"Can you believe it?" June was able to hug and walk at the same time on their way back to the car.

"No. I'm stunned. Speechless."

Jackson followed behind them, not too far away, but far enough to appear separate from them. His hand was in his coat pocket, clutched tightly. Frank and Nova were the people he could to talk to, but the old Farrah he married when they were young was the one he wanted to talk to first about anything in his life. He wanted it to change. He needed to create more space between them.

At the end of the cement ramp Farrah stopped and looked back for him. His head was down and he almost didn't notice that she was in his path. His case still had to be formalized in writing, but Caressa Lamour and the conference center didn't want any more bad publicity.

"Hey," she said.

He inhaled the chilly air through his nose. "Yeah?"

"Um. I'm not sure how this changes anything. Ya know with our situation and our finances. I think we need to sit and talk, but honestly, I'd really love to do it without lawyers. I've kind of had enough of them for a while."

"Yeah. Maybe. I'll text you later."

"Okay."

She had hoped for more but wasn't going to get it. She needed to respect his pain and unwillingness to forgive her. She was rather used to not getting what she wanted. Breaking the habit of him being there every day even for small talk was harder than she imagined it would be. The good old days were long behind, but the memories of them masked a lot of the neglect she felt in their final years as a couple. The idolizing stage — where one forgets the bad things and only wants to remember the good.

Before he had the chance to walk further away, she tried again.

"I was hoping we could just do it now and get it over with. Then if you want, have a drink with me and June. Call Frank too. Invite him to Happy's."

"You want to hash out the details of our divorce at a bar? With your girlfriend?"

"She's my roommate goddammit. And yes, why not? We can't agree on things when we're sober so we may as well try something else."

June resented being blamed for their problems. She was an easy scapegoat, yet one that made no sense at all. She was not the one Farrah fooled around with at the Caressa Lamour retreat.

"Hey, I have an idea." June pulled out her keys and clicked the remote start button to warm it up. "Why don't you two go to Happy's and work on your shit while I go home and answer emails? How's that? Exciting enough? Dull enough? Take your pick. Because quite honestly, I'm sick of you two fighting, especially now, when there's nothing to fight about!"

They watched June quicken her pace and aggressively open her driver's side door.

"She has a point. We could just go alone and do this. Let's go and get it over with. Then we celebrate apart, away from each other, with whomever you choose." Since it looked like June was going to drive off without her, Farrah needed Jackson for a ride at the very least.

"Fine. My car is over there." He pointed to the far right side of the parking lot.

When Farrah slid into the passenger seat, she noticed it was different. The seat had been adjusted. Someone else had sat in it, but who? It could've been their daughter, but Farrah didn't believe the simplest theory and she would refute Occam's razor where matters of her broken heart were concerned.

Her mind, as always, went to the most outlandish place. She immediately thought that Jackson's dating life must have been going well enough that someone else had been in his car. She reached underneath the seat for the latch and moved herself forward a couple inches and grabbed for the lever on the side to raise the backrest.

Jed, the owner of Happy's, waved at them as they walked through the bar. His blue flannel shirt was a departure from his frequently worn red. Jed didn't have a wide range of men's fashion in his wardrobe, but he was a sweet and pleasant barkeep. He greeted them and said to have a seat wherever they wanted. It was an odd time before the busy happy hour crowd but after the late lunch crowd.

Jackson didn't look Farrah in the eye much. He played around with the mini flipboards of the drink and food specials.

"Do you know what you want?" she said when he put the menu down.

"Beer."

"Oh. Okay. Well, my treat. I mean, it'll go on my credit card until the money comes in."

"Which means I'll pay for everything until the money comes in." He was unintentionally smug.

"Fair enough. I was just trying to do something nice."

231

The waitress was intercepted by Jed. For a couple of his old favorite customers, he took their order personally.

"What can I get ya? Cosmo?" He knew Farrah and June's favorite order, but couldn't predict if she would have something else being there with Jackson instead.

"You know what? I will be different today. Something good finally happened so I'll have a lemondrop martini today. Probably two or three, Jed. Just to give you a heads up."

"Well, I guess you're not driving. What can I get you, Jack?"

"The honey lager on tap will be fine."

After Jed delivered their drinks, they said they weren't interested in food and he didn't disturb them except for Farrah's refills. It was obvious from the expression on Jackson's face that he wasn't there to socialize and have a good time. Farrah smiled, even though it was forced, mostly in trying to convince herself that the settlement was the first step in her life finally turning around from the nightmare it had been for a couple years.

"Farrah, if you get too buzzed, you can't possibly agree to divorce terms rationally."

She finished her second martini. Her hands were sticky from the sugar. "I'm fine. And I want us to part in respectful, healthy ways. I want both of us to be satisfied with what we decide."

What they decided was that they had no interest in combining and then evenly dividing the sudden fortune because of the fifty-fifty distribution of assets per New Jersey divorce law. They didn't have the money before when they were together and it wasn't something either expected to ever receive.

"What I would like, if you're agreeable, is that I would pay off Nova's education and she can go on for a Master's degree or a Ph.D. if she wants. And I'd also like to buy your share of the house." Besides the doodle Farrah inked on the corner of a paper napkin, she wrote "college" and "house" and then circled them.

"That's okay with me. I kind of thought you'd want to move, start fresh." His pint glass had the same three sips worth of beer in it that had been sitting there for thirty minutes. He swirled it around, but if he had finished it, he'd order another and staying there drinking with his soon-to-be ex-wife was not a good plan.

"I considered it. I might spruce up the place. Maybe add a usable garage that I could actually park inside. But it's got everything else I want... in a house that is. What are your plans for the money?"

"Well, it's not enough for me to up and quit my day job, but at least I know I'll have some retirement money. Stocks are in the toilet these days. I think I'll take a vacation first. Then become a real partner to Frank and buy into his special effects shop. He's so busy. We could use a good workshop and a real base of operations."

"That sounds fun. The business advice people always spout is that if you love what you do, you'll never work a day in your life. I'm really happy to hear that you love working with him."

Jackson didn't say anything new about his role with Frank. Frank was the artist, the sculptor and engineer behind all the wicked props. Jackson did some basic things like mixing epoxy foam and pouring goop into molds. He started to handle the bookkeeping too since Frank, ever the artist, hated that kind of thing.

"Let me see if I can get Jed's attention and pay this bill. Why don't you text June to come on over? When she gets here, I'll take off. You two can keep celebrating. I'm telling Jed to cut you off at four though."

Finally, her smile was genuine.

CHAPTER THIRTY-TWO

WHOEVER said money can't buy happiness never had to worry about whether or not they could eat that day. Farrah knew how to be frugal. She and Jackson had been doing that for years. Struggling. Stressed. Depressed.

Maybe money didn't bring enlightenment, but it sure as hell would take away the biggest obstacles in her life. It was even better that she could share this one positive moment with her best friend.

Farrah's settlement was more than she could have hoped. She didn't even think of her life as being worth that much especially since she hadn't had life insurance for so long. Equating her life to dollars was a mystery to her.

When the Caressa Lamour and Shawnee Conference Center legal teams made the offer, she wanted to sign the deal before they were even finished speaking. The companies were each responsible for half. Naturally, her own lawyer wanted to hold out for more.

It wasn't enough to never work again, but it was enough that she wouldn't lose her house after the divorce. And at least she'd be able to do the work she loved without the anxiety of whether she booked eight appointments or three in any given week. She wouldn't have to worry about missing clients because of unpaid sick days or if she wanted to take a couple weeks and travel. As long as it was work she loved, she would didn't mind being busy.

The companies were able to convince Farrah that they could not be held solely responsible for the cyber attacks on bank accounts, doxing, and harassment she and Jackson received. The damage was done by individuals not under the control of a single employer or with any group. Life on the internet was chaos. The companies still offered something for the suffering she and Jackson endured for those weeks. Since Jack hadn't been there at the conference, his vulnerability was the lowest as his settlement reflected.

Given the physical threat against Farrah, coupled with all the other problems and the fact that she had actually tried to save their CEO's life, her final dollar amount seemed adequate. Of course it came with a non-disclosure agreement.

"I'm happy for you that you got even more." Farrah raised her glass to toast June.

"Hey, who knew dying for a few seconds would pay off? I wonder if I'll get superpowers like that guy in *The Dead Zone*."

June's case was practically the same, but because she needed to be revived after someone drowned her, she was offered a substantial settlement.

The lawyers had even considered suing the radical animal rights organization because their recalcitrant dogpiling on social media was responsible for so many people swept up by the mob mentality. Farrah and June didn't want to bring them into it much to the lawyers' dismay (a missed opportunity for a percentage of the award).

Farrah savored the end of her fourth cocktail. No reason to suffer an extreme hangover at her age. "I've already been thinking about what we can do to counter the enviro-terrorism of that radical animal rights group."

"I'm relieved we agreed on not suing those nutjobs. It's too stressful going through this. And they have big name celebrities that endorse them. I'm not interested in that kind of fight."

"Here's my idea, we take some of our settlements and donate it to some local no-kill animal shelters or to maybe those from areas hit by tornadoes and hurricanes. And we can even pay people individually who need to crowdfund their vet bills. Nova taught me about those sites where individual families post their funding needs and people from anywhere in the world can chip in."

"Jeez, woman, where have you been? You only just learned about that?"

"About a year ago, when she told me that's how she paid for her name change."

That lawsuit chapter of their lives was finally closed. They basked in the good news for as long as they could before returning to reality. They still had a houseguest who feared for her life and her mental state.

"I want to do something for Lenore too."

"You've done a lot for her and we only just met her a couple weeks ago. You gave her shelter and safety and you've been her chauffeur." June finished her Irish coffee and switched to water. "I want another piece of pie."

"You can have all the pie you want. But about Lenore, I know it sounds irresponsible since we only just met her, but we've gotten to know her. She's been living with us. And to be honest, I've kind of liked having the house full of people who aren't fighting." Farrah waved over to the server to get her attention and told her another piece of chocolate pie was required for June.

"Extra whipped cream!"

"Are you taking tomorrow off?"

"I suppose I could. Screw them if they don't like it. I'm not in love with my work the way you are. And in thirty days I'll be able to think about taking a long vacation and maybe leaving government work for good."

"All right, we've been out long enough. Let's get back to Lenore and not accidentally rub it in her face that we've had a victory while her life is in the toilet." June signed off on the credit card receipt and included a massive tip for the server who took over once June arrived.

When they got back to the house, they were surprised to find Detective Morrison keeping Lenore and Star company.

"Hi? Did we interrupt something?" Farrah was disheveled and didn't care how her hair stood on end with static electricity and that her cardigan was buttoned wrong. She had a great buzz going and knew neither of them should have driven home. That guilt would hit her in the morning.

"This is only a semi-official visit. Lenore called me because she was scared and didn't want to disturb your little celebration." He politely stood as Farrah and June entered the living room.

June chose the antique caned chair, her slight frame unlikely to make it creak the way Morrison's had before. Lenore was in the large extra comfortable chair. That left the coziness of the couch for Farrah and the detective. He sat first while she fluffed the throw pillows. Her drunken uncoordinated ass flopped so closely to him she almost ended up in his lap.

"Can I get you something? Maybe some water or black coffee?"

Farrah looked back into his eyes and thought for a second that he was only speaking to her and that they were alone.

"No. No." Her head moved like she had to get reacquainted with her own home, her line of sight catching on random things. The framed photo of her hugging Nova on high school graduation day. The glass votive candle holder on the coffee table. The original watercolor painting by a local artist of a ginger cat that resembled Miles.

She finally looked back at him. "Why are you here?"

"Oh boy," he said. "Maybe we'll wait to catch up when you're sober. June, can you get her to bed?"

"She's fine." June relished the awkward intimacy as it grew. "So, detective, I didn't realize you were also personal security."

"He's here because I called him. I got more text messages. I know I should change the number, but it's my life. I shouldn't have to do that. And you guys were out and I got scared."

"It's specific this time. It's a good thing she called. The messages have escalated to include dates, times and locations where they plan on assaulting Lenore. I'm not taking this lightly."

The news was startling and sobered Farrah right up. Not completely. She couldn't walk a straight line, but her thoughts definitely cleared up.

"What can we do?" Farrah asked Morrison with her face far too close to his ear for a professional conversation.

He inched away from her, not to be rude, but to exercise courtesy.

"You'll be fine all together tonight. The texts warned Lenore that her 'Satanic coven will be in the under fire tomorrow,' their words, not mine."

"If they think they can threaten my shop and my people, they better watch their own backs." Star's anger moved through her entire body. Her neck lengthened making her seem even taller. Her bejeweled wrists and hands waved in the air showing no way, no how would she sit idly by and be insulted, threatened, or be quiet without a fight when loved ones were in harm's way.

"I suggest you try to get some sleep tonight. I'll have patrolmen around both places where Lenore works, plus here, and at her apartment which we know they are already familiar with. I'll check with her building's management again to see if they can somehow get a security camera up there first thing in the morning. But chances are, this person knows Lenore is staying here. They seem to know her whereabouts."

"It's that dating app on her phone. I swear that thing is just creepy!" Farrah had forgotten about the app Nova showed her but thinking about the geographic locations of Lenore's main spots, jogged her memory.

"If your phone is tracking you in any way, and let's face, they track all of us all the time," Morrison said, "you should turn it off and take out the battery. Stick with someone else who has a phone at all times. The four of you make sure you have hard copies of emergency contact information and check in with each other."

Morrison and Star left for their own homes. Star said she'd be at the shop at nine in order to make sure everything was cleaned up from the late night workshop.

Without any massage clients booked for Wednesday, Farrah had the whole day free to stick by Lenore's side. It was a relief to let the anxiety of worrying about missing appointments off her shoulders. It was only one area of concern though.

She couldn't sleep soundly. Overnight she came up an idea to present to Star. Since part of her massage training included not only Western medical approaches to treatments, but also Eastern practices and energy work, it might be the sort of thing that she could do from Star's Blessings. They already had Reiki there. If there was room for Farrah to utilize her inclusive approach to chair massages or energy work, maybe she could find more love for the work that she thought would be a fulfilling career. Plus, she wouldn't have to wait for the spa expansion.

CHAPTER THIRTY-THREE

JUNE took another day off of work. She had neither guilt nor regret. She had given her situation enough thought and decided that she would quit her county job as soon as the check cleared from the settlement. She made a list of financial advisors to ask around about, because even if it meant living on a budget, the grind of a day job was something she was ready to put behind her. She even considered going back to college and finally getting that advanced degree in anthropology, though she had no idea what to do with it.

At that moment however, all that mattered was protecting Lenore and finding out who was behind the terrorism against her. June got up at her regular time as she would have for work. Farrah and Lenore were already in the kitchen.

"Silly me thinking I could ever beat you to the coffee pot."

"I added some chicory to it today if you pick up an earthy flavor." Farrah was partial to adding a cinnamon stick to her own cup, but once in a while dressed up the whole pot with something like chicory root.

"Look, I'm even having some. I feel like I can never drink tea again without being afraid of being poisoned." Lenore held up the mug with bold print stating, 'Coffee is my boyfriend.'

Farrah put the almond milk carton on the counter since June would need it. She practically tripped over Miles who rubbed against her ankles. 'Twas feeding time for the marmalade cat. He could have waited another hour, but everyone was up so that had to mean it was breakfast time.

"It feels really weird that I have all you guys and the police surrounding me like I'm some kind of important person." Lenore tried the coffee with only almond milk before adding agave to it for sweetness. "Hey, maybe while you guys are hanging out as my guardian angels, we can do something fun like make incense. Ostara is coming up. I'm sure Star would love to have something new for sale."

"Don't you have to be a pagan to do that?" June found all of Lenore's practices interesting, but she had never done any of the craftwork herself. She loved having her tarot cards read, but thought of incense as something used by pagans, Wiccans, Catholics and Buddhists.

"Star's shop is interfaith. Anyone can help. It's all about your open heart and intentions."

"Hmmm, I'd like my intentions focused on getting someone arrested for making your life a living hell." June didn't gloss over it. Not when it came to her life or her friends.

"That would be incredible, June. Thanks for looking out for me. What do you say, Farrah? Are you in?"

"If you think Star would be okay with us being there and getting into her supplies, I'm all in. I also have no idea what to do, so you have to be our leader."

"Priestess. Even though I'm the youngest here, I have the most experience. You can be our Crone though if you want, Farrah. Are you passed childbearing age?"

243

It was an innocent question, but she felt betrayed by the shocking label of old crone. "Uhh... ummm... No. No, I'm not. I doubt I'd successfully bear another child, but I'm not menopausal just yet. Give me a few more years. Like maybe eight or ten."

Lenore had to keep busy or she would have another breakdown. Before anyone had the chance to object, she pulled out Farrah's oldest all-American cookbook and began whipping up the batter for pancakes.

"You still need rest. You shouldn't be busting your butt to cook us breakfast and work your jobs." Farrah reached for the whisk in her hand, but she pulled it back too quickly.

Farrah and June relished the savory pancakes and the kitchen assistance. Fluffy, doughy goodness hit the spot on Farrah's hangover.

The great news they received the day before had to mean things would turn around for all of them. If Lenore felt well enough to make pancakes, her body and her mind had to be improving. The medications had been sucking the life out of her. Taking them only as needed so she could enjoy friendship and community was another healing step.

Lenore went up to shower. June had already finished in the bathroom before breakfast. She and Farrah cleaned up the kitchen when a jingle interrupted them.

Farrah's phone screen lit up from a text message. She peeled the dishwashing gloves off her hands and checked it. Detective Morrison said he arranged for them to have a patrol escort and uniformed officer with them if they planned to leave the house. She relayed their plans about all three of them going to Star's Blessings.

"This is so weird. Don't you think so?" June dabbed the tablecloth with a soapy sponge to get out some syrup.

"You spilling syrup? That seems normal."

June threw the soapy sponge at Farrah who was fortunately not dressed yet in clothes for going out of the house.

"Honestly, I think the past year of our lives has been pretty surreal. And it'll keep changing so hopefully the weirdness starts to feel more like wonderfulness."

In front of the house, a Riverside PD patrol unit pulled up to the curb. Farrah noticed it out the front windows on her way upstairs to get ready. She shouted over to June to let her know and then texted Morrison so he could be relieved that the patrol officers were doing their job. It was hard to see through the windows, but Farrah thought she recognized the figures of officers Alvarez and Groff who assisted with Lenore's apartment vandalism.

The weather called for dressing in layers of leggings, a tank top, a button-down shirt and a sweater. She didn't feel like messing around with her hair since it was still cold enough to wear a knitted hat. It'd end up in a frizzy mop from the static anyway. She pulled a hair scrunchie onto her wrist for when the time came for a ponytail. Since the ice melted sufficiently, she felt safe wearing a pair of tall boots with a slight chunky heel. At this point in her life, anything that wasn't flannel pajamas and slippers was fancy dress up.

Piling in June's SUV, the ladies headed downtown with their police escort behind them. June turned into a parking lot that would allow them up to a full day for a small rate. Before she parked and paid, Officer Alvarez knocked on her driver side window.

"Don't park here. You'll be under our watch all day so we're going to have you park close to us directly in front of the store. Don't worry about the meters. We'll make sure no one else tries to ticket you."

They said thank you and lead the way down Center Street to Stockton Street.

Officer Rosie Alvarez led them inside Star's Blessings and introduced herself to the proprietor. She left Officer Groff outside in the car. The premises were secure and the only people there were ones who were supposed to be there, plus Farrah and June.

The back of the shop was extremely cramped quarters with shelves of supplies and merchandise. There was a small workshop area with a round table and four chairs. Other folded chairs were collapsed and leaned against a wall. There wasn't anything resembling a proper office for Star; she used a small ledge behind the main counter where she sat on a stool but could keep an eye on anyone entering.

"We do our rituals back here around this table but it's also where we make a lot of things for sale in the store," Lenore said.

Farrah heard Alvarez in the main room tell Star that she would be standing right out front. The bells over the door jangled as she exited. They chimed again a minute later as a customer entered. It wasn't the best system in terms of security. Farrah wished there were cameras and monitors then realized how nice it must be to feel safe enough without them.

Lenore prepared for making incense. She pulled out some jars of dried herbs and black dyed wood pulp. The labels were handwritten and lovingly stained with years of use: St. John's Wort and black peppercorns.

"I'll be right back. We keep the whole cloves and dragon's blood resin behind the front counter."

June leaned towards Farrah after Lenore went through the Dutch door. "Dragon's blood?"

Lenore came back into the workshop/storage room with her arms full. "We won't be using rosemary because that also triggers memories and quite frankly, I cannot wait to forget all about this awful period of my life. But I did grab the rue and sage."

"Almost sounds like we're making soup." June took the sage from Lenore's crooked elbow and popped open the glass jar to smell the contents.

"Hopefully it will smell as good. I've made some that aren't pleasant at all," Lenore confessed.

"What's this?" Farrah picked up the small five milliliter bottle of liquid labeled banishing oil. "Smells like cilantro."

"It mostly is. Cilantro is used in banishing and also love spells depending on how it's combined. Star whipped that blend up specifically for getting rid of evil energies."

The final things to be placed on the table were small paper bags, officially branded Star's Blessings labels, markers, and the largest mortar and pestle that they had ever seen. It was eight inches of solid granite, charcoal black with white speckles.

"Bubble, bubble, toil and trouble." June pulled out a chair and showed she was ready to go.

They didn't measure the ingredients. Lenore eyeballed how much of each she wanted and put all the herbs into the mortar. Grinding them up took plenty of elbow grease so they took turns. The pulp was added with nine drops of the banishing oil which Lenore ground together with the herbs for the last step.

"It's more than enough for one personal use so we'll bag up most of the batch for sale. For that, I do need the scale in order to keep them consistent." Lenore pushed back from the table and looked around until she spotted the digital scale on a shelf near the herb inventory.

Farrah organized the stuff better on the table. "Why don't we do this like an assembly line? Lenore can measure, I can bag, June can label."

"Why do I have to label?"

"Because your handwriting is ten times better than mine."

June accepted her challenge and started making the labels. "What are we calling this? What should I write?"

Lenore squinted with a half-smile. Farrah loved how she looked when she was feeling like herself and not the depressed dishrag Joel turned her into.

"Let's name it after powerful guardian goddesses. Zorza Protection and Banishing Incense."

"Who's she?"

"They, not she. They're two sister goddesses. One that protects the gate of the sun god's palace in the morning when he leaves and one that takes the shift after he returns home."

June congratulated Lenore for knowing so much about arcane history most people forgot after final exams.

Anukset, the long-haired Calico cat jumped up on the table at the precise moment a loud crash blasted from the front of the store.

CHAPTER THIRTY-FOUR

THEIR reflexes sent all three women cowering to the floor and using the table for protection. Anukset leapt off the table before she even had time for all four paws to land. She took off for the safety of the employee bathroom and hid behind the toilet.

"STAR!" Lenore called repeatedly for her boss and closest friend.

With the Dutch door's top half open, they could see smoke wafting through the store.

"STAR!" She tried again. And again.

Lenore began to crawl from under the table towards the door when June grabbed her by the leg and dragged her back.

"What are you doing! Are you crazy! You can't go out there!"

"Lenore wait for the police! They were right outside. They know we're back here." Farrah couldn't possibly console her after an explosion like that.

Maybe it was because of Star's enchantments on her shop or just luck but, as far as explosions go, it was small enough that they could still hear and mostly see through the rooms, but things had caught fire. Finally, they heard Star's voice call out for Lenore.

Lenore kicked away from June's grasp. "We have to see if she needs help!" She managed to get up on her feet and reach the door.

June and Farrah were right behind her. They entered the main shop and were surprised that it didn't look as bad as it sounded, though there were small fires at the front that needed to be put out. Before they knew what happened, neighboring merchants were there with fire extinguishers getting it all under control before the sirens from the firehouse two blocks away finished blaring.

"Watch the glass!" Star yelled. Her arms straight out like she had to hold off a herd of wild boar stampeding through the store.

"What the hell happened?" June said.

Officer Alvarez came through what used to be the large front window. She walked over the shards that once read: "All are welcome here."

"I need you ladies to get back into the storage room, away from this glass. EMS is setting up in the alley behind the stores. You'll be examined and treated there.

"Officer, did you see who did this?" Farrah said.

Less tactfully, June began her own questioning. "Yeah, what the hell happened? You were supposed to be keeping watch! Where's your partner? What did you see?"

"Ladies! Get in the back room. Now!" Rosie Alvarez had a commanding voice and intimidating presence over the civilians. Her radio piped through a lot of voices chattering about locations and a chase.

Star ushered June, Farrah, and Lenore into the relative safety of the storage room where they were when the Molotov cocktail busted through the front window.

"Let me prop open this door and make sure we can see when the EMTs are here." Star had a brick near the door to the alley that she used frequently for propping the door during deliveries and days when she had to work in the stuffy storage space with one pathetic old window.

Alvarez came in the back to tell them that the ambulance was a block away.

"But we aren't hurt," Farrah said.

"You should get checked out anyway. I need to stay up front and keep people away from the scene. The fire seems to be out, thanks to your neighbors having quick access to fire extinguishers." Star said she wanted to thank them again for saving her store, but agreed it would have to wait until after the commotion died down.

Lenore had already been shaking from all the adrenaline and then when she heard the different sirens approach, she burst into tears.

Farrah had no idea how she was holding herself together considering what a weepy mess she normally could be. Worrying about someone else seemed to have given her some stamina and resilience to the dismay of the situation. Plus, she wasn't alone. She had June close by and what little she knew of Star Turner, she liked and trusted. Alone, she would have been fetal, sobbing and hyperventilating. If the three older women could keep their heads on straight, then Lenore would have a fighting chance of not breaking down completely. With the best of luck, maybe their fortitude would rub off on her at least a little.

An EMT poked her head into the room from the alley. She said if they were all able to walk, they could go to the two rigs for examination. They had pen lights shone in their eyes, followed rubber gloved fingers from left to right to check for head trauma, and had their vitals taken. The medics heard that one of them in particular was the likely target of the attack and decided that Lenore should be kept inside the ambulance for her own safety. Star sat with her assured that Farrah and June would help the police keep people from entering the store.

The sidewalks immediately filled with gawkers taking pictures for the internet and live streaming the agony of the businesswoman. Alvarez made them keep their distance and ordered them to the far side of the street. Soon other patrols arrived to set up barricades and yellow tape; and even the arson investigator showed up despite the incendiary device clearly being intentional. Not much mystery there other than to track down who did it.

"As much as I think all the people taking pictures are vultures right now, maybe there's a chance one of them has footage of something useful," Farrah said to June.

"We should ask Alvarez to find out if any of them were here before the bomb was thrown."

"Maybe she'll let us start to clean up too. I didn't realize fire extinguishers made such a mess. And all those other merchants seemed eager to keep helping Star."

They found Alvarez talking with a sergeant in the cordoned off part of the street right in front of the store. She told them to butt out in no uncertain terms and that, of course, the police would ask questions to everyone around. They were used to the moderate kindness of Detective Morrison and not the brashness of the patrol officers.

"The cat!" June pointed to the alley and saw the fluffy ball scurry under a car. "She must be terrified!"

Farrah knew she'd be a wreck if Miles ever took off. "And Star is in the ambulance. Damn! See if you can coax her out and maybe get her into your car or into one of the other shops."

None of them noticed the cold for a while until things began to quiet down. Farrah went back into the storage room and got her coat. She brought June's out to her and then headed towards the busy police, afraid to interrupt them again. They were taking their own sets of photos, interviewing pedestrians and the other shopkeepers. From the way it looked, it was the crime of the century. For a small town, it probably was.

"Officer! Officer Alvarez!"

"What now, Ms. Wethers?"

"I was wondering if we could start cleaning up the mess and maybe find some plywood or cardboard to tack up over the big hole in the wall."

"I think we have all the evidence we could expect. We have the rest of the department, neighboring patrols, and the state police in pursuit of the car."

"Oh? So you got a good look at it?"

"Black SUV. Tinted windows. A driver with a passenger, both faces were covered. The window rolled down. The Molotov was hurled at the building. Groff was right behind them immediately as they took off while I stayed to check on all of you."

She was missing the high speed action. Farrah figured that was why the officer was bitter.

"So can I get started then?"

"Yes."

Farrah may have been there on Star's behalf, but the shopkeepers on the block knew her better. There was a trust already established. Tom Vanderbirk of Van's ice cream parlor had a jolly demeanor and jumped at the chance to help. He closed his store and brought over a couple of brooms then wrangled Josie Koch, the chef of Sadie's Bar and Grill, from her morning prep duties. Josie brought over a stack of folded boxes that would have been recycled anyway.

Farrah found duct tape in the back room along with a retractable box cutter. She dug around for the garbage bags, another broom and a dustpan. She let Tom take the lead in giving out assignments. She was more than happy to take sweeping and vacuuming chores while the others worked on removing the broken window pieces and boarded up the hole.

It was perhaps, the fastest they worked since the south branch of the river flooded in 2011. There were, of course, merchants who kept their distance. They didn't seem to mind gossiping about the blaze, but they were "too busy" to help. Too busy on a closed off block meant they were only consumed with being looky-loos. Not everyone appreciated Star's polytheistic spirituality.

Officer Alvarez came in Star's Blessings to inform Farrah that she was taking down the barricades and joining the rest of the team who had finally caught the assailants.

"Who was it?"

"No idea. They didn't say over the radio."

"You're opening the street up so quickly. I kind of thought there would be more evidence to gather or something."

"We saw who did it. We have all the evidence we need. Plus, some of the other business owners were complaining that they were losing out on customers with the street closed. You'll be fine. Ms. Turner can come down to get a copy of the report for her insurance. Carry on."

And she was gone before Farrah could process the news.

"I got her!"

June wasn't wearing her coat when she came into the shop from the back entrance. She held it in her arms in a rolled up ball.

"The cat?"

"Yeppers! She's in here. I closed the back door but wanted to make sure there was no way for her to get out through the window before I let her go."

"Hang on. Close her in the storage room. Make sure her food and litter are back there. We still have a lot of glass to clean up. And then we need to go."

"Go where?" June reconnected the top of the Dutch door to the bottom half and made sure it was secure before letting Anukset out of her clutches.

"They caught the people who did this. We can finish up here as best as possible for Star."

"I'll text her to make sure Lenore is okay. The EMTs decided it was best to take her to the ER for some sedation. She was completely distraught again just like with the miscarriage. So you want head to the hospital?"

"No. I want to go to the police station and find out who has been terrorizing her."

June tried explaining to Farrah that the police would probably have their building surrounded by news cameras, reporters, and tons of citizens looking for a simple glance at people in handcuffs with jackets over their heads as they had their walk of shame. Farrah didn't care. She believed that her connection to the case and with Detective Morrison's help, she was privileged.

Tom and Josie went above and beyond to pitch in cleaning up the mess. Just like everyone else, including Farrah and June, they took before and after pictures of Star's Blessings. Tom double-checked that the cat was fine and the doors were locked so Farrah and June could depart.

"We have one car. Do you want me to drop you off at the police station and I'll go check on Lenore?"

June buckled her seatbelt and out of habit reached for the coffee cup in the holder. It was empty. She shook it and even looked under the lid to be sure as if the last sip of ice cold coffee would make the day any better.

"Sure. It might be easier to get just one of us inside the police station anyway."

CHAPTER THIRTY-FIVE

BEFORE June pulled the car up to the police station, Farrah texted Morrison. She was surprised he responded at all, no less as a real phone call instead of texting back. She pleaded to be let inside to talk.

His voice gave away his aggravation. Fortunately, it wasn't about her.

"Yeah, you wouldn't believe it, but the Stateys have taken over the interviews."

"Must be because of all the media attention. We're a couple buildings away creeping along and the street is mobbed."

"Listen, it'll be a stretch for me to justify letting you in here without Lenore. She's the victim. I could've at least said you were her caregiver or something. But without her, I don't know what I can come up with for you."

June pulled over and let Farrah hop out. She waved as she drove off. Farrah had to step wide over a puddle of melting black slush from the sad dregs of the plowed snow.

"Don't I count as some kind of witness? I've been with her through most of this including that nasty little bombing."

"All right. I guess that'll be enough when O'Donnell asks me what you're doing here."

Often lacking grace and poise, Farrah tripped over a cable from one of the news crews. She attempted to apologize, but was met with anger from the woman who didn't want her shot ruined.

"Hey, lady! Watch where you're going!"

"Sorry."

"Sorry? This is the biggest story this region has seen in a hundred years. If any of you yokels mess it up for me, I'll be stuck in this affiliate station hell forever!"

"Good luck with your Pulitzer." Sarcasm was not held back one bit. It was her town and damned the breaking news cycle that interfered with her own life again.

How did everyone get to the police station so quickly? Helicopters still circled overhead. They were crucial in the chase down the interstate. Whether it was good planning on the part of the bombers or sheer dumb luck, Stockton Street crossed to Center which ended right at the ramp to one of New Jersey's largest highways. Normally the only helicopters above Riverside were CEOs of the big pharmaceutical companies getting quick rides in and out of New York City or medical choppers. No doubt about it, this event would be talked about for the next hundred years like Bitchy Reporter Lady said.

She elbowed through the crowd of citizens, blogger-activists, and the rest of the camera crews. Morrison told her to go through the city administration offices and snake through the corridors to get to the stairs and then meet him on the second floor where there were other conference rooms, the town council chamber, tax offices and the municipal court offices.

As she walked by the offices, she saw everyone away from their desks and looking out the windows. The part-time mayor and some of the council members left their day jobs to be right there at the pulse of the activity.

"Can you believe it?"

"But she looks so normal."

"He'll lose his license and go to jail."

"Only because he's not a white guy."

They weren't even trying to whisper.

"Psst. Over here." Morrison leaned out a threshold and called Farrah over.

"This is nuts. How are you holding up?"

"I'm doing okay. Thanks for asking. No one ever asks if the cops are okay unless they've been shot."

"Oh. Sorry. Did anyone get hurt? There was so much going on and Alvarez kept us sequestered for a long time."

"Only minor injuries from the broken glass at the scene. But there was a lot more damage because of the chase." He showed her into the small conference room and closed the door behind her. Then he explained that an officer from the next town crashed his patrol car during the chase and was badly injured. He had to be evacuated by helicopter with the passenger of another car in the wreck. Both were in critical condition and there was no word whether they'd survive.

"Oh my god. That's awful. Have the families been notified?"

"The county sheriff's office is handling that."

Farrah filled him in on her side of the story all the way up to June dropping her off and heading to see Lenore at the hospital.

"Now that I've told you everything. Your turn. I recognized the description of the SUV. It's obviously Joel DeSantos, but was it his wife Nikki helping him?"

"Nope. I was surprised too. It was that ultrasound tech working in his office, Marlena Ramirez. They were having an affair for a long time."

"Wow. What a pair."

"He's been sticking to his story that he never slept with nor impregnated Lenore Lexington. Now that she miscarried, there's no way to prove otherwise. They're going to try twisting this into the most bizarre case of self defense I've ever seen."

"Self defense? But how?"

Morrison laid out what he had been told by the state police. Joel and Marlena confirmed their affair and some of his story was consistent to what Lenore said. He intended to leave Nikki and get a divorce, only it wouldn't be to live happily ever after raising a family with Lenore. He and Marlena planned to run off to Florida once his divorce was final. They grew up together as kids down there.

As far as Lenore, Morrison explained they stuck to their previous versions of the story and told the police that she was a troubled, psychotic patient who imagined the affair with Joel because the real baby daddy abandoned her.

"That's bullshit and you know it."

"I agree. It's a matter of what can be proved in court and you know that as well as I do."

He offered to get her a soda or coffee from the first floor break room. She accepted on the condition that they use the trip down there to nonchalantly get her close to the action. She didn't fear for her life in the police station; another privilege she was well aware of. She wanted a good look at the people who were so evil that they could make her friend think she went insane.

Officers who weren't even on duty had come in by that point. No one wanted to miss the chance to see DeSantos and Ramirez fingerprinted, interrogated and cuffed to tables especially when word spread that an officer was severely hurt chasing after them.

Alvarez stood next to the coffee machine waiting for a fresh batch to finish brewing making no effort to move out of the way of the busy hands of the department secretary who wiped off the mess on the counter and tables. She greeted Morrison and left without saying anything to Farrah.

"Cassie just started a new pot," Alvarez said to them. "Never saw so many people in this building before."

"Me neither and I've been here a long time." Morrison shook the red and white whole milk container on the counter and muttered about it being empty. Alvarez slid the canister of powdered creamer over to him. "I hate this stuff."

"So, you're here to look at the fish too?"

Farrah didn't have a clue what Alvarez meant. The nod of the officer's head towards the wall that separated them from the main police office finally gave her the idea she was talking about the prisoners in the interrogation room with the special one-way mirror.

"They're not together, are they?" Farrah asked.

"Hell no!" Alvarez said. "He's in there now. She's sweating it out in the office handcuffed to the bar on the wall."

"You didn't give her a chair, did you?" Morrison's experience was that prisoners should be made uncomfortable for as long as possible so that when someone offered them anything like water or a chair, they'd be grateful for the compassion and hopefully become inclined to cooperate.

"No one did, as far as I know. Groff was the first of our guys to make contact with them. But the troopers took over pretty quickly."

"You still want to see them?" Morrison asked Farrah.

"Yes. I think I do. I want to see with my own eyes that their little reign of terror is over and show that I will not let Lenore back down to their ludicrous accusations."

"If you're sure — come with me. Now, listen, you're not to say a word. You can see that she's in custody for peace of mind and that's it. I don't know if you'll be able to see the mirror to see DeSantos."

He never bothered to make them cups of coffee. His hand went to her back to guide her out of the break room back into the hallway. Alvarez noticed.

Two officers were right outside the closed door. One in uniform and on duty; the other in plain clothes getting caught up on the situation. The uniformed one politely opened the door for his superior to walk through.

As Morrison entered, he saw their normally quiet office had been transformed into a major command center. The problem for him was that the state police were the ones at the top of that command. His chief's uniform stood out with the stark white shirt against the ocean of blue in the room.

"Wait here," Morrison said quietly to Farrah. He left her side and went over to the chief. They exchanged words without any signs disclosing the subject matter. Then the chief looked over at her and his face was far from happy.

While Morrison was busy, Farrah kept herself as close to the wall as she could get which meant grazing a bank of filing cabinets. She stretched her neck to look around the towering troopers in her way. She caught a glimpse at the other side of the room of the dark-haired woman responsible for so much of Lenore's pain.

Marlena Ramirez.

Farrah was all too familiar with jealousy and had years of her own struggle with it. She could not imagine being such a sociopath that she would go on a crusade to destroy another woman all because of a man. She didn't know what it was, but it was definitely not love.

She tried to use the other bodies in the room as a barrier, but Marlena spotted her looking. A smile? Or was it a sneer? It was some kind of mix of the two. Her eyes were slightly veiled by the bangs no longer held by bobby pins like she wore on the job to keep them off her face.

Their eyes locked on each other. Ramirez moved her mouth, miming words.

"I see you."

The sinister grin returned. If Farrah hadn't been surrounded by a throng of trained police armed to the teeth, she would have been scared to death. The type of scared that would normally have her panic-stricken and looking for some place safe to hide. She looked away unconsciously and ducked behind the tallest body near her. Her hand automatically reached up to her face and shielded her own eyes as if her inner voice told her, "Don't you dare look."

It's not like Ramirez was a Gorgon. She didn't have magical powers to turn someone to stone. But that shit-eating grin with those pearl white teeth behind blood red lipstick — it was the sort of stare that would haunt Farrah's nightmares.

CHAPTER THIRTY-SIX

JUNE reported back via text that Lenore and Star were fine. Knowing that the culprits were apprehended by the police made them feel tremendously better. The detail assigned to watch over them was canceled and Lenore was released to go home with yet more prescriptions in hand (which she probably wouldn't take).

Farrah agreed that home was a better option than dragging them to the overcrowded police station. June was more than happy to chauffeur them to the house, but Star wanted to return to her shop to see the damage and immediately call her insurance agent.

"Wethers!"

She looked up from her phone and saw Detective Morrison waving her over to meet Chief O'Donnell. Two foreboding state troopers impeded her path, not on purpose, but because there wasn't much room in the office space designed for four desks and records storage.

"Sorry. 'Scuse me. Sorry." As soon as she cleared getting by one, another was in her way. Cop clones seemed to pop up out of nowhere in their morning glory blue uniforms.

Farrah alternated looking towards her goal, Morrison, and the perp against the other wall, Marlena. The rage it had to take to destroy a toy doll and hang it on Lenore's door seemed like something a psychotic woman would do, not the boyfriend looking to break up with her. Farrah longed to find out which of the two was the real mastermind of the harassment. Not that it mattered in the long run – it was over and Lenore was safe.

She was one step away from Morrison, when Marlena screamed, "I'm not going to jail!" She had only one wrist cuffed with the other bracelet attached to the bar instead of the having the chain passed around it. That unfortunately left her with one hand free.

"Get down!" Different voices barked the same command. It was chaos. Farrah ducked with Morrison covering her. *Were they supposed to get down or were the troopers ordering Marlena to get down?* Farrah didn't know and when she looked up, the deepest terror she had ever known filled her body.

Marlena managed to swipe a pistol out of the holster of a nearby municipal officer. Farrah tried to look up and watch. Morrison pushed on her head trying to keep her vital brain bucket as out of sight as possible. From what she could decipher in that second, Farrah believed it was the gun of Officer Groff.

"I didn't hurt anyone!" Marlena screamed. She pointed the lightweight Glock-19 around the room to fan off some of the cops. It worked. They backed up, but all of them had guns drawn on her. If she even flinched, she would be riddled like Swiss cheese.

"Stay down," Morrison said in Farrah's ear. He stood up, unarmed and held up his hands.

"Don't move!" Marlena's left hand looked comfortable holding the pistol, but the way she waved it around wildly showed she wasn't ready to target anyone in particular. That was until Morrison took a couple steps forward around the statuesque uniformed cops in the room.

"Ms. Ramirez, you don't want to do this. You don't want to put your own life in more jeopardy."

"Don't come any closer!"

She was grossly outnumbered, but for most of the municipal cops, this was the first time they ever had guns pointed at them. The tension all around was palpable.

"No one wants to get shot here today, Marlena. Not even you. Right? You don't want to die today, do you? But these officers are prepared to do that if you put their lives on the line." Morrison kept his voice at a normal speaking volume. His hands stayed up so she could see that he wasn't threatening. Of course, he didn't need to; he had all the help necessary covering every inch of the office.

"Her! Get her!" She pointed the barrel of the gun in Farrah's direction.

Farrah slowly stood with her hands up mimicking Morrison. She wasn't in the mood to die for once. She finally had something good happen in her life and she was looking forward to using the settlement payout to improve her situation. It's not like she never thought the family would be better off with her, but having a gun in her face unlocked a survival instinct just like when she was threatened with a knife at the Caressa Lamour conference. The instinct meant she had no desire to leave her daughter motherless. She had no intention of dying without saying goodbye to June and Jackson either. *Not today, Satan.*

"What do you want?" Farrah tried to sound like she wasn't about to pee her pants. Bile emptied into her stomach and flopped around. She lowered her hands when they began to tremble.

266

"You're gonna get me out of here. Someone give her the keys to these cuffs. You gonna unlock me and the two of us are getting out of here."

Morrison had already considered that Marlena wanted a hostage. Choosing the only civilian in the room was the obvious move. It was not an area he would negotiate. No hostages. No civilian casualties. There was still a massive chance for bloodshed though.

"She's not going anywhere with you. If you want a hostage, why not pick me? Look... I'll take out my gun and I'm going to put it right over here." He removed his firearm from under his armpit and put it on the closest desk. He also made sure to block Marlena's clean line of fire, prepared to take a bullet for Farrah if it came to it. Unfortunately, as a detective, he switched to wearing plain clothes and rarely put on his Kevlar vest. Any of the other officers in the room would make for a better shield.

"Not you. You're a cop! Someone hand her the keys! Now!"

Meanwhile, the officers in the interrogation room with Joel had no idea there was a showdown on the other side of their door. They heard the yelling, but figured a bit of raucous, loud-mouth behavior was to be expected from someone who threw a Molotov cocktail at a quaint small business.

The chief was in the back of the room, also without a bulletproof vest. However, back in his office suite, his secretary Cassie sat watching the security cameras with the court clerk Ellie peering over her shoulder. What exactly does one do when the people you normally call for help are the ones who need the help? The dispatch center wasn't going to be helpful. Instead, Cassie flipped through her contact list in her email system and called the state police headquarters. They had SWAT, something small towns lacked. The fact that state troopers were in danger allowed Cassie to get through immediately.

The phones began to ring on every desk inside the police office. Cassie transferred a negotiator and waited for someone to answer.

"After four rings, voicemail picks up," Morrison said.

"So!"

"I just think that call is probably one you want to answer."

Third ring.

The gun he put down was right next to a phone. He reached over the gun slowly. Marlena watched. The rest of the cops kept their eyes on her.

"I'm picking up this phone. It's okay. It's okay." He grabbed the receiver and held it up so she could see he wasn't making some kind of daring play.

"Detective Morrison... Uh huh... We have a situation. No one is hurt. No one is going to get hurt if everyone just keeps calm." Morrison looked over at Groff inferring, *Don't you dare jump on her to get your gun back.*

Farrah moved inch by inch closer to Morrison. She wanted to be near him. She couldn't protect him or herself, but there was no one else in the room she longed to be next to. Her movements were barely perceptible. Marlena was too fixated by what he was saying.

"Who is that? Who are you talking to?"

He didn't give away any information that she would understand. He kept his answers to "uh huh" and "that's right" then ended the call with "you got it." He pushed the speaker button on the phone and placed the receiver down.

"Here's what gonna happen..." Morrison kept his hands visible to show that he didn't see any reason to pick his gun up with fifteen others drawn on her already. "The state police are dispatching their SWAT team. Now believe me when I say, you don't want them busting through these windows. None of us want that. There'll be tear gas and smoke and we'll all be miserable. And you will not get away from this building. No one is uncuffing you. No one is shooting anyone. Do you understand what I'm saying? This is over. You are done."

Words came out of Farrah's mouth before it registered in her brain. "Marlena? Don't ruin your life because of Joel DeSantos. We're all sure you only did what you did because you love him and because he told you to, right?"

Marlena looked stunned. "Yes. Stay back!" She fanned the Glock back around at all the uniforms who crept closer to her. They backed up, but only a couple inches so she felt like she got her way.

"We do anything for the men we love, don't we?" Farrah could barely keep down the food and coffee that churned in her stomach.

"I love him. I would do anything for him. You're going to let me go and you will bring him to me. You, nosy bitch, you are going to make sure we get out."

"Why would you want to do that, Marlena? Why protect the man that is in that room telling the police that all of this was your idea. Why try saving the man that wants you to take the fall?"

"He wouldn't do that. He loves me! He was leaving his wife for me!"

"Oh, sweetie, you do know he lied, right? He was having an affair with Lenore too and he told her the exact same things. He's not worth it. I promise you. There are better men out there."

The fake man-hating, sisterhood lovefest captivated the police and the clerks watching from the other room. All of the people in the room knew the tactic and knew precisely why Farrah said what she did. There was no way Marlena Ramirez would have any dating options for a long time to find a better choice than the conniving Joel DeSantos.

There would have to be active gunfire for the newly arrived SWAT team to bust through windows where so many cops were already holding their own. The chief saw their truck and vans pull up.

Chief O'Donnell spoke up. "Look, Ms. Ramirez, the SWAT team is here. You are not leaving this room with that gun or with your boyfriend."

Morrison took that prime opportunity while Marlena was distracted by the chief to charge at her. She gave a good struggle for a woman handcuffed to a bar with one hand. As he grabbed her hand wielding the pistol, he flicked the safety on with his thumb a second before feeling her fingers clamp down tight. She tried to pull the trigger not knowing the switch was moved. Reality began to sink in and she let go. By then, four other officers were on top of them, each trying to be a hero.

The cluster broke up and allowed one of the uniformed officers to cuff her more securely. The chief went outside and immediately found the SWAT captain in charge. No windows had to be broken. No tear gas or smoke. It was dangerous, but the fact that no one was hurt was what made the showdown a genuine victory.

"Are you okay?" Farrah would have tried hugging Morrison had they not been in a crowded room of his peers. Instead, she stroked the back of his shoulder.

"I was going to ask you the same thing. Still want to see the other one or have you had enough excitement?"

"I'm done. I'm so done. Get me out of here. Please." Every inch of her trembled with fear.

In the hallway, a voice called out to them. Cassie and Ellie came running from the administrative office.

"Is everyone all right? Do we need to bring the squad in?" As an administrative assistant, Cassie had never seen any real police action, but she had spent her five years there butting her way into activities where she didn't belong. Her scope of work included secretarial duties for the chief and all the officers. Filing. Answering the phones. Making copies. Dealing with the public in person when they want to yell about their speeding tickets at which point she would send them to Ellie's office.

"No injuries. Everyone is fine. The chief is outside handling things. You need to stay out of our office for now. No one without police training or their lawyers gets in until those two are hauled over to lock up." Morrison knew Cassie's desire for action and adventure. For her own safety, he had to discourage her from getting in the way with her interference.

As Cassie and Ellie turned around and went back to Cassie's office, Morrison and Farrah heard, "But she's not a lawyer," barely disguised as a whisper.

CHAPTER THIRTY-SEVEN

FARRAH took a seat close to Morrison in the conference room where they were earlier. A couple glasses of whiskey would have made them tremble less from adrenaline and definitely would have soothed the awkward tension. It was hard for her not to vomit.

"What now?" She didn't want to leave without getting some answers to bring home to Lenore.

He patted her hand. It was the best either of them expect for comfort. No public displays of affection in the police station.

"I'd offer you some water or coffee, but to be honest, this building is still chaos."

"That's okay. I don't need coffee. I'm shaking so bad from the excitement. I need a Valium."

"As for what's next, well, they'll finish being interrogated and we can now add more charges to her case. The prosecutor will be thrilled. We have cameras in that room. The clerks were watching the whole thing. There were fifteen or sixteen cops, plus you. She is definitely going to face some big charges."

"I want you to know that I don't think she's some innocent peach who was taken advantage of. Not like Lenore. Marlena seemed well aware of what she was doing and made her own bed."

Morrison calmed her worries. "We knew what you were doing. I was furious with you. Don't get me wrong. I wanted to be the one to talk her down or at least one of the women in the room who was wearing a bulletproof vest. But let's just be grateful that she didn't shoot you for running your mouth, okay?"

As they discussed the cases, Farrah found out that the police had also found the critical footage they were after of Marlena buying three burner phones from three different stores. The dates of the harassing texts Lenore received were after those purchases. It was thin and circumstantial, unless they recovered the phones showing the texts. It could Lenore was not a severely mentally ill person who sent texts to herself.

Most of the cops moved outside to soak in the appreciation and gratitude of the public who praised them for getting two violent people off the streets. The chilling air did all of them some good.

Riverside didn't have any fancy public relations office or equipment so it was Chief O'Donnell who invited all of the press and the public that could fit into the town council chambers for a formal statement and photo opportunities. The cops lined up much like elementary school hall monitors to guide people in an orderly fashion to the elevator or stairs.

Morrison poked his head out of the conference room's back door which lead directly into the council chambers since it was used for their closed door executive sessions away from recorders and audiences.

Farrah heard the buzz of the crowd. "Don't you want to get in there to face the press and your adoring fans?"

"You deserve to be in there just as much as I do. Do you want to go in?"

Farrah chuckled and gave him a firm "God no!"

What they wanted didn't matter though. The chief texted him to get his ass in chambers and bring "that busybody" along.

Chief Oliver O'Donnell and Mayor Allen Mayberry managed to soak up the spotlight. Neither Farrah nor Morrison stepped up to the podium. They posed for some photos with all the officers who had been in the room though and gave polite "no comment, ask the chief" responses.

Farrah's unease had never been given a chance to settle. She wanted to be home in pajamas sipping a drink and curled up under a blanket. Flashing cameras and microphones did not help her.

She didn't know if she should try smiling to mask her bitch-face of fright and nerves. *Was smiling appropriate after having a gun pointed at my face? What would June do? Is crying allowed? Do I need some of Lenore's tranquilizers?*

The press conference took forty minutes. Morrison offered her a ride home, but said he couldn't stay. Too much paperwork and the chief had already scheduled meetings for the ranks. It was a long day.

Before she got out of his car, a sense of bravery far different from standing up to a gun-wielding lunatic surged through her. "Hey, now that this is all over, how about that dinner invitation? Are you free Friday night? I'll check with the girls and see if they're up for it."

"I'll tell you what, keep me posted. Let me know what they say. And maybe if they aren't up for the company, you and I can go out and get a quiet dinner on our own."

"Without guns pointed at us, I hope."

"It's good to have goals."

The nausea finally passed once Farrah was inside the house among her friends and comforts. She spent the time she needed leaning on June's shoulder crying while Lenore worked in the kitchen to come up with something edible. She managed to whip up a rice casserole with the dairy free cheese she found in the fridge. Joel and Marlena behind bars had given her one kind of peace she needed.

They looked like a group of sorority sisters of the misfit variety, each one in comfortable clothes, cross-legged on the living room furniture, eating a cheap piping hot meal. Farrah's phone vibrated on a regular basis once gossip got out about her ordeal. Lenore never turned her phone back on once she had been advised to take out the battery. She finally agreed to get the number changed and even get a different phone to be sure there was nothing else hidden in the software apps.

June's voice of reason came out insensitive and invalidating. "He can't hurt you anymore. He can't track you. He's in jail. They are done for and they are never coming close to you again."

"June, if she wants to take every precaution, don't discourage her. She's been through enough."

"Yes, I have. I'm not taking any more chances. I gave that asshole the benefit of the doubt a hundred times. Speaking of, did the police confirm that he's really going to jail?"

Farrah finished her bite and swallowed a sip of water before she answered. "They'll be locked up throughout their trials. Phil seemed confident they wouldn't allow bail. What happens there with juries, we can't begin to guess. A lot of juries have let some very bad people go."

Lenore returned to playing with her food rather than eating it.

"But, as Farrah said, the police have them in custody and after the general public was put in danger at Star's shop and then cops themselves were threatened, so it's kind of a slam dunk."

"Do you mind if I stay here a little longer? I'm not ready to go back to living in that apartment." Her voice returned to a weak and pitiful tone. She looked like an orphan pleading for scraps and a mat in the barn to sleep on.

Ever the maternal one, Farrah would not let that slide. "Stop worrying about that. We told you that you could stay here for as long as you want. In fact, if you want, tomorrow we can pick up the rest of your things and you can just move in completely."

"What? For real?" The excitement didn't magically erase the black circles under Lenore's eyes, but it was a start.

"You betcha." June stretched out her arm for a high five smack with Farrah. "Don't worry about breaking that lease either. A good attorney can scare the crap out of that landlord to make sure you don't owe the remainder."

"Speaking of attorneys, I think half the voicemails on the house phone are lawyers that tracked down the number." Farrah wiped her mouth before finishing off her drink.

"What do lawyers want?" Lenore asked.

"You. They want to represent you. It seems there's interest in civil suits against Joel and Marlena."

June and Farrah exchanged the look that said it was time to let Lenore in on one of their theories. The stress and the emotional pain caused by the harassment and Joel's denial of being the baby's father could have had real physical effects including the cause of the miscarriage.

276

"You think they're responsible for me losing the baby?"

"We do. We watched what you went through," June said.

"Your body took a huge toll. Plus, with him being the unethical dirtbag he is continuing in the role of your ob-gyn, he most certainly did not have your interests in mind when advising you," Farrah said. Her words hung in the air like a neon billboard.

"Patti Lu Montgomery was one of the lawyers who called. We know her. She's good. She'll take excellent care of you. Family law is her specialty so with the right team, we believe that she'll be able to show that the family you were planning was destroyed by him."

They didn't push. It took a few seconds, but Lenore processed the news as best she could. "I don't know if I want to relive all of this, but he needs to be punished. He needs his license revoked and my little girl does deserve some kind of justice for never having had a chance."

"Don't forget, he also poisoned you with the tea. I'm so glad my mother figured that out or you would have kept drinking it," June said.

Farrah divulged all she knew about the ma hwang effects which wasn't much, but it was enough that Lenore would not have to spend one more night blaming herself for her miscarriage or clinging blindly to a man's empty promises.

"The doors of his office will never reopen. The business manager will be the point of contact for the authorities. Phil said the investigation would begin first thing in the morning. They'll be up late tonight getting warrants and subpoenas and all the crap."

June put her cup of hot Earl Grey tea on the coffee table, a rare departure for her. She was often the encouraging voice to the others, but she had her own fears and doubts too. Joel DeSantos and Marlena

Ramirez weren't a threat to her or their home. It was a matter of this new family accepting that they were safe at this point.

"While we're all together, there are some things I want to tell you too."

Lenore had given June a tarot reading when they met. She was right about the relationship between June and Hellen. Maybe more of what she talked about that day behind the gauze curtains of her tarot nook was ready to come out.

"Is it about your ex-husband?"

"Frank? No. Not really. I will be seeing him on Saturday though. It's just for lunch. I want to tell him these things too. In person."

"You have me scared now. What's wrong?" Farrah moved closer and put an arm on June's shoulder.

"Okay, well. It's all good news, I think. Not bad news. First, is that once the lawsuit money clears, I'm quitting my job. I told you that already. But I've decided to take the time to travel to look for my sister." She braced her hands on her crisscrossed knees for support to keep talking.

"That's great!" Lenore said. "What about that one woman who contacted you? Is it her?"

"Are you going to meet her?" Farrah was surprised too.

"It's not her. But I've had a few more email inquiries. And maybe it's none of them, but I want to do the search as best as possible. Get into some vital records offices and trace back where my birth father, Han Kwan-ho could be and if he can lead me to her."

They wished her the best of luck. Farrah had thought about her own new chapter in life and for once, didn't immediately offer to tag along with June to help her out. It was a personal journey for June and with her strength and wits, she'd be fine traveling alone.

"Was there something else? You have a look."

"There is. I don't know how to say this either."

"We know you're bi. You don't need to go through a big coming out to me." Lenore tried to assume that's what a difficult conversation would be, but she was wrong.

June smiled and let out the smallest bit of relief. "Nope. I know you guys know that. Before I search for my sister, I'm going into rehab. In Arizona."

"Rehab? What the hell for?" Farrah could have tried harder to be supportive, but June and rehab were two things she never expected unless it was of the physical, coming out of surgery kind.

"Yes, Farrah. Rehab. I know you and I have always unwound with a couple of drinks at the end of the day while we talk, but it's more than that. I guess I hid it pretty well if my closest friend in the world didn't see it."

"I have no idea what to say." Farrah wondered if she was somehow responsible for contributing to this secret.

"You can do this, June. We both have complete faith in you and we will do whatever you need." Lenore proved she had every intention of repaying them for their kindness and hospitality.

"Have I been making this worse for you? Have I pressured you into drinking?"

"No! I promise." She smiled and put a hand on Farrah's lap. "You are never responsible for my actions. And like I was saying, it wasn't just our cocktail hours. I was drinking at lunch a lot and if I couldn't sleep, I'd have something. It never seemed like much. A glass or two. But I've done a lot of thinking about it and it's been alarming." She admitted how reckless it was for her to drive while buzzed so often.

She told them that if it wasn't for the expectation of money, she wouldn't even consider an in-patient facility and would have done it through a twelve-step or outpatient program. She already told Hellen and Jae, another tense family conversation.

The treatment center she chose wasn't like a hospital either. She carefully selected a place where celebrities, politicians, or executives went for nervous exhaustion, sex addiction, or a myriad of other problems. June wanted to approach her next chapter in life with newfound direction and clarity, not medicated or wearing ugly patient pajamas. She let her friends know that she would be on a wonderful dietary plan with plenty of exercise and group activities, even horseback riding and swimming. It was more a vacation with therapy but without temptations of alcohol. Of course, Farrah was going to worry anyway.

"So that's my plan. What about you, sweetie? What are you going to do now that you'll be able to buy the house and worry a little less than normal?"

Farrah smiled at June then Lenore. In the back of her troubled mind, she felt that creeping sensation of guilt nagging at her. Her mind was used to being stressed and causing different symptoms that ranged from aggravating to debilitating.

"I think Jackson and I will be in a good place to be civil now since money won't be a factor for either of us to want from the other. The best part is that with Nova and her boyfriend taking those internships and living in an expensive city for the summer, I'll be able to give her a decent allowance so I know she's eating properly. Maybe even get her a nice used car."

"Give her your old car! It's over ten years old for crying out loud!" June had been urging her to lease a shinier car for a while, but with unstable income from massage therapy, Farrah never considered it.

Farrah laughed. "I suppose I could finally upgrade my car so you're not embarrassed to be in it. A nice hybrid would be a relief, but I don't know how they are in the winter. I guess it'll give me something to research."

She also had new business plans. With the expansion and possible manager position of the spa being a long way off, Farrah and Star worked out a deal for her to participate with chair massages and energy work at the botanica. It broadened the Reiki that Star's Blessings already offered and meant that Farrah could learn more about different religious practices and meet new people. It would give her a reason to leave the house and feel more employed than she did trying to drum up business for Riverside Wellness Spa.

From across the coffee table, Lenore reached over and tapped Farrah's hand. The petite witch moved to the floor and sat closer to the bowl of tortilla chips and salsa to eat with renewed vitality.

"How about that new romance I read in your cards? I think you're ready to move on properly after all the disasters you've been through."

Tingles of nerves shot through Farrah, only this time, she wasn't terrified for her life. It felt more like feathery wings tickling her arms and dancing up to her neck making her shoulders shrug while she smiled.

"Okay, I will not hide it any longer. I think I have some feelings for Phil."

"No duh," June said.

"Hey! It's nice for once to have someone that isn't ignoring me or trying to kill me and in fact would have taken a bullet for me. I honestly don't know if we have anything besides coffee drinking in common."

"But?" Lenore pushed.

"But, I am willing to find out. In fact, I asked him to come over for dinner with all of us so that it would be less like a date. If that's all right with you guys."

"Less pressure. I'm okay with that," June said.

Lenore agreed and immediately starting brainstorming a menu sans alcohol. "It'll be a fun family dinner, calm and relaxed with plenty of laughing. Can I invite Star?"

"Of course! She's part of the family now too."

How their families would change throughout the years hadn't been something Farrah thought of before. She expected it to be her, Jackson, and their daughter forever. Life had other plans for them. Fortunately, part of that included introducing her to the right people to define a new family.

ACKNOWLEDGMENTS

I know this story of Farrah and June is quite different than the previous two WhoDunIts. Essentially, I want people to take away that *family* is however you define it; and if getting out of toxic situations seems impossible, it's not. As Shonda Rhimes said, "Your tribe of people are out there in the world, waiting for you."

Thanks as always to: Joe and my parents who make sure that the cats and I are cared for every day. Neliza Drew, Thomas Pluck, Natali Heuss, Josh Neff, and Twitter friends who checked in on me. The NaNoWriMo Cabin that welcomed me and shows each other lots of support. Thomas Boatwright, for producing another stunning cover and sharing cat pictures.

I'd also like to thank all the creators who have come on my podcast, Vodka O'Clock, to talk about their processes of making art, writing, acting, and all that entertaining stuff. I find talking to people about their work motivating. I hope that listening to the show provides that motivation for others.

Lastly, tremendous thanks to the backers at Patreon who have allowed me to follow my dreams in arts and entertainment.

ABOUT THE AUTHOR

Elizabeth Amber Love (sometimes credited as Amber Love) is the author of The Farrah Wethers Mysteries: *Cardiac Arrest, Full Body Manslaughter* and *Miscarriage of Justice*. In 2015, Love had a short story in PROTECT volume 2, *Protectors: Heroes*. She hosts the Vodka O'Clock podcast and occasionally writes comics and short stories.

If you appreciate a lot of cat pictures and selfies, you're welcome to follow Amber Love on Twitter @elizabethamber and Instagram @amberunmasked.

www.ingramcontent.com/pod-product-compliance
Lightning Source LLC
Chambersburg PA
CBHW011444170626
46816CB00008B/2503